Bonereapers

Books by Jeanne Matthews

Bones of Contention
Bet Your Bones
Bonereapers

Bonereapers

A Dinah Pelerin Mystery

Jeanne Matthews

Poisoned Pen Press

Copyright © 2012 by Jeanne Matthews

First Edition 2012

10 9 8 7 6 5 4 3 2 1

Library of Congress Catalog Card Number: 2011942728

ISBN: 9781590586181   Hardcover
      9781590586204   Trade Paperback

Poisoned Pen Press
6962 E. First Ave., Ste. 103
Scottsdale, AZ 85251
www.poisonedpenpress.com
info@poisonedpenpress.com

Printed in the United States of America

*For their many and varied contributions to this book,
I thank Gail Boyer Hayes, Jeanne Kleyn,
Joe Winston, Sal Gordon, and Joe Massucco.
And for his extreme indulgence and insightful editing,
I thank my husband,
Sid DeLong.*

Acknowledgments

Medieval Folklore, An Encyclopedia of Myths, Legends, Tales, Beliefs, And Customs, Volume 1: A-K; Carl Lindahl, John McNamara, and John Lindow, Editors; ABC-CLIO; Santa Barbara, California; Denver, Colorado; Oxford, England.

The Norse Myths, introduced and retold by Kevin Crossley-Holland, Pantheon Books, New York, 1980.

Great Norse, Celtic, and Teutonic Legends, Wilhelm Wagner, Introduction by W. S. W. Anson, Dover Publications, Inc., Mineola, New York, 2004.

Larousse, Dictionary of World Folklore, Alison Jones, Larousse, 1995.

Norway, Lonely Planet, Anthony Ham, Miles Roddis, Kari Lundgren, 4th edition.

Poetic Edda, English Translation, Olive Bray, 1908.

Yet I had planted thee a noble vine, wholly a right seed: how then art thou turned into the degenerate plant of a strange vine unto me?

—Book of Jeremiah, Chapter 2, Verse 21

Between August and December, 1349, approximately two-thirds of the population of Norway perished from the Black Death. Historians believe that the plague arrived on Norwegian shores when an English trading ship carrying a cargo of wool and a crew of dead men ran aground on the western coast near Bergen. But legend holds that the Great Pestilence was brought by a pair of mysterious travelers, a man and a woman. The man carried a rake. The woman carried a broom. Where the man raked, those lucky enough to slip between the teeth of the rake were spared. But where the woman used her broom, all were swept away to their deaths.

Chapter One

"Doomsday? No, no, no. That's a gross exaggeration, a scary catchword cooked up by another disaster salesman like yourself. You journalists just can't help yourselves."

Senator Colt Sheridan, R-Montana, fat-cat wheat farmer and presidential hopeful, remained annoyingly fresh and full of himself after the nearly nine hour flight from Washington, D.C to Longyearbyen, Norway. Dinah Pelerin shifted uncomfortably in her front-row seat and tried not to groan out loud. Three speakers had delivered their remarks and sat down, but the gentleman from Montana gave no sign that he was ready to cede the podium. He had spoken for over twenty minutes and now he was fielding questions from the media while Dinah shivered from the cold.

The disaster salesman was undaunted. "So this trip isn't because you're worried about an agricultural Armageddon?"

"It's about international cooperation." Senator Sheridan spared the man a pitying shake of his head, as if resigned to the deliberate stupidity of the media, and his eyes returned to the cluster of TV cameras and the home audience that mattered. His practiced smile radiated reasonableness and sincerity. "It's about insuring the continuation of the finest wheat crop on the face of God's earth, Montana red. It's about American leadership and making sure that American moms never have to send their kids off to school without their favorite cereal."

A large assemblage of Norwegian government officials, members of the Alliance to Rescue Civilization, the Global Crop Diversity Trust, concerned scientists, and interested citizens crowded into the harshly lit, inhumanly cold arrival lounge of the Svalbard-Longyearbyen Airport to welcome the U.S. dignitaries who had brought with them an assortment of seeds for storage in the Svalbard Global Seed Vault. It was popularly known as the "Doomsday Vault" whether Senator Sheridan liked it or not. He had brought a box of Montana winter red wheat berries to be added to the nearly twenty million seed varieties already on deposit inside the fortress-like facility on the frozen Arctic island of Spitsbergen. He had also brought his Norwegian-born wife Erika and his fellow Republican and best buddy in the Congress, Senator Whitney Keyes of Massachusetts.

Senator Keyes lounged in a chair behind Sheridan and projected a genial but dignified reserve. With his elegantly tailored suit, his mane of luxuriant dark hair, and his just-off-the-yacht élan, he reeked of privilege and Ivy League prestige. Keyes was a fiscal conservative and a vocal proponent of tax cuts, industry deregulation, and small government. But the normally liberal voters of Massachusetts had been won over by his Kennedyesque appearance, his moderate views on social issues, and his record of generosity to the poor and underprivileged. Following his marriage to the widow and heiress of a billionaire British oil magnate, the senator had founded a charitable organization dedicated to building nutrition and health centers in third world countries. It was he who had arranged this event in Longyearbyen, presumably to showcase Senator Sheridan's commitment to safeguarding the world's food supply and to soften his somewhat jingoistic image. Senator Keyes had brought with him a box of New England pumpkin seeds and a dewy-eyed intern from Boston named Tipton Teilhard III who looked like he was twelve years old.

The third member of the delegation, Senator Norris Frye, D-Hawaii, had not volunteered for the mission. He had been deep sea fishing off the coast of Maui when President Obama, eager to show that the Democrats also care about international cooperation and insuring the variety of children's cereal products, called him to service. Nursing a painful flareup of gout and an all-too-apparent sense of imposition, Senator Frye had brought offshoots of the rare Hawaiian hapai banana and, in the absence of a qualified botanist willing to leave sunny Hawaii and pop off to the North Pole in late December, he'd brought Dinah. She had been tapped as his "technical consultant"—in case anyone had the bad manners to ask him a question about bananas. At least, that was the story Senator Frye believed and it was Dinah's job to make sure he kept on believing it.

For the past six months, Dinah had been studying ethnobotany at the University of Hawaii in Hilo, focused on the complex relationships between ancient Polynesian cultures and the plants they cultivated and on a complex romantic relationship with the nephew of her department head, Eleanor Kalolo. A full-blooded Hawaiian with a passion for preserving endangered native plant species, Eleanor harbored a deep suspicion of the Seed Savers Exchange managers who had been pestering her to send her prized collection of heirloom seeds to Svalbard for safekeeping. She didn't relish the idea of storing her agricultural heritage on foreign soil inside of a frozen mountain and under the control of people she didn't know and couldn't keep tabs on. But as founder and chairwoman of the Native Peoples' Horticultural Cooperative, she felt it was her duty to learn what this Doomsday Vault was all about, which was where Dinah came in. Eleanor didn't travel. The mountain—or else a first-hand report on the mountain by someone she trusted—would have to come to her.

"You find out if these Seed Saver know-it-alls who want my samples will keep their promise to protect them," she'd said in a voice of rumbling command. "Senator Frye has asked me to give him a special cultivar from my collection to donate on behalf of the Hawaiian Seed Savers Exchange and he wants to take along somebody who knows something about it. I'm gonna give him you. You'll be my plant. You can tell me if this crazy ice cave in Norway is on the up-and-up."

A visit to the North Pole in the middle of winter had sounded slightly mad to Dinah, but mad at just the right moment. She needed a jolt of something different. Island living had lately made her feel lazy and hemmed in and her entanglement with Eleanor's marriage-minded nephew had begun to feel…well, entangling. She'd turned thirty-two in October. Time was scorching past and she hadn't done half the things she wanted to do. She wanted to return to her first loves—archaeology and mythology and world travel. She wanted to discover the ruins of a lost city, or rescue some storied relic from a careless farmer's plow, or record the last speaker of a dying language. This trip would give her time to think and decide whether to unmoor herself from Hawaii and sail on, or trim her sails and her dreams and settle down. She'd bought a book of ancient Norse myths and legends to re-inspire her and she was looking forward to learning about the famous Svalbard Seed Vault.

She didn't expect to uncover any defect in the vault or misconduct in its management. The local people who'd been soliciting Eleanor's seeds may have rubbed her the wrong way, but Norway was renowned for its cleanliness, efficiency, high ethical standards, and commitment to world peace. Moreover, it stood to reason that a U.S. presidential candidate wouldn't make a highly publicized trip to declare his support for the project if it hadn't been carefully vetted. She would play her part as Senator Frye's assistant and, when the opportunity arose, ask a few questions about the reliability of the vault's new cryopreservation chamber, which was supposed to maintain unorthodox seeds like bananas at ultra-low temperatures to prevent them from drying out and losing viability, and she would inquire discreetly about the bona fides of the vault's managers. Other than that, there would be little for her to do except read and think.

It crossed her mind that Eleanor wasn't concerned about her seeds at all. Not the plant variety, anyway. She wanted Dinah to marry her nephew, Jon, and have babies. She'd probably sensed Dinah's restlessness and packed her off on this boondoggle to give her time to reconsider Jon's proposal of marriage. But Dinah had been reflecting on the dubious blessings of marriage since she was ten years old. She came from a family where the marriages tended to be ill-starred, contentious, and short. If she had inherited any of her mother's characteristics—and it was already pretty clear she'd inherited the restless gene—Jon would be well advised to retract his offer and give her a pass.

Having grown up in the sultry heat of southeast Georgia and stuck to places with a mild climate, Dinah had no serious cold weather experience. Eleanor had given her a few hundred dollars to outfit herself for the Arctic, and during her layover in Washington she'd gone shopping for cold weather gear. She'd bought a navy wool pea jacket with chichi red buttons, a pair of fur-lined winter boots, wool gloves, wool socks, and a raffish ski cap with earflaps and two long, braided tassels. She'd felt cheerful and ready for her adventure at the top of the world. And then she stepped off the airplane in Svalbard into the thirteen-degrees-below-zero Polar Night and her enthusiasm shriveled.

The cold hadn't quelled Senator Sheridan's enthusiasm. He gestured behind him to the American and Norwegian flags mounted side by side. "It's not just my hope, it's my promise to forge better working relationships and broader cooperation among the nations of the world. We can learn a lot from each other. I'd like the folks watching back home in America to know why it is that little Norway can afford to build this extraordinary vault for the benefit of future generations. Norway isn't the richest country in Europe for nothing. Its trillion dollar surplus comes from offshore drilling and it's time we in the United States stop dragging our feet and start drilling more wells off our shores."

A reporter in full-length fur coat raised his hand.

Senator Sheridan recognized him with a confident wave. "Yes, sir. In the second row."

The man stood. "There is currently a trade gap between the U.S. and Norway. You import more from us than you export. Do you advocate stiffer trade restrictions?"

"No way. I'm a strong advocate for free trade, always have been. I've helped to enact some of the least restrictive agreements between the U.S. and its trading partners, including Norway. If elected president—"

Dinah tuned out the oratory. She had an inherent distrust of politicians. There were those who would say she had an inherent distrust of everyone, but politicians had proven themselves to be particularly untrustworthy. Even so, Senator Sheridan was an undeniably handsome man with a boyish energy and a disarming, down-to-earth manner when he wasn't politicking. On the flight over, he had told a funny anecdote about doing jumping jacks to keep warm while waiting for the school bus during the bitter cold Montana winters. Dinah wished he'd lighten up and lead the people freezing their behinds off here today in a few jumping jacks.

"Do you advocate gene modification?" The reporter who'd needled him about an agricultural Armageddon cut in without being recognized. He was a scruffy character with an accent that rose at the end of every sentence, which made him sound angry, and a press badge that read "Dagbladet," which looked like a swear word. He had a long, lupine face with pock-marked cheeks and wild, Einstein hair. "American companies have applications pending to sell their patented genetically modified grains to Norway. Are you here to promote those applications?"

Sheridan's eyes narrowed. "I'm here to donate unmodified Montana wheat seeds to the Svalbard repository. But global population is outpacing food production. With seven billion mouths to feed already, genetically modified foods may be one way to achieve food security."

"That sounds like an advertisement for Tillcorp Industries," goaded the reporter. "Tillcorp is one of the biggest contributors to your campaign and they've made selling their genetically engineered products a major goal in Europe and the rest of the world. Are you here to spread international cooperation and good will or mainly to advocate for Tillcorp?"

A disapproving murmur rippled through the ranks of the government officials seated on a makeshift stage behind the podium. The minister of agriculture thrust out his lips and glowered. Whitney Keyes darted a sharp look over the tops of his half-moon glasses. Norris Frye, whose gout-inflamed toes had kept him in bedroom slippers and off the stage, sat up smartly on Dinah's left, all ears.

Senator Sheridan glared at the reporter. "What's your name, fella?"

"Aagaard. Brander Aagaard."

"Well, you can put this in your pipe and smoke it, Mr. Brander Aagaard. Colt Sheridan advocates for the hard-working farmers of this world. He advocates for responsible research and development that'll make our staple crops resistant to disease and pests and for policies that'll keep global markets stable and predictable."

The agriculture minister stood up and applauded as if that concluded the program. Looking ill at ease, the other officials followed his lead and so did the senators. Dinah joined in. Her fingers felt like icicles, at risk of breaking off with each clap, and she was increasingly desperate for a visit to the ladies' room. She noticed that Erika Sheridan, who sat primly on her right, was also showing signs of impatience. Her curtain of blond hair hid her face as she stared into her lap and worried her wedding ring. Twenty-five years ago, Erika had been the lead singer for Fata Morgana, the hottest rock group in Europe in the '80s. On the long flight over the North Atlantic, she and Dinah had played numerous games of gin and Crazy Eights and Erika had talked about her life before and after Colt Sheridan. They had met while he was a Rhodes scholar living in Oxford and, after a whirlwind romance, she left Fata to follow him to Montana. The way she hid her face and fidgeted with her rings made Dinah wonder if she was completely on board with her husband's presidential ambitions.

When the applause died, the agriculture minister, a big, beefy man with lips like sausage links, cleared his throat significantly. "Well said, Senator Sheridan. We are all in agreement on these matters. Stable markets. Research. Yes, and now I'm sure that Senator Sheridan and his party are weary from their long journey and anxious to be shown to their hotel."

Senator Keyes extended his hand to the agriculture minister. "Thank you, Herr Dybdahl. We appreciate this warm reception here in the Kingdom of Norway and look forward to more substantive discussions with you and your cabinet at the dinner tonight." He nodded deferentially to Sheridan. "Do you have anything you'd like to add, Senator Sheridan?"

Sheridan waved an arm across the audience. "If there are no more questions…"

"I've got one," said Aagaard. "Tillcorp can buy genetic deregulation in the U.S. simply by donating to you Congress people. Is the fix in for them to have free access to experiment with American seeds stored here in Norway?"

"What do you mean, 'the fix'? There's no fix here. Not anywhere." Sheridan appealed to the sensible people watching him on TV back in America. "My vote's not for sale. Never has been, never will be."

"If you're not lobbying for Tillcorp, why did you bring the president of Tillcorp and his lawyer with you on your plane?"

"How the…?" Sheridan scowled and a note of uncertainty crept into his voice "You're way out of line, fella. I'm here at the invitation of the Norwegian Government. To do my part, to do my country's part to guarantee the planet's food security." He turned angry eyes to the row of ministers behind him, as if to demand that somebody give this rabblerouser the heave-ho. The senator obviously wasn't accustomed to the aggressive style of European journalists.

Dinah wasn't accustomed to associating with politicians or the reporters who egged them on. The antagonism seemed mutually calculated to stir up their particular constituencies. The Norwegian ministers exchanged looks of embarrassment, but seemed unsure how to handle the situation.

Aagaard pressed his advantage. "Is Tillcorp's presence a secret?"

"Let me through. Move. Move aside."

There was a commotion at the rear of the room.

"Out of my way. Move, move!" A small, pudding-faced man with a few tufts of grayish-red hair tried to shove his way past the guards at the door. His English had the same singsong pitch as Aagaard's. "They have to be stopped. They're destroying God's creations. They rob the earth of its precious fruits!"

A shout went up from somewhere in the crowd. "Look out! He has a gun!"

"Let me through. It's the Americans who are dangerous. Atrazine! Alachlor! They've brought the death gene."

There was a scuffle. Norris Frye turned sideways in his chair and half-stood to see what was happening behind him. Dinah craned her neck, but Norris blocked her view. She glanced back toward the stage as a dot of red light flashed against the window to the left of Senator Sheridan. The dot jittered across the wall behind the stage, herky-jerky as a moth. She stood up and looked around for the source, but all she could see was a knot of men in coats and suits flailing their arms and trying to subdue the protester. Everyone was focused on the altercation at the back of the room. She turned back to the stage as the red dot bobbled across a corner of the Norwegian flag, lit momentarily on the microphone in front of Sheridan, flitted across Senator Keyes' lapels, and landed onto Herr Dybdahl's face.

"Kristus!" Dybdahl's hands flew to his face and he staggered backward into the arms of the other officials. "My eyes!"

Senator Sheridan shrank away from the podium and gaped at the fallen agriculture minister. "What the…What…?"

Erika jumped up and ran toward her husband. Norris Frye slid to the floor at Dinah's feet and covered his head.

She bent over him. "Senator, are you hurt?"

"Get down," he hissed. "It's a terrorist attack!"

A frightened mob stampeded toward the exit.

"I can't see," cried Herr Dybdahl as his fellow ministers eased him to the floor.

Dinah watched open-mouthed as Brander Aagaard snatched up his camera and began to snap pictures. Several other reporters did the same.

Senator Keyes took Erika by the arm and tried to drag the Sheridans out of the line of fire. "Let's get out of here, Colt. This way."

"What was it?"

"A laser, I think. Come on now."

Looking dazed, the Sheridans followed Keyes to the far side of the room.

Norwegian police blocked the exits.

Even as he was pinned against the wall by a large policeman, the little pudding-faced man continued to cry out his warnings. "Like the Romans who sowed the fields of the conquered with salt, they'll starve us, I tell you."

A loud male voice shouted, "Go back to your seats everyone. Nobody leaves." He shouted again in Norwegian.

The two Secret Service agents who'd accompanied the senators on the flight from Washington jogged down the aisle toward the stage, guns drawn and pointing every which way. They spotted Norris Frye huddled on the floor in the fetal position and pulled him up and away toward the other senators. They appeared not to notice Dinah.

A Norwegian policeman gesticulated with some kind of telescopic baton. "Back, back to your seats. Everything is under control."

Brander Aagaard put down his camera, pulled a pack of cigarettes out of his jacket pocket, and slouched into the chair left empty by Senator Frye. "Your American Secret Service is crap." He lit a cigarette and blew a pungent stream of smoke toward the stage. "Or maybe they asked the *angriper* who he was aiming for and when he said it was the herring eater, they moved aside to give him a clear shot."

Dinah needed a bathroom too urgently to argue about either the epithet or the target, but the way the protester seemed to feel about Americans, she would've sworn he was aiming at Senator Sheridan.

Chapter Two

The enormous stuffed polar bear inside its glass cage looked straight at Dinah—meaningfully, it seemed, as if it were trying to tell her something. Something not soothing. She downed another slug of aquavit, spelled Akevitt on the bottle that Brander Aagaard had produced from the pocket of his parka. It tasted like cough syrup, but it was the only nerve medicine in sight.

The senators had been whisked away immediately by the Norwegian police and the Secret Service agents, leaving Dinah to fend for herself. Her plea for a toilet had finally been granted, albeit reluctantly. A female officer had patted her down and shepherded her into the restroom. Now she was standing at the rear of a long line of people waiting their turn to be processed and dismissed. Unfortunately, the Secret Service had insisted on presenting all of the Americans' passports together upon their arrival and they still had hers. She was pissed off and paperless and she didn't know which hotel had been booked for the delegation or where they'd gone. She pulled her inadequate wool pea jacket more tightly around her and hoped she'd find an understanding person at the front of this line.

"Who are you?" Aagaard asked. He had latched onto her the minute she came out of the bathroom. "Are you an aide to one of the senators or do you work for Tillcorp?"

"Neither."

"What then? What are you doing here?"

"I'm here to answer questions about bananas."

"Be serious."

"At thirteen below, after watching a man struck blind by a laser, who isn't serious?"

"You're avoiding my question. What's this *skitt* about bananas?"

Dinah assumed that she had learned her first Norwegian word and, the way this trip was shaping up, she foresaw multiple uses for it in the future. Aagaard wasn't sharing his liquor for nothing. He was pumping her for information. Sour as she felt over being abandoned, she had no desire to see herself quoted in *Dagbladet*. She stuck to her script. "Bananas were the first fruit cultivated by humans and they're the world's fourth largest fruit crop. Actually, the banana tree is an herb and the banana is the fruit. Banana seeds are recalcitrant. They can't survive drying and freezing like orthodox seeds, but at ultra-low temperatures…"

"*Skitt.*"

No kidding. She took another gulp of aquavit and turned the tables on him. "What do you know about the protester? What did he mean about Americans being dangerous? Is there an anti-American movement here in Norway?"

"Not anti-American. Anti-Tillcorp. Anti-gene-modification. We Europeans aren't as willing to gamble with the world's DNA as you are. More than one organization is opposed to Tillcorp's drive to patent Mother Nature's creations and concentrate control of the food chain in corporate hands."

Dinah hadn't been formally introduced to the Tillcorp execs on board the senators' U.S. Air Force jet, although Erika had pointed them out, saying only that they were "Colt's corporate friends along for the ride." The jet was equipped with two private suites, one in the nose and one in the tail, modeled Dinah supposed, after Air Force One. She, Erika, the Secret Service agents, and Norris Frye had kept to the open seating area in the center. Senator Sheridan had sequestered himself in one of the suites for almost the entire duration of the flight. Whitney Keyes and his intern buzzed in and out periodically carrying armloads of files and documents. The CEO of Tillcorp, Jake Mahler, was bald and barrel-chested with wily eyes and a transparent appreciation of his importance to the universe. He and his attorney, an attractive, businesslike woman named Valerie Ives, drifted out of the other suite and visited Sheridan from time to time.

She said, "If the protester is anti-Tillcorp and he believes that Senator Sheridan is aiding and abetting them, then that laser beam was probably meant for Sheridan."

"It'll make better copy if he was going after a government minister or one of the Diversity Trust people."

"Why?"

"People go after Americans for all kinds of reasons—Iraq, Afghanistan, those subprime mortgage derivatives that you bundled and fobbed off on the rest of the world. But an attack on the Norwegian minister ties directly to the seed vault."

"Is the seed vault controversial?"

"It's aroused a lot of suspicion. The Norwegian government paid for it to be built, but a number of shady billionaires and foundations have poured millions into the project. The Global Crop Diversity Trust oversees the operation of the facility, but the Internet is full of rumors about the Trust's dishonesty."

"What kind of rumors?"

Aagaard's eyes grew leery. "Are you a writer of some kind?"

"No."

He took another drink of Akavitt and apparently decided she was harmless. "Some believe that Trust operatives have infiltrated indigenous seed banks in order to donate part of their stocks to the Svalbard Vault, but they conceal the fact that once seeds are deposited in Svalbard, they fall under the control of the United Nations' FAO treaty, which was designed to facilitate access by corporate breeders."

"FAO?"

"Food and Agriculture Organization. It's supposed to protect farmers' rights to their specialized knowledge and commercial use of traditional crops. But the conspiracy theorists say it's nothing short of theft, a massive seed grab to benefit international agribusinesses. FAO gets most of its funding from a tax on seed patents."

Dinah could see that her report to Eleanor would be considerably more involved than she'd bargained on. "It sounds a bit sinister."

"It is. Some blame the Norwegian government for being in bed with the corporations, some blame the Trust for misappropriating their donors' seed collections, and some blame the corporate breeders."

"And some see Senator Sheridan as a tool of Tillcorp," she said, wishing she'd spent less time gabbing with Erika about rock-and-roll and Norwegian mythology and more time delving into her husband's relationship with Tillcorp. "Are genetically modified seeds stored in the vault along with the natural seeds?"

"I don't think so, not yet anyway. The plant breeders don't want that. Too much paperwork and disclosure and they'd run the risk of losing their intellectual property rights in their hybrids."

"What *do* they want then?"

"I'm not sure yet. When I find out, it'll be the scoop of the century."

A Norwegian woman in a police uniform pulled Dinah out of line. She wore her golden hair in braids pinned tightly on top of her head and her attitude was as crisp and starchy as her uniform. "Come with me, please."

She escorted Dinah to a tiny, glass-enclosed cubicle and motioned her into a white plastic chair behind a white plastic desk. The woman sat down across from her and stared. Through her glass enclosure, Dinah could still see the polar bear staring back at her from its glass enclosure.

"Passport, please."

"I was on the plane with the American senators. The Secret Service agents have my passport."

The woman frowned. "What is your home country?"

"America. The United States."

"Naturalized?"

"No. I was born in the U.S. Georgia."

"Are your parents Arab then?"

"No. My mother is a Seminole Indian."

The woman frowned more deeply. "From what part of India come these Seminoles?"

"They're not...They are Native Americans." Dinah was growing exasperated. Her dark hair and eyes couldn't help but stand out in a nation lousy with blonds, but this jumped-up Goldilocks seemed to regard her non-Nordic features as per se terroristic.

"What is your name?"

"Dinah Pelerin."

"Full name."

"Dinah Loyce Pelerin."

"Will you open your purse, please?"

Dinah handed over her sporty red Hobo bag, which matched the buttons on her pea jacket, and watched as the woman removed and scrutinized each item. Tissues, chapstick, wallet, iPod, compact, lipstick, hairbrush, toothbrush, pen, notepad, keys, aspirin, peanut butter cheese crackers. She held up the puka shell Eleanor had given Dinah to wish her a safe voyage and examined it minutely.

"It's for good luck. Please, if you'll just contact Senator Norris Frye, at whatever hotel he's staying, he'll vouch for me. I'm his technical consultant. Really. I'm here to talk about Hawaiian bananas."

The woman instructed her to wait and strode out of the cubicle. She marched past the polar bear's cage and paused to confer with two male cops, also blond. One of them opened a cell phone. She saw that Brander Aagaard had reached the front of the line. Blowing smoke out the side of his mouth like a diesel truck, he brandished his press credentials to some sort of military cop in a red beret. The cop's forehead corrugated into angry folds. Dinah didn't have to hear what Aagaard was saying to know that he was being obnoxious. She massaged her temples, which had begun to throb. What kind of chicanery was going on here? Was Aagaard being a provocateur or did he have evidence that seeds could be checked out of the Svalbard vault for experimentation? That was precisely what Eleanor had sent her to find out.

If only it weren't so cold. She kneaded her chilly arms and envisioned herself somewhere far, far away, stretched out in a snug, soft bed piled high with blankets.

After what seemed like an eternity, the woman returned and informed her that she had been cleared to leave the airport.

"But where…?"

"Your senators are staying at the Radisson. One of the military officers will drive you."

The Radisson. Dinah almost whimpered with relief. She should have known that a bunch of VIP senators wouldn't undertake a winter junket to the Arctic unless their creature comforts could be assured. She picked up her purse and stood up. As an afterthought, she asked, "Have you heard whether the agriculture minister is going to be all right?"

"He is in hospital. We have no report on his condition yet."

The two-mile drive from the airport into Longyearbyen didn't afford much in the way of sightseeing. It was three o'clock in the afternoon and black as coal, the commodity which had been mined here since the beginning of the twentieth century. In the seventeenth and eighteenth centuries, Spitsbergen Island—the largest in the Svalbard archipelago—had been visited primarily by whalers and Russian trappers. But the island was rich in coal and in 1905, an American tycoon named John Munro Longyear bought out the Trondheim-Spitsbergen Coal Company and renamed it The Arctic Coal Company. The town that grew up around the mines became known as Longyearbyen, "*byen*" being the Norwegian word for city. Today, with the addition of the airport, a university, a research institute, tourist facilities, and the Doomsday Vault, Longyearbyen had become the largest town in the Arctic, boasting a population of just over two thousand hardy souls, all of them in excellent health. There were no dead people in Longyearbyen. Because the permafrost prevented bodies from decomposing, no burials were allowed. According to what Dinah had read, dying was for all intents and purposes illegal. Anyone who felt sick enough to die was required to get out of town pronto.

In front of the merrily lit Radisson Blu Polar Hotel, her driver opened the door for her and walked her across the snowy walkway to the entrance. A sign posted inside the foyer requested her to remove her boots, so she lined them up on a rack with scores of others, slid her cold feet into a pair of the hotel's clunky clogs, and scuffed into the lobby. The huge stone fireplace drew her like a magnet. She stood with her back to the fire for a few minutes and took in the ambience—modern, nicely furnished in the bland style of most hotels, and brilliantly lit. The Blu Polar could have been located anywhere in the world except for another sign that was posted on the wall above the front desk.

To all our guests, the risk of polar bears in the restaurant isn't very big
So can you please hang your weapons in the weapons cabinet?
(Rifles, guns, revolvers)

The Secret Service wouldn't have surrendered their guns. In fact, Dinah would be surprised if they hadn't confiscated every other gun on the premises. The agents had already checked her in and the hotel staff had stowed her suitcase in her room. She accepted her key card from a smiling blond receptionist, burrowed her feet more firmly into the clogs, and scuffed off toward the elevator.

As the doors pinged opened, Tipton Teilhard III bustled out while typing something on his iPad and nearly knocked her over. Dinah had almost forgotten the intern's presence among the senators' entourage. He had an irrepressible cowlick and an air of hectic breathlessness.

"Oh, sorry," he said. "I wasn't looking where I was going. I'm on the way to the kitchen to get Senator Keyes a sandwich."

"Couldn't he order one from room service?"

"Oh, he's got far more important things to think about, the weight of the world on his mind, really. I know what he likes and it's my duty to look after his day-to-day needs. It's more a privilege than a duty. He's an absolute political genius, a true statesman. I wish he were the one challenging Obama in the fall. He has a perfect resumé—successful businessman, two-term senator, member of the Foreign Relations Committee, philanthropist. But Whitney's more of a policy wonk and behind-the-scenes kingmaker. I couldn't have asked for a better mentor."

"Do you plan to run for office one day, Tipton?"

"Oh, yes. I'll start with the House, the way Senator Sheridan did. During the second term of the Sheridan Administration after I've got four years of insider knowledge under my belt. It's all about relationship management and leveraging one's social capital. My mother was Ambassador to Lithuania under Bush Two and she serves on the Board of the American Council for the Arts with Cynthia Keyes and Portia Warren."

"With so many social assets, it sounds like you'll be a shoo-in."

"Oh, thank you, Dinah." He beamed, seemingly deaf to sarcasm.

Tipton bustled on and Dinah rode up to the second floor. She had her doubts about the prospects of a twerp who started every sentence with "oh," regardless of his social assets. But his slavish devotion to Whitney Keyes and his work for the Sheridan campaign would probably pay off in the long run.

Her room was at the end of the hall on the second floor and the bright interior lifted her spirits. The walls were splashed with colorful murals of Viking ships and crenellated castles and, most importantly, a plush down comforter covered the bed. Before she took off her coat, she bumped the thermostat to high and went to the bathroom and ran a tub of hot water.

While her bath was filling, she scouted out the mini-bar. She wanted something to take the cloying taste of aquavit out of her mouth. There was a selection of beers she'd never heard of, but Russian vodka predominated. She found a can of tomato juice and mixed herself a Bloody Mary, no rocks. Drink in hand, she opened her suitcase and grabbed an insulating silk turtleneck, a pair of wool socks, and a flannel shirt and repaired to the bathroom. She dumped a bottle of gardenia scented bath gel into the water and tested the temperature with a finger. Perfect. She set her drink and her book of Norse myths on a stool beside the tub, stripped off her coat and the numerous but insufficient layers underneath, and climbed into the hot water.

"Ahhh." She laid back and let the hot water and the vodka seep into her frozen veins. After a few minutes, she began to thaw. Her headache subsided and her thoughts reverted to Herr Dybdahl. As horrible as it was to have one's eyes burned by a laser, it could have been worse. Someone in the crowd had seen a gun, or imagined he saw one. If the protester had had a gun instead of a laser, Dybdahl might be dead. Senator Sheridan, too. If it had been one of those guns with laser sights, or a semi-automatic blaster with an oversized clip that could fire dozens of shots in a few seconds, the entire assembly might have been murdered, their bodies already loaded onto a plane for shipment south, to a burial place in softer ground.

Dinah shivered and immersed herself to the neck in the steaming water. The last two years of her life had been haunted by murder, first in Australia and last summer in Hawaii. Those events still gave her nightmares and she hoped with all her heart that she would never find herself in the vicinity of another murder.

She took a sip of her Bloody Mary, dried her hands, and reached for her book of Norse mythology. She hadn't read five pages when the first murder transpired. Literally, the first murder. The Norsemen believed that the earth was created by an act of murder.

In the beginning, there was nothing but black emptiness bounded on one side by a region of fire, Muspelheim, and on the other by a region of ice, Niflheim. At the dawn of time, a few sparks of fire escaped and melted some of the ice, which formed into a primordial, hermaphroditic frost giant named Ymir. The sweat under Ymir's arms dripped and formed two more giants and one of his legs mated with the other to form a third. Other giants emerged and somewhere down the line a giant cow, Audumla, came along and licked a salty block of ice into the shape of a man, Buri.

Dinah drank another sip of her Bloody Mary. Hermaphroditic frost giants? A primeval cow licking blocks of ice into human form? What a twisted imagination those Vikings had. She read on, transfixed.

Buri, who possessed the reproductive attributes of both male and female, mated with himself and begat Borr. Borr represented a break with Ymir's brutishness and a genealogical advance toward humanness. He eventually mated with Bestla, a benign frost giant who exemplified the nourishing forces of Nature and out of this union was born the triumvirate of Norse gods—Vili, Vé, and Odin.

But there was still no earth—only fire and ice, with a space of dark, lawless emptiness in between. The gods were constantly at war with Ymir and his marauding gangs of frost giants, as well as giants of other races—fire giants and mountain giants. The gods longed for a pleasant, orderly universe. But unlike the Judeo-Christian God, they couldn't create something out of nothing. They needed raw materials to work with. They looked around and saw Ymir, whom they hated, and a light bulb went on. They saw in the giant everything that a well-structured world would need and, in short order, they murdered him for his parts. They fashioned the earth out of his skull and ground up his flesh to make dirt. The blood gushing from his wounds became the lakes and the seas. They made his teeth and bones into the rocks and mountains, his thick and curly hair into the trees, and his brains into clouds.

Dinah closed the book and turned on the hot water tap with her toes. Norse mythology was not for the squeamish. Offhand, she couldn't recall another creation story that was quite so grisly.

Arriving in Norway to shouts of "death gene" was a pretty grisly introduction to the country. The protester's words were directed at Americans, but what had he meant? Was he talking about seeds? It was common knowledge that Tillcorp had developed seeds that didn't reproduce after a first planting.

They produced a single, sterile crop. If a farmer wanted to grow another crop the next season, he had to purchase another batch of seeds from Tillcorp. Designing the seed to self-destruct was how Tillcorp protected its patent. But if she'd understood what Aagaard was saying, once the seeds were deposited into the Svalbard vault, they fell under the control of the U.N. and corporate breeders could plunder them at will.

She turned off the water and soaked for a while. Should she call Eleanor and brief her? Eleanor hadn't laid out her concerns with any specificity, but she would definitely want to know if the seeds on deposit with Svalbard could be removed and rendered sterile. At this point, Dinah didn't know if the protester was a raving wacko or a male Cassandra. Likewise, Brander Aagaard. She decided to wait until the facts were in before raising Eleanor's blood pressure. In the meantime, she needed a nap. There was plenty of time before the scheduled state dinner, if it hadn't been canceled, which it probably had. In that case, she would be able to sleep straight through until tomorrow. She crawled out of the tub, dried herself off, and snuggled into her nightshirt.

It's never what you expect, she thought, and fell into bed, cocooning herself in the soft depths of the down comforter.

Chapter Three

A door slammed so hard that it rattled the wall.

"Jerusalem!" Dinah sat bolt upright in bed.

An argument was raging in the room next door. "For chrissakes, get back in here and be quiet."

"Let go of me, Colt. You can't stop me."

"Grow up and get over it, Erika. You're obsessing over a phantom."

"She's not a phantom. Hannalore…"

Something crashed and the voices died away. Dinah let out a breath. It sounded like a domestic fight rather than a terrorist assault. Had the senator hit Erika or vice versa? Should she call hotel security or the Secret Service guys? Dear God, what idiot had assigned her the room next door to the big cheese and his missus? They should be ensconced in the VIP suite with armed guards stationed outside their door. Maybe the senator was afraid the VIP treatment would tarnish his image as a regular joe and man of the people.

Dinah nipped across the room and pressed her ear against the wall. Nothing. Not a peep. And no sound of anyone rushing to the scene. Surely, she wasn't the only one who heard the ruckus. In another minute the cavalry would come charging down the hall to find out what was happening. What time was it anyway? She went to the window and peered out between the drapes. It looked like midnight, but her watch showed six p.m.

The quiet began to sound ominous. Just because a man was running for president didn't mean he didn't beat his wife. Maybe Erika was afraid of him and that's why she'd seemed so fidgety and nervous at the press conference. Dinah pictured her lying hurt and bleeding. The least she could do was knock on their door to make sure she didn't need help. She threw on her Radisson robe. But before she had the sash cinched, someone knocked on her door.

Expecting Erika to stumble in with a split lip or a bloody nose, she flung open the door.

"I hope I didn't get you out of the shower." It was Erika, all right, but she showed no ill effects from the slamming and smashing. Her eyes were dry, her demeanor unruffled, and she was dressed in a sexy, body-hugging black-and-white ski outfit that belied her fifty years. She held out a small paper bag. "You came from Hawaii so unprepared for the Norwegian winter. I brought you this silk pullover and a balaclava. I packed a spare and you said you didn't have one. It'll keep your nose from freezing off if you go outside."

"That's so thoughtful, Erika. Thank you." Dinah took the bag. "Won't you come in and chat for a while?"

"Sure. For a few minutes. After being so cramped on the plane, I thought I'd go for a walk to loosen up. Would you like to join me?"

Was there a plea implicit in the invitation?

"Let me think about it for a few minutes. I'm still thawing out from this afternoon."

Erika came in and sat in an armchair next to the window. Her face, sliced thin by her straight blond hair and foreshortened by bangs to her eyebrows, seemed designed to hide her emotions.

Dinah perched on the edge of the bed. She was happy to provide refuge, but a walk in the frigid polar night, even with a balaclava to keep her nose from freezing off, didn't appeal. "Do you think it's safe to go out without a security detail after what happened at the airport?"

"That's nothing to do with me." Her tone was emphatic, almost belligerent, as if she were serving notice. She pushed her hair back and rested her hands on her knees. "Anyhow, no one would recognize me in the dark and with my face covered."

Dinah forbore to point out the obvious, namely that a man had shouted out heated grievances against Americans and, just possibly, tried to blind her husband. His nearest and dearest, however well disguised, should not go wandering about the streets unprotected.

Talking with Erika had been fun and easy on the plane, but now Dinah felt awkward. She was curious about what had caused the row and who this Hannalore might be. But it was none of her business, probably as organic and irrational as any other marital spat. The naming of a third party was reminiscent of the jealous brawls she'd overheard between her mother and her various stepfathers. She changed the subject. "I don't know how people make it through the winter here in Longyearbyen. I read that the sun sets in late October and doesn't rise again until mid-February."

"Yes, but during the summer, the sun shines around the clock." Erika dropped her eyes and lapsed into silence.

Dinah cast about for another subject. "Will you be visiting your home town while you're in Norway?"

"No. Notodden is far to the south, south even of Oslo."

"Do you still have family living there?"

"My parents are dead. My sister might be there still. We lost touch. Notodden is tiny. She probably married and moved away."

"You don't know if your sister is married?"

"I haven't seen her in years. Neither Colt nor I have any family." Her mouth curved in a wistful smile and the outer corners of her blue eyes crinkled into crow's-feet. "He used to say that we are each other's child."

Dinah knew that the Sheridans had no children, a fact that made the senator an unusual and rather daring candidate for president. His opponents never failed to call attention to his lack of a stake in the next generation. Dinah didn't like to parse a simple declarative sentence too finely, but "used to say"? It sounded as if Erika were remembering her husband's affections as something in the distant past.

"You must have friends in Norway. The members of Fata must get together now and then for old times' sake."

"The band was at the height of its popularity when I fell in love with Colt and moved to the States. My decision caused a lot of hard feelings and the band broke up. They wouldn't want me at their reunions." She rubbed her legs briskly and stood up. "I came to apologize, Dinah. You must have heard us quarreling next door. I hope it didn't upset you. Colt and I are both exhausted. He's been campaigning in every little town in Iowa and that man with the laser…the incident unsettled him. Things like that probably happen a lot to the president. If Colt wins, he'll have to get used to it."

Dinah noted the singular pronoun. "You don't want him to run?"

"He's always wanted to serve his country. But when he left Oxford and went home to Montana to run for the House, he found that his education and experience abroad were a detriment, a sign of snobbery and elitism. He's spent his entire career trying to live down the happiest time of his life." She dipped her head and her hair fell forward. "Of course, having a foreign-born wife has always been his main detriment."

It was a poignant thing to say. Whether she felt that way because that's how Sheridan felt was unclear. Having grown up in a small town in rural Georgia, Dinah understood how leaving for greener pastures can be construed by some as snooty and highfalutin, a rejection of the home folks' values. Sheridan's fancy education in England and his Norwegian rock-star wife might be viewed as pluses in some quarters, but evidently not all. Dinah skated past what was obviously a sore point. "Did you and Colt spend a lot of time together in Oxford?"

"Fata did a concert there and someone invited Colt and some of his friends to a party backstage after the show. Colt and I fell in love at first sight. I went back to Oxford as often as I could between gigs, but I wanted us to be together all the time. He took a leave of absence from his classes to follow the Fata tour to Spain and Portugal. Since then, what I want hasn't mattered all that much to him." She laughed, as if to signal she didn't really mean that.

Dinah didn't know how to respond. Erika was using her as a sounding board, but if it was marriage counseling she needed, she'd knocked on the wrong door. "Marriage is complicated. Or so I imagine."

"You are right. In Norway, we have a saying, *å svelge noen kameler*. It means to swallow some camels. Do you know it?"

"'Strain out a gnat, but swallow a camel.' It's from the Bible. The Pharisees observed the little rituals, but disregarded the big things like justice and mercy."

"It means something else here. If you swallow some camels, you've made concessions. You've given up something that you want for the common good."

"I like that definition," said Dinah. "But a camel would stick in the throat unless you were sure that what you were giving up was something you could do without."

"That's very wise. How can such a ruthless card player be such a sympathetic listener?"

"Just versatile, I guess."

She dropped her chin again and her hair closed around her face. "You mustn't take my ramblings to heart. People say a lot of foolish things they don't mean during the long night."

Dinah took that as the last word on the Sheridans' marital discord and if it wasn't, she wasn't in a state of mind to hear more. She covered a yawn. "I don't think I'll join you on that walk. I'm going to take a nap."

Erika got up and moved toward the door. "Will you be going to the dinner with the Norwegian ministers?"

"Hasn't it been canceled?"

"No. Herr Dybdahl's assistant telephoned and the minister insists that the function go ahead as planned. He has a corneal flash burn, like you get with snow blindness, but his vision won't be permanently affected. He's in a lot of pain and won't attend the dinner, but his assistants and several of the vault's personnel will be there. None of the other wives plan to go, so Colt has let me off the hook. But Valerie will be there and I'm sure she won't want to be the only woman."

It sounded to Dinah like the place she needed to be to pick up scuttlebutt about the vault. "I've never been to a state-sponsored dinner. I'll definitely go."

"Good. After my walk, I'm going to order supper in the room and try to catch up on my sleep. Tomorrow Colt and Whitney will meet with the managers of the seed vault over breakfast and in the afternoon we'll tour the seed facility." She picked up the wool pea jacket Dinah had thrown across the foot of the bed. "Is this flimsy thing the only coat you brought?"

"It looked warm as toast in the shop window. And you have to admit, the buttons are adorable."

Erika opened the door and smiled back at her. "You should turn down the thermostat, Dinah. Too much warmth will only make it worse when you have to go outside."

Chapter Four

"Is it true that bananas are radioactive?" asked Herr Dybdahl's assistant, a ravishing blonde with eyes the color of morning glories and an expression of rapt interest.

"Now, now, Ursille. It can't be or monkeys would glow in the dark." Norris Frye chortled and patted her hand. He had recovered from his fright at the airport and had been flirting openly with Ursille from the moment they sat down to dinner.

"But that is what I have heard," said Ursille. "Is it not true, Dinah?"

Dinah swallowed a mouthful of mashed rutabaga and washed it down with red wine. She was trying to chat up the geneticist on her left, a man named Peder Halverson, and she resented the interruption. "Small amounts of the isotope potassium-forty occur naturally in bananas, making them very slightly radioactive. It's hardly enough to measure and the banana…"

"Some say it's an aphrodisiac," chortled Frye. The senator knew more banana lore than he'd let on. He dug into his reindeer steak with gusto and Dinah noticed the band of white, naked flesh on the ring finger of his left hand. "Ever been to the U.S., Ursille? You'd love Hawaii. We call it the Aloha State. I could show you sights that would amaze you."

Dinah returned her attention to the geneticist. He was a fleshy man with a bulbous nose crisscrossed with red and blue spider veins like streets on a city map. "How long have you been in Longyearbyen, Peder?"

"Not yet one year."

"What is it that you do, exactly?"

"Genetics."

"What kind of genetics?"

"I have rendered Hungarian oats immune to the Fusarium. The same technique will be applicable to millet. With the new genes I have inserted, spoilage will be retarded."

"You do this work for the Svalbard Vault?"

"No, I am employed by…" His words were drowned out by a cacophony of riotous laughter in the main hotel dining room.

The senators' dining area had been sectioned off by mirrored privacy screens, but the screens didn't shut out the noise. And with fourteen diners at the senators' table and multiple conversations, some of them in Norwegian, Dinah found it hard to hear.

"What did you say?"

"The Griegs Foundation. We study the effects of Stachybotrys mycotoxins in wheat, maize, and vine fruits."

"It must be fascinating work, tinkering with genes and DNA. Will you be experimenting with the wheat and pumpkin seeds that the senators brought for deposit in the vault?"

"*Nei*. It is strictly *forbuden* unless…"

There was another burst of noisy laughter.

"Unless what, Peder?"

A gaunt-faced man sitting across the table from Halverson said something to him in Norwegian and the two of them began to jabber excitedly, forgetting Dinah. She would have to pry the answer to "unless what" out of somebody else.

At the far end of the table Colt Sheridan, Whitney Keyes, and Jake Mahler of Tillcorp were engaged in a discussion with a man who had something to do with the Global Diversity Trust whose name she'd missed. Senator Sheridan still looked confident and presidential, but Dinah thought she detected a trace of unease in the way he kept eyeing his watch. Tipton Teilhard III ignored his food and appeared to be taking notes on his iPad.

She strained her ears. Mahler said something about cigars, which seemed to elicit frowns all around. After that, all she heard from that end of the table was an undifferentiated drone. Directly across from her, the gaunt-faced man had drawn Mahler's attorney, Valerie Ives, into the conversation with Halverson. She sounded fluent and friendly, but she didn't seem happy with the seating arrangement. Her eyes kept skewing down the table to Mahler. After a while, almost absent-mindedly, she transitioned to English. "Is the market for reindeer expanding since the Chernobyl disaster, Herr Gjertsen?"

"*Ja*. Not much radiation in the lichens and mosses now. *Reinsdyr* meat is good for human consumption. High-protein, low-fat, tender like *smør*…how do you say, Valerie?"

"Butter."

"*Ja*, tender like the butter and very ecologically sound. Only the Sami can keep herds. Nobody else. It's the law." Gjertsen had been introduced at the beginning of the meal as a food safety bureaucrat of some kind. Dinah hoped it was his concern about excessive fat content and not radiation poisoning that kept him whippet thin.

"WikiLeaks? What the hell?" Mahler's voice carried like breaking glass.

Valerie's head snapped up. Dinah looked down the table. Senator Keyes was shushing Mahler with a finger to his lips.

Dinah pricked up her ears. WikiLeaks was the organization that published classified government information from anonymous leakers and whistleblowers.

Mahler kinked his lip and gave Keyes the back of his hand. "It's your problem now. You hotshots best clamp a lid on it. It can't go any farther."

"Is your *reinsdyr* not *godt*?"

"What?"

Herr Gjertsen leaned his long, bony face into Dinah's. "Is the taste of your steak not to your liking? Lots of iron and zinc and B vitamins. It's very healthy."

"I'm not really hungry." She wasn't, but even if she were, she couldn't bring herself to eat the remains of Dasher or Dancer or Donner or Blitzen. "The time change has confused my stomach."

"*Ja, ja.* You will be hungry tomorrow night when we have seawolf. *Spesiell.* Very special and nutritious. You will like."

Dinah squeezed out a tenuous smile. What kind of God-awful creature was a seawolf?

"He means Atlantic wolffish," said Valerie. Apart from a curt "hello," it was the first time she'd spoken to Dinah. This sudden outbreak of friendliness made Dinah wonder if she'd poked Gjertsen under the table and the two of them were creating a diversion to prevent her from hearing any more clinkers from Mahler. Valerie looked to be somewhere in her late thirties, with steely blue eyes, thick but artfully groomed brows, and a sharpish nose. Her hair was several shades lighter than her brows and she wore it layered with backward facing curls, a sort of ersatz Farrah Fawcett.

Norris Frye had also noted Mahler's remark. It had distracted him momentarily from his flirtation with Ursille. Valerie smiled at Frye. "Have you ever eaten seawolf, Norris?"

"Can't say that I have."

"It's called stone biter in Iceland because of its fearsome fangs. They eat mostly crab and shellfish and they taste delicious. The chef here at the Radisson prepares them in a wonderful Thermidor sauce, isn't that right, Herr Gjertsen?"

"*Ja, ja. Fortreffelig.*"

Waiters had begun to clear away the plates and Ursille tinkled a little bell. "If you will please to follow me, *kaffe* and *krumkake* is now being served in the bar." She raised her arms like a kindergarten teacher and waited for everyone to push back from the table and stand to attention.

Senator Frye was the first one up.

Herr Gjertsen held up his hand to one of the waiters and stood up. "I must supervise. Please to excuse."

Dinah watched the exodus with interest. Colt Sheridan and Jake Mahler, their heads together like parrots, strolled out in deep conversation. Although shorter and less physically imposing than Sheridan, Mahler placed a hand on Sheridan's back in a way that implied that he was the alpha dog. Whitney Keyes trailed after them and, unless Dinah was mistaken, the look in his eyes betrayed a glitter of malice. But whether it was directed toward Mahler or Sheridan or both, she couldn't tell.

Valerie lingered over her wine. "What did you and Mrs. Sheridan talk about on the flight from D.C.?"

"Music, mostly, and her days traveling around Europe as a performer. She told me a few Norwegian superstitions." Dinah wondered if she could winkle any answers out of Valerie. "You speak Norwegian very well. Were you born here?"

"My grandparents are Norwegian and I've traveled here on behalf of Tillcorp many times. We don't have a field office in Scandinavia, but it's important to maintain our lines of communication with local officials."

"What kind of business does Tillcorp do in Norway?"

"Norwegians like to be on the cutting edge of new technologies and that's what we offer. Tillcorp is a world player in agriscience and technology."

"One Norwegian doesn't approve of the company's new technologies or its presence in the country."

"You mean that lunatic in the airport?" She scoffed. "He's a known troublemaker. The police shouldn't have let him get past."

"How is he known? Does he represent a group opposed to Tillcorp's work with gene modification?"

"I'm sure he was acting alone. Jake thinks he's the same psycho who's been stalking him from place to place all over Europe, wherever he gives a speech. He's never been violent before, or even caused a disturbance. He must've been drunk or stoned."

Dinah cut to the chase. "Does the vault allow companies like Tillcorp to study the seeds? To tamper with their DNA?"

"Only the depositing country can reclaim its seeds or give permission to another country or entity to reclaim them."

"So the U.S. could permit Tillcorp to check out its seeds?"

"In theory. But it doesn't happen." One fire-engine red fingernail ticked against the table and she leveled her steely blues on Dinah as if evaluating an adversary. "I saw you talking to that reporter Aagaard at the airport. What did he say?"

"He seems to think Senator Sheridan is here to lobby the Norwegian government to grant Tillcorp greater access to the vault."

"He doesn't know what he's talking about. Tillcorp should be applauded for its pursuit of scientific advancement and Colt Sheridan is a visionary for supporting the company's goals."

"So Tillcorp *is* pursuing greater access?"

"A smart business is always pursuing more advantageous terms." Her eyes narrowed to slits and her fingernail pecked faster. "What did you tell Aagaard about Senator Sheridan?"

"Nothing. All I know about the senator is what I've read in the newspaper."

"You should have understood that Aagaard was fishing for something damaging to print about Senator Sheridan."

"I understood. I also understood that you and the senators had run out on me and his was the only friendly face in the crowd."

Valerie blotted her lips with her napkin, leaving a red stain. "I hope you understand that you are not at liberty to hold private conversations with any member of the press unless one of the senators or myself is present to advise you."

"You're the first person who's mentioned it."

"Somebody should have. This is a diplomatic mission. There are competing interests to be balanced and sensitivities to be considered."

Dinah bristled. "I'll ask Senator Frye if my conversations are restricted."

Valerie dropped her napkin onto her plate like a dead rat. "If you're here for some purpose other than to advise Norris on questions of botany, you'd better think twice." And on that note, she strode off to the bar.

Chapter Five

Dinah sat for a while and seethed. It was obvious that Senator Frye had no further need of her expertise this evening and she had no taste for *krumkake* or further admonitions from the likes of Valerie Ives. The woman might be a good attorney, but she had a serious charm deficit and her answers to Dinah's questions had been decidedly equivocal. If the seed vault had been a bastion of the world's seed stocks until now, Tillcorp was scheming to change that and Colt Sheridan seemed willing to lend the power of his office to help them.

The wait staff removed the mirrored room dividers and left her feeling exposed. The dining room had emptied except for her and a pair of lovers who occupied a table in the back corner. They gazed adoringly into each other's eyes and fondled each other's hands. They seemed to be in a world of their own, a perfect world that needed nothing more than their mutually requited love.

Dinah shook off a twinge of nostalgia and headed back to her room. On her way through the lobby, she stopped and peered out through the glass panels of the front door. She hadn't noticed when she arrived, but rows of blue Christmas lights had been strung around the entrance. It had started to snow and, in the glow of the twinkling blue lights, it looked like a scene in a shaken snow globe. All of a sudden, she felt unaccountably sad, as if Judy Garland were warbling "Have Yourself a Merry Little Christmas" in her ear.

For pity's sake. She gave herself a mental slap. There was no sense second-guessing herself. Christmas was over and she'd done the right thing when she told Jon no. She didn't have the stick-to-it-ivity—or face it—the moral courage for marriage. And she didn't think she would have the good grace to swallow many camels.

As she came abreast of the Sheridans' door, it opened and Erika stepped out. She was dressed in the black ski pants and a thick white parka with reflective silver stripes down the sleeves. She started when she saw Dinah.

"Erika, where are you going at this hour?"

"Only for a short walk."

"Another walk? Didn't you get enough of the cold?"

"I need some fresh air."

"It'll be fresh, all right. It's snowing like mad."

"Dinah, you mustn't say that you saw me. Colt will stay up 'til all hours talking politics with Whitney and Jake and it will just vex him if he thinks I've gone out without his approval. I'll be back before he comes up to bed"

"He'd be right to be concerned for your safety, Erika. You don't know if that protester has buddies in Longyearbyen, other crazies with lasers or guns. Judging from the weaponry in the rack downstairs, guns seem to be commonplace. And don't forget the polar bears. I saw a warning sign with a picture of a bear on the way into town from the airport."

"Longyearbyen is one of the safest places in the world. There's no crime here and bears rarely stray into town."

"You should at least let the Secret Service guys know you're out of the fold."

"I'm not a sheep and they're not Secret Service. They're Jake Mahler's hired bodyguards. This is Norway, not Afghanistan or Iraq. Colt won't get Secret Service protection until and unless he becomes the nominee."

Dinah felt duped. The men looked like government agents with their dour expressions and their earbuds. They acted as if they were vested with the full authority of the U.S. government.

And one of the imposters still had her passport. "Why does Jake Mahler need bodyguards? Were they expecting to be greeted by anti-Tillcorp demonstrators?"

"I don't know what Jake was expecting. But he has no right to spy on me and neither does..." She dropped her eyes and adjusted the fingers of her gloves. "If you like, I'll tap on your door when I get back. But please, you didn't see me, okay?" She pulled a black balaclava out of her pocket, slipped it over her head and face so that only her eyes showed, and pulled up the parka's fur-lined hood. "I'm a mirage. Like Fata Morgana."

If neither the cold nor the bears discouraged her, there was nothing Dinah could do but watch her flee down the hall and disappear into the stairwell. Strange creature, Erika Sheridan. Had she lied about having no friends in Norway? Maybe she was off to a secret tryst with one of her old band mates. Between card games, she'd sent a number of text messages. Well, so what if she was off on a frolic? It was her country, her prerogative, and her husband was preoccupied with other matters. Dinah wondered if politics and carrying water for Tillcorp were his only interests. A woman named Hannalore had figured in a lamp-smashing marital fracas. Was she his mistress? A one-night stand? Or as Sheridan seemed to contend, a phantom of Erika's imagination? Whatever. It was pointless to make assumptions about a marriage that had lasted as long as the Sheridans'. She just hoped that Erika returned before she was missed. Charming as she was, Dinah didn't fancy having to cover for her.

Back in her room, Dinah chained her door and kicked off the clogs. The room was finally toasty and she tossed her sweater on the bed.

Something thudded. Like the thud of a plastic bottle dropped on a tile floor. Like the thud of a plastic bottle dropped on *her* bathroom floor.

Jerusalem's bells. What fresh grief was this? She hotfooted it to the door and unhooked the chain. She'd learned from the Sheridans that screaming and breaking things roused no help.

Hand on the knob, she eased it open and stepped into the hall, ready to run for her life.

The bathroom door opened. "Ms. Pelerin. Wait. I'm a policeman."

Unable to resist, she glanced back. He was tall and spare with thick brown hair clipped short, prominent cheekbones, tawny skin, and wide-set brown eyes. He could have been an Apache.

"Sorry if I frightened you." He flipped open a wallet and displayed an official looking ID with a photo. "I shouldn't have entered until you were present, but I didn't know when that would be and I'm pressed for time."

She took another step backward. "You were in a hurry to search my room?"

"I'm searching the rooms of everyone who was present at the airport today. I just came from the Sheridans' room."

"Show me a search warrant. In English."

"I don't need a warrant. There was an attack on a Norwegian government official and the officer who interviewed you at the airport thought you might be in Norway under false pretenses."

"What?"

"Will you please come back inside and answer my questions?"

Furious, she swept back into the room. "Let me see that ID again."

He held it out to her. The photo matched. She was apparently dealing with Detective Inspektor Thor Ramberg.

He put the ID back in his inside jacket pocket and took out an American passport. Hers. "Your passport indicates that you've traveled recently in the Philippines."

"What of it? I'm an American citizen. And while it's none of your business, I was in the Philippines two years ago with an anthropological expedition, studying the customs of the indigenous tribes on Mindanao. All of whom are more polite and considerate than the Norwegians I've met so far, by the way. Now give me back my passport."

He handed it her back to her without a glimmer of apology. "I assure you, this is a routine inquiry, Ms. Pelerin. I will be questioning both diplomats and non-diplomats who arrived with you. Are you an employee of Tillcorp?"

"No. I'm in your country at the behest of Senator Frye."

"Do you work for Senator Frye?"

"No. I work for the University of Hawaii. I'm here as Senator Frye's temporary assistant." She felt a spurt of generalized resentment. "And the only compensation I get for freezing my buns off is a round trip ticket, a coat and boots that feel like they're made out of paper, and two nights lodging in a hotel where apparently anyone can waltz into my room whenever they please. Just what is it you're looking for?"

"A laser pointer."

"Like the one that protester shot at Herr Dybdahl?"

"The same one. It wasn't on Herr Eftevang when we searched him, nor has it been found at the airport. Either he passed it to an accomplice or someone picked it up and walked off with it in the confusion."

"Well, I didn't swipe it. I haven't the foggiest who this Herr Efte...what?"

"Eftevang. Fritjoe Eftevang."

"I've never heard of him and I haven't a clue what he did with the laser."

"He claims he didn't do anything with it. He claims it was someone else in the crowd who fired the beam. Think back. What did you see?"

Dinah sank into the armchair and tried to recall. What was it that Aagaard had called the protester? *Angriper.* It must mean somebody with a gripe, an aggressor or assailant. Whatever. The *angriper* had made so much fuss that, like everyone else, she'd assumed he was the source of the beam. But it could have come from the man who shouted "he has a gun." The people around him would either have ducked or turned to look at the protester, perhaps giving him time to whip out the laser, fire at the minister, and pocket it again before anyone saw. "It all happened in an instant, or seemed to. A man shouted 'gun,' the guards tackled the protester, I saw a spot of red light flash in the window behind the stage. It bounced around willy-nilly until it landed on the minister's face." She spread her hands, palms up, like what do *you* think?

His face was impassive. "Did you look back to see where the light was coming from?"

"I tried, but I couldn't tell. Senator Frye was looking back at the protester and he blocked my view. I suppose if he didn't see the laser, and the people on the stage didn't see it, then it must have come from the side. I didn't realize what it was until Herr Dybdahl cried out and collapsed."

"Did you observe Brander Aagaard's reaction at any time? Did he give any indication that he anticipated the attack?"

She stared in surprise. "No. I mean, I can't say. Do you think he knew...?"

"I'm investigating every possibility. Longyearbyen has attracted a group of *forførers*..."

"What?"

"People who think they can mock the police. They will find themselves much mistaken."

She wasn't sure if he lumped her in with the *forførers* or not, but his arrogance irked her. What kind of investigative experience could the guy have acquired way up here in the boondocks where polar bears outnumbered people? And what's more, she didn't believe for one second that he had the right to enter anyone's room without a warrant. If he tried prowling through the senators' rooms, they'd raise holy hell. This was probably the crime of the century in Longyearbyen and Thor Ramberg was looking to make a name for himself and maybe get promoted to a more temperate, cosmopolitan *byen* down south. She said, "Your investigation can't benefit from anything I have to say. If you suspect Herr Aagaard, I suggest you question him directly."

"I have and will again. During your flight from the States, did you observe anyone in possession of a laser?"

"Of course not."

"Did you see or hear anyone on the plane contact another person here in Norge, in Norway?"

"Not to my knowledge." Erika had texted somebody, but Dinah didn't know whether the somebody was in Norway or the U.S. or right there on the airplane with them. She definitely hadn't fired the laser.

"From where you were sitting in the airport lounge, could you see either of Mr. Mahler's bodyguards?"

"No. And aren't you going a bit overboard with your investigation? That laser may be more powerful than's legal, but it's probably no bigger than a ballpoint pen. The protester could've dropped it into a furnace grate or a waste bin before the police got ahold of him. Why do you believe his story? He was angry, ranting. He thinks Tillcorp wants to destroy God's creations. Valerie Ives says he's been stalking Jake Mahler."

Ramberg's eyes glinted. "The laser wasn't fired at Jake Mahler."

"Do you think Senator Sheridan was the target?"

"No. I think the beam reached its intended target. And I believe Mr. Eftevang when he says he didn't shoot it. He seemed to me an idealistic sort of man."

"But what conceivable reason would anyone else have to assault a member of the Norwegian government? Mr. Mahler and the senators could have no earthly reason. They're here to curry favor with the Norwegians."

"If you are unfamiliar with the animosity between Mr. Mahler and Herr Dybdahl, I suggest that you question Mr. Mahler directly."

So she had irritated him. Good. He was a blister of the first order. "It seems obvious that Herr Eftevang was the culprit. He's probably part of some radical green movement and his anger was stoked by Internet rumors about the Norwegian government facilitating access to corporate breeders or some such. I'm sure if you start over again and grill him more thoroughly, you'll get a confession."

"I have no witnesses and no evidence and Eftevang had the right to speak his opinion freely. It was an open forum and likening Americans to the Romans cannot be deemed as hate speech. I was forced to release him."

"How irksome that must be for you. But seeing as how you've found no evidence in my room, I'd appreciate it if you'd take your Gestapo tactics someplace else."

He gave her a sardonic look. "Norway was invaded and occupied by the Germans in nineteen-forty. We know something about the Gestapo. You may find me lacking in delicacy, but do not compare my tactics to the Gestapo."

He started for the door and she got up and followed him.

His hand was on the knob, but he turned back to her with a frosty half-smile. "You'll be here longer than two nights."

"And why is that? Do you intend to arrest me?"

"Blizzard's blowing in. No planes in or out until it clears."

She shut the door behind him with a bang, rechained it, and boosted the thermostat as high as it would go. Thor Ramberg gave off more chill than an iceberg.

Chapter Six

What kind of a name was Thor anyway? Had his parents christened him with the name of the Norse god of thunder or had he, in his overweening arrogance, adopted the moniker? She undressed, nestled under the duvet with her book of Norse myths, and scanned the index for references to Thor.

Thor, it seemed, was the greatest of the Norse gods, the most revered and the most beloved. His father, Odin, had created the earth, which would give anyone a big head. But Thor was different. Whereas Odin championed warriors and the nobility, Thor stood up for the little people, the farmers and peasants. Odin strutted about with a raven on each shoulder and amused himself by inciting wars and deciding on a whim who should win them and who should lose. By contrast, Thor liked law and order and stability. Thor came across as a reasonable sort of god. Dinah wasn't so sure about the reasonableness of his namesake. She thought about him snooping around her room. Had he pawed through her suitcase, too? He must have.

There was a knock on the door. "*Hallo.* Service for the turndown, *behage.*"

"No need," called Dinah.

"And extra towels and tomato juice, as you requested."

Dinah dog-eared the page about Thor and let the maid in. Blond, blue-eyed, and petite, she could have doubled for Reese Witherspoon. While she changed the towels and restocked the mini-bar, Dinah reflected on an article she'd read somewhere about eye color. Apparently, ten thousand years ago, everybody had brown eyes and blue eyes were the result of a mutant gene. She wondered how Thor Ramberg had dodged this mutant gene that seemed to have colonized most of Norway. He must have mixed ancestry.

"Will there be anything else?" Reese asked.

"Nothing you can help me with. Thank you."

When she had gone, Dinah refastened the door chain and went back to reading about the original Thor.

His wife Sif was another blonde. One night while her husband was off making thunder and she was sleeping, the mischievous trickster Loki sneaked into her bedroom and lopped off her shining tresses. The lady woke up to a very bad hair day. She was distraught and Thor was royally pissed. He would have murdered Loki, but Loki promised to replace every golden strand. And he did. He conned a pair of dwarf goldsmiths into spinning Sif a brand new head of hair so fine that the slightest puff of air would ruffle it. While their bellows was hot, the dwarfs forged other marvelous gifts for the gods—a magic spear for Odin, a magic boat for Frey. Somewhere during the description of Thor's magic hammer, Dinah dropped off to sleep.

"Where the hell have you been?"

Once again, the sound of raised voices coming from the room next door awakened her. Overheated and thirsty, she hauled herself out of bed, turned down the thermostat, and went to the bathroom for a glass of water. Evidently, Erika hadn't made it home before Colt and he was giving her what for. Had she not warned him that the walls had ears or didn't she care?

What time was it anyway? Dinah picked her watch off the counter and was astounded. Six a.m. Had Erika stayed out all night or were they resuming a quarrel they'd begun earlier in the evening? If so, Dinah had slept through it. She walked back into the bedroom and opened the drapes. It was pitch black and in the winking blue lights, snow whirled past her window in a maelstrom. Good God, how did people cope with this climate when they didn't see a sunrise for months on end?

"Don't lie to me, Erika. Did you meet him? Did you tip him off about Jake?"

Dinah stretched and put on a pot of coffee to brew. The Sheridans' marriage was fraught with drama. How much of it derived from personal issues and how much from politics she could only guess. But from what Dinah had seen and heard so far, the former songbird of Fata Morgana led her husband a merry chase. She would make a remarkable First Lady.

Starving, Dinah reviewed the directory of hotel services and amenities. "*Frokost*" was served from six-thirty until ten-thirty. She dressed in the first few layers she intended to wear on the tour of the seed vault and sat down to drink her coffee and wait until the restaurant opened. If the weather didn't improve, maybe the tour would be postponed.

The Sheridans were holding it down this morning or maybe they'd kissed and made up. It was impossible not to speculate about the cause of their conflict. She inferred that the "him" Erika had tipped off was Brander Aagaard. Who else could he have had in mind? Aagaard's question about Jake Mahler had definitely thrown him off balance. But how would a Montana senator's wife know a *Dagbladet* muckraker and why would she feed him information that would embarrass her husband? One thing was certain: whoever tipped off whom, Iceberg Ramberg considered everyone who was in the airport lounge yesterday a suspect in the assault on Herr Dybdahl.

At six-thirty on the dot, she tucked her passport in her purse for safekeeping and sallied out the door to breakfast, riding her clogs with growing proficiency. As she entered the dining room, she saw Senator Keyes and Jake Mahler already seated at the table where the lovers had sat last night. Engaged in what appeared to be a troubling conversation, they didn't look up. Before sitting down, she scoped out the buffet table. It was laden with smoked fish, pickled herring, boiled eggs, cheese, and bread. There were also individual boxes of muesli and a pitcher of milk. She'd hoped for a few slices of fruit, but after all, it was December at the North Pole. She would have to make do.

The long table set up for last night's fete had been dismantled and she took a small, out-of-the-way table and sat facing the entrance with her back to Keyes and Mahler. If Senator Sheridan came down and joined his two friends, perhaps Erika would sit with Dinah and dish. A winsome young woman with blue eyes, deep dimples, and a lilting accent asked if she would prefer *kaffe* or *te*.

"*Kaffe*, please."

She poured a cup and gestured toward the buffet. "*Frokost.* What you say in English, breakfast. Please help yourself at the *koldtbord*."

"Thank you." Suddenly, Dinah felt guilty that she hadn't bothered to learn the words for please and thank you. "How do you say thank you in Norwegian?"

"*Takk.*"

"*Takk.* And thank you very much?"

"*Tusen takk.*"

Dinah read her nametag. "*Tusen takk, Greta.*"

The girl smiled and breezed off to the next table.

Dinah sipped her coffee and thought about what she would do to entertain herself today if the Svalbard tour had to be nixed due to the blizzard. Bitterly cold as it was, she supposed she ought to take at least one short walk through the town just to say she'd done it. She'd never be in this neighborhood again, that much was sure. She returned to the *koldtbord* and loaded her plate with enough protein to insulate her against the elements and was on her way back to her table when the Sheridans rolled in, smiling and holding hands like newlyweds. Or actors in a play.

Erika acknowledged Dinah with a suggestion of a smile, but walked past her without a word. Colt led her straight to the Keyes-Mahler table. The men stood up and there was a chorus of commentary about the blizzard before they all sat down. Erika expressed disappointment that the weather prevented them from seeing the aurora borealis.

Dinah sat down and devoted herself to her *frokost*. She chalked up Erika's aloofness to the fact that she'd revealed too much about her husband and his entourage for comfort.

Valerie Ives, Norris Frye, and the two non-Secret Service bozos trooped into the dining room next, talking a blue streak. They filed past Dinah and seated themselves at a table adjacent to the Sheridans. An animated buzz of conversation ensued. Dinah listened for a mention of Thor Ramberg and his invasive and possibly illegal search, but the only words she picked up were "change of plans" and "delayed departure."

Dinah finished her muesli and was about to slink away unseen when Tipton Teilhard III appeared in the doorway looking like a little lost boy. He had wet down his hair, but the cowlick on top of his head remained stubbornly perpendicular and his Brooks Brothers suit looked ridiculous when everyone else was decked out in ski outfits. He chewed his lower lip and hesitated, as if debating whether it would be okay to interrupt the grown-ups. Dinah flashed him a big smile and motioned him to her table.

"Oh, hi." He looked stressed. "Everything's a total shambles. Senator Sheridan is supposed to be in Iowa the day after tomorrow to get ready for the caucus and now our whole agenda is up in smoke."

"It's not your fault if the weather won't cooperate, Tipton. The blizzard probably won't last long. The tour of the seed vault can be put off until tomorrow and the senator will make it to Iowa with time to spare. Sit down, why don't you? Have something to eat."

Tipton drooped into the chair across from Dinah. "I've left a dozen messages for our campaign chairman back in D.C, but he's not answering. Whitney will be livid, not that he'd ever let anyone see. Oh…my…God. His strategy was brilliant. Sheridan's speech to the Club for Growth last week positioned him squarely between the wingnuts crying foul about overregulation of business and the wingnuts whining for a business czar to implement still more burdensome rules. The trip to Longyearbyen was the frosting on the cake for Colt, the perfect setting to highlight his pro-industry, pro-conservation, pro-science and technology views. And then that Norwegian crackpot showed up. My mother won't believe it."

The pretty girl with the coffee traipsed by and Dinah held out an empty cup for Tipton. The girl poured him a cup and refilled Dinah's.

"*Tusen takk.*"

"You are welcome." She smiled and sailed on to the next table.

Tipton tried to finger-comb the cowlick into place, but succeeded only in making it worse. "I don't drink coffee."

Dinah was about to ask him if he would rather have a glass of milk when he pulled a bottle of Pepto-Bismol out of his jacket pocket and poured himself a capful.

She said, "You're overly concerned. The senators all seem to be in good spirits this morning in spite of the ruckus. Frankly, I'd have thought they'd be outraged that the police barged in here last night and questioned them and their Tillcorp friends. At the very least, I'd have expected Ms. Ives to insist on seeing a warrant before their rooms were searched." She backed up. "Were their rooms searched?"

"Oh, yes. Whitney was adamant that we put our best foot forward. He doesn't like to make waves." Tipton chugged the Pepto and shuddered. "Now it's the mother of all waves."

"What do you mean?"

"I can't think how to tell him."

"For pity's sake, tell him what?"

"That stupid policeman released the protester. Into the streets, for Christ's sake." He closed his eyes and shimmied.

"Jerusalem. What did he do? Did he attack the agriculture minister again?"

"Murdered."

"Herr Dybdahl is dead?"

"No. The protester. Somebody found his body in an alley this morning. Behind some sleazy pub, stabbed in the chest. Oh, Christ, it's a publicity nightmare. There's no way to spin this without the words Tillcorp and genetic engineering cropping up next to Colt's."

Chapter Seven

"Murdered?" Erika made an ugly, strangling noise and covered her mouth with both hands. Her eyes were riveted on her husband's face.

Sheridan glared back at her with what Dinah read as bafflement and fury. Fury, anyway. "A homicide. I must be jinxed. What next?"

Val reached out and waggled Sheridan's arm reassuringly. "It'll be all right, Colt. We'll handle it." The look in *her* eyes portended more rough waters for the Sheridans' marriage. The manicured hand on the senator's sleeve was a blatant assertion of ownership.

Dinah tried to read Erika's reaction, but almost immediately she lowered her head and her hair covered her face like a veil.

Senator Keyes' élan had deserted him and he seemed vacant, unable to comprehend. "How could he have been murdered? What did the police say? Was he involved in a fight? Tipton?"

"They wouldn't tell me, sir. The man I spoke with said that Inspector Ramberg would be coming to the hotel later this morning to interview everyone."

"Not everyone," said Valerie. "You won't have to submit to questioning, Colt. There are protocols about questioning diplomats."

"If I may?" Tipton emitted a diffident cough. "Colt Sheridan is perceived as a straight shooter. Not to be, oh, you know, up front would seem…"

Keyes shook off his bewilderment. "Good thinking, Tip. This isn't Russia or France. Norway's got no negatives back home. Not to cooperate with the local authorities investigating a murder wouldn't play well in the media."

"I agree," said Sheridan. He, too, had regained a semblance of calm and self-control. "You're not well, Erika. Going to pieces over the death of a stranger. I shouldn't have let you come with me on such a tiring trip. You need to go and lie down."

Mahler hadn't budged from the breakfast table or shown so much as a flicker of emotion. He held a rye cracker between his front teeth and his cell phone against his ear, on hold for somebody named Tom. He took the cracker out of his mouth and signaled to one of the bodyguards. "Lee, see Mrs. S to her room, make sure she's comfortable, and stay with her until you hear otherwise. Rod, you go up and fetch Senator Sheraton's briefcase. He's probably got the names and numbers for all the spin doctors he'll have to contact."

Dinah caught Erika's eye as she passed by. She'd gone blank, passive. Off to the Tower, thought Dinah. By royal command.

Spurred to action, Keyes dispatched Tipton to reserve a meeting room and bring him his laptop. "And Tip, make sure Colt's press secretary in D.C is up to speed. See if Dybdahl's people have any background on this Fritjoe Ef...what was it?"

"Fritjoe Eftevang," said Tipton. "I'll do a computer search." And he was up and away like a retriever after a Frisbee.

"That kid is gung-ho," cracked Mahler. "What do you do, put uppers in his Ovaltine?"

"He's the best assistant I've ever had," said Keyes. "He has a habit of taking everything I say as crucial to the health and welfare of the republic. And he's a computer whiz."

Valerie seemed to take this as a personal slight. "I was the best assistant you ever had. You like that little kiss-up because he's constantly telling you what a genius you are and stroking your ego."

"We all know that you'd never cater to a man's ego," twitted Mahler, looking pointedly at Sheridan.

She blushed bright red.

If Sheridan picked up on the allusion or the blush, he pretended not to. He sawed a finger across his chin and paced.

"Eftevang. I've heard that name somewhere before. What was he? Who'd he work for?"

"He was a recurring pain in the ass," said Mahler. "One of those kooks who thinks everything's a secret plot against humanity. He showed up whenever and wherever I did, beating his breast about the intrinsic value of natural organisms and the risk of creating human allergens. One of those people who can't see the forest for the trees."

Sheridan smacked a fist into his hand. "That prick Aagaard. He's probably salivating over this. *Sheridan Protester Knifed in Alley*. He'll slime us and it'll spread from Oslo to every other news outlet."

"To be accurate," said Keyes, "he was protesting against Tillcorp."

Mahler sneered. "By all means, keep it accurate, senator." He pointed a cracker at Valerie. "Find out which news outlets are covering our visit and put out a feeler to the friendlies. If anybody's slimed, let's make sure it's Eftevang. Can you handle that, Val?"

"You know very well she can handle it," said Keyes, as if to atone for his previous slight. "She'll craft the story. By the time it crosses the Atlantic, if Colt's name appears at all, it'll be a passing mention in the last paragraph."

"Let's hope she can keep the company that pays her salary and funds Colt's campaign out of the story, too," said Mahler. He laughed. "If she needs help, I'm sure Tipton will be happy to pitch in."

Valerie ignored him. "Are you okay, Colt?"

"What? Yes, sure."

She seemed to waver, as if she didn't trust Mahler and Keyes to take care of him while she was gone. "Don't worry, Colt. We're a long way from Iowa. We'll be fine." She gave his arm a consoling little shake and left.

Senator Frye's eyes followed the back-and-forth as if he were watching a tennis match. "I don't get it. Why the fire drill? What does this nutty Norwegian's murder have to do with us?"

Sheridan rounded on Norris. He seemed taken aback, as if he'd forgotten the Democrat was there. "It's got nothing to do with *you*, Norris. You're not sticking your neck out to run for the highest office in the land. Your life's not under a microscope and every word you've ever uttered twisted and blown out of proportion. You're not forced to defend yourself against false insinuations by cheap-shot reporters and Democrat lies. Admit it. The only reason you're here is to keep an eye on me and report on any mistakes that your man Obama can use against me."

Frye's chin jutted and his chest swelled. "I'm here for the reasons you stated in the press conference. International cooperation and protecting the world's food supply."

"In a pig's eye, you are."

"Easy, Colt." Senator Keyes laid a hand on Sheridan's arm. "Norris isn't your enemy."

Mahler snapped his fingers for quiet and growled into his cell phone. "That you, Tom? Well, get him. Tell him we took some verbal abuse from a conspiracy nut at the press conference yesterday and now he's dead. We need to get out in front of the story, control the message." He looked up, saw Dinah staring at him, snapped his fingers again, and pointed.

Senator Keyes responded with the alacrity of a bouncer. "Dinah, Norris. Forgive our rudeness, but you can see that we have a public relations problem here. Senator Sheridan has a lot at stake. You know how twisted stories can get, especially when they involve a major corporation and a presidential candidate. Would you two mind leaving us to deal with it in private?"

Norris sniffed. "Your candidate is being paranoid, Whitney. If this is how he reacts to every crime that happens in a town where he shows up for a photo op, pretty soon people will start to believe he's a serial killer."

"I'm sorry you feel that way, Norris. Colt and I hold you in high esteem as both a colleague and a friend."

"Now who's lying?" Norris spun around, snagged Dinah's arm, and hobbled out of the restaurant with her in tow. When they reached the lobby, he dropped her arm and flopped into one of the leather chairs in front of the fireplace. "Well, well, well. That was interesting. What do you make of Sheridan's behavior?"

"He seems exceedingly perturbed. They all do."

"If you ask me, Colt and Whitney know something they're not telling. Did you see the way they looked at Mahler? They're spooked. This Eftevang had been badgering Mahler for a long time. I wouldn't put it past that man to order a hit on anyone who interfered with his boy's procession to the White House." Norris chuckled, then grimaced and pulled a bottle of Aleve out of his pocket. "Damn big toe is killing me. I'm going to rest here for a few minutes and then go back to my room. Maybe I'll give the hotel sauna a try. If they reschedule the tour of the seed vault, I want you to go in my place. You can give me a full report."

Dinah didn't doubt that he was in pain, but she suspected that the lovely Ursille and a bottle of Viagra might also figure in his afternoon plans. She would like to believe that her senator wasn't so petty or spiteful that he would resort to partisan smears in connection with a murder. But he was already reaching for his cell phone. Maybe Sheridan's paranoia was justified, after all.

She said, "I'm going to go out for an hour or so."

"In this blizzard?"

"The outside weather can't be any more blustery than the inside weather."

"Suit yourself. What's your phone number?"

"My cell isn't a global phone. It doesn't work in Europe. I'll check at the front desk for messages when I get back."

She crossed the lobby and started up the stairs. Politics wafted over everything like a bad smell. Norris' gibe about Mahler ordering a hit was unfounded and totally off-the-wall, not to mention mean-spirited in the extreme. And it didn't enhance Sheridan's or Keyes' stature in her eyes to hear that a man's death meant no more to them than a public relations problem.

On her way up, she met Rod carrying Sheridan's briefcase on the way down. She didn't fault herself for having mistaken Rod and Lee for Secret Service agents. They fit the stereotype to a T. Medium height, medium build, medium coloring, no distinguishing physical traits, and a Doberman-like alertness. On the flight from D.C., they'd kept to themselves, reading magazines and taking turns catnapping. She studied Rod more closely as he passed. Norris had planted a seed of doubt in her mind. She couldn't help but wonder if Mahler's bodyguards doubled as hit men.

The memory of Erika's stricken face stirred more doubts. She'd been out last night. Had she witnessed the murder? No. She wouldn't have sauntered into the restaurant all smiley-faced and fresh after seeing someone stabbed to death. But maybe she'd met with Eftevang before the murder. Could that be why Colt was so wrapped around the axel? Holy moly! Maybe it wasn't Brander Aagaard he'd accused her of meeting, but Fritjoe Eftevang. But how would Erika know him and, if she did, why in the world would she meet with him? Dinah's thoughts brimmed over with questions and whatever was eating Erika, she needed somebody to sympathize.

She hesitated outside Erika's door. Well, nothing ventured…

The other guard, Lee, answered her knock. He was a couple of inches taller than Rod, but they could have been brothers. Same thin mouth, same thin nose, same thin hair.

"I'd like to talk with Erika, please."

"Mrs. Sheridan doesn't wish to be disturbed."

"Is she ill?"

"She's resting."

"I won't stay long."

"Look, she doesn't want to be disturbed, okay?"

The door was closing when Erika peeped around his shoulder. "What is it, Dinah? Did you bring a message from Colt?"

"No, Erika." Did she expect that he would send a gofer to apologize for him? "You looked so shaken when you left the restaurant. I thought I'd come and sit with you for a while."

"I guess it would be all right."

Lee folded his arms across his chest and widened his stance. "Senator Sheridan said you should rest."

Erika skimmed a sideways look at his face. "Colt's right, of course. I have to take care of myself or I'll get a migraine."

Dinah didn't believe her. "Exercise is always good for what ails you. I'm going for a walk. Come with me."

"In a blizzard?"

"It'll be invigorating. Like you said, too much warmth isn't healthy."

"That's not exactly what I…Wait!" Erika's eyes brightened. "I want you to take my parka. You'll freeze to death in that pea jacket you brought." She went back inside the room.

Lee stood in the doorway with his arms across his chest. His eyes were as hard and unreflective as slate.

"Must be a full-time job protecting Mr. Mahler," said Dinah. No comeback.

"You must have had previous encounters with Mr. Eftevang. Valerie says he's been a real nuisance."

A muscle in his jaw twitched.

Dinah frowned. The hit man hypothesis began to seem less far-fetched.

"Here you are." Erika reached past him and handed her the coat. "The hood is lined with mouton and the body's down-filled. It will keep you warm."

"Thanks, Erika. I'll return it this afternoon."

"No hurry," said Lee, and closed the door in her face.

Dinah retreated to her room. Outside her window, the blizzard Ramberg had forecast was swirling in the blue lights. Her thoughts swirled as furiously as the snow. What was going on next door? Was Erika being held incommunicado by her husband or was she cutting off communication of her own volition? Dinah slumped into the chair and propped her feet on the window sill.

Why had Eftevang's murder rattled the Sheridans? A raft of possible explanations scudded through her head. Maybe Eftevang knew an embarrassing secret about the senator or Erika and had threatened to expose it. Or maybe he knew something damaging about Tillcorp and Sheridan's dealings with the company and was on the verge of passing whatever it was to

WikiLeaks. What had Mahler said? *Clamp a lid on it. It can't go any farther.* What had he meant by that? During the press conference, he and Valerie had been seated near the back of the audience. Dinah wished she'd seen their faces when Eftevang charged the podium yelling, "They've brought the death gene."

She sat up and took another look at the outside world. The snow was coming down so fast and so thick that it covered some of the lights. The heat put out by the little blue bulbs couldn't melt it fast enough. It was hard to think of a storm of this magnitude as an aggregation of separate, unique snowflakes, but that's what it was. Perhaps that was the story with the human storm roiling around her. It was an aggregation of unrelated problems that just happened to converge in the same place at the same time.

With no one to talk to and nothing to do, she was in limbo. She supposed she should call Eleanor with an update, but all she could think about was Eftevang's murder and Erika's predicament and she had no idea if these matters had anything whatever to do with the seed vault. She decided to wait and call Eleanor after the tour of the vault, if it ever took place. In the meanwhile, she had told Norris that she was going out and, if she was going to enjoy a taste of this bracing climate, now was the time. She dressed and took her excess of curiosity and nervous energy downstairs.

Encased in so many layers she could barely bend, she fitted the chemical toe warmers she'd bought at a sporting goods store in D.C. into her boots, bundled herself into Erika's parka, pulled the balaclava over her face, pulled up the fur hood, and set out to explore the mean streets of Longyearbyen. Her primary destination was the public library where she hoped she would find a computer. She didn't want to risk being caught trolling for information about the Sheridans or Jake Mahler on the Radisson's computer.

The first breath she drew outside the shelter of the Radisson seared her lungs and the welter of flying snow stung her eyes. She buried her nose in her collar and squinted down the street to her left. The town was lit up as if it were night, which of course it was, even if it was morning. She made binoculars out of her hands to little effect. Through the blur of white, she made out a jumble of yellow and blue and red and green squares, like pixels on a fuzzy screen. More from inference than from vision, she decided that the colors were houses. Boxy houses with peaked roofs arrayed on a hillside overlooking the main street. There were also colored rectangles that looked like railroad flatcars, probably apartments for the coal miners or the scientists and researchers who cruised in and out of town conducting various studies. A red steeple seemed to float atop the torrents of white, an ethereal reminder that the world's northernmost settlement had not slipped the boundaries of Christendom.

A snowmobile sped past her, throwing up a cascade of snow in its wake. Leaning into the wind, she trudged after it. Every few steps, she stopped to brush the snow out of her eyes and get her bearings. There were plenty of lighted signs and store-front displays. The denizens of Longyearbyen did not want for goods or services. It hadn't occurred to her that there would be so many shops and businesses. There was a sports outfitter, a pizza parlor, a pharmacy, a bank, a combination supermarket and department store, more hotels, even an art gallery. If there was a library, she could avail herself of a computer and answer a few of the questions that nagged her. There might be news articles or blogs about the friction between Tillcorp's CEO and the agriculture minister and the American media was sure to have dug into Colt Sheridan's relationship with the company. She might even find something about Eftevang if he was as big a troublemaker as Valerie said.

Erika's gasp of horror and dismay puzzled Dinah most of all. Had she seen something when she went roaming last night? Dinah wished she'd asked the man on duty at the Radisson's front desk for the name and location of the pub where the murder had taken place. He probably knew all about it. In a town this size, it wouldn't take long for news of a murder to spread.

She struggled against the headwind for another few blocks without seeing any evidence of the crime scene—no police tape, no sign, no barriers. And if there was a library, it was lost in the snow. Her eyeballs felt as if they were turning into gelato. Somewhere at the end of the street was the wharf and beyond that stretched the icy waters of Adventifjorden, or Advent Bay. The fact sheet posted on the Radisson notice board warned guests not to venture beyond the wharf unarmed because polar bears do not hibernate like their brown and black cousins. They range along the shores of the bay all winter, hunting tirelessly for seals. Or, if the opportunity arose, negligent tourists. A group of young campers had been mauled near Longyearbyen only a few months ago.

It was impossible to gauge distances in this blizzard. The streetlights didn't help. Everything looked surreal. On the next corner, she discerned the words KAFFE & KANTINE in coruscating red neon and decided it was time to defrost and ask directions. She put her head down and waded through the snow toward the sign. By the time she reached the door, her nose felt brittle as a China cup. She pushed inside, blinked away the snow, and prayed that the establishment didn't require that she take off her boots. She shrugged out of Erika's parka, pulled off her balaclava, and shook her hair loose.

"Is that you, Dinah Pelerin?"

She looked around the dingy, dusky little café and saw Brander Aagaard slouched over a table near the back. His face was wreathed in cigarette smoke and he squinched his eyes as if he were drunk or nearsighted. "Come and sit down. What is it you Americans say? We can scratch each other's backs, yes?"

She stuffed her gloves and ski mask in the pockets of the parka and hung it on a peg beside the door. "Hello, Herr Aagaard."

"We Norwegians are the rustic strain of Scandinavians. We don't stand on ceremony. I am Brander. Shall I call you Dinah?"

"How do you know my name?"

"It's my business to know things. Would you like a cup of coffee?"

"Yes, please."

He held up his hand to a man behind the counter. "Two more coffees, Lars. And another bottle of Akevitt."

"Right. Okay. *Et øyeblikk.*"

Dinah edged her way between the tables, pulled out a chair, and sat down. "Have you heard about the murder of the protester? Are you investigating?"

"Is the Pope Prussian?"

She took that for a yes. "Where did it happen? Do the police know who did it? Have they made an arrest?"

"In the alley behind the Beached Whale, directly across the street. No one claims to have seen who did it and no, there has been no arrest."

Aagaard plucked a pen from his rat's nest of hair and opened his notebook. "Did the news of the murder disconcert your American senators?"

If an admission of something that obvious counted as back scratching, she would scratch. "Yes, of course they were disconcerted."

"What did Sheridan say?"

"He was afraid…he thinks you'll use the situation to slime him."

Aagaard put down his pen and rumpled his hair with both hands. When he looked up, his grin was diabolical. "You'll have to do better than that if you want me to tell you about the thief of their peace."

Chapter Eight

"It takes a warped sense of humor to hang a name like Fritjoe on an innocent child," said Aagaard, pouring a tot of Akevitt into his morning cuppa. "It means thief of peace and he has fulfilled his prophecy admirably."

Dinah calculated how much grief she might bring on herself if she talked to this bird. Valerie's admonition not to talk to him was practically an inducement to do just the opposite and, whether from a lack of patriotism or personal dislike, she didn't feel any loyalty to either Senator Sheridan or Tillcorp. Aagaard probably had multiple sources. Nothing she said would necessarily be attributable to her. Even so, she hedged. "You go first. Who was this thief of peace?"

"Fritjoe Eftevang was a stringer for a Swedish alternative newspaper and an all-around gadfly."

"He was your competitor then."

"Not on the same level. I write for a major Oslo daily. But he and I occasionally vied for scoops."

"You both seemed to have learned that Senator Sheridan would be bringing the Tillcorp CEO on his visit to Svalbard. How did you find out?"

"Jake Mahler's not known here in Norge, but he gives speeches all across the continent. I recognized him when he came off the plane."

"And you wanted to make Colt Sheridan squirm."

"I want to make everyone squirm. Squirming liars make good copy. I would have gone after Sheridan if he'd brought another campaign contributor with a scheme to sell. I'd have gone after him if he'd brought his mistress. Happen to know if he has one?"

She tried to remain expressionless. "No."

He laughed and drizzled more Akevitt into his cup. "Too much to hope that he'd bring her on the same trip with his wife. Anyhow, Fritjoe was more single-minded. Lots of companies genetically modify seeds and patent them, but for whatever reason, he was fixated on Tillcorp. 'They've taken out a patent on hunger,' he said. Fritjoe could wind himself up to a very emotional state."

Dinah pictured his look of feverish excitement as he lunged through the crowd. Were there others who shared his passionate intensity? She said, "Environmentalists in the U.S. worry that modified seeds can blow astray and cross-pollinate with neighboring crops. And they're concerned about the overuse of herbicides, which makes weeds more resistant and the herbicides have to be made more and more toxic to control them. Does Europe have a problem with superweeds or cross-pollination? Is that what he meant by 'a patent on hunger?'"

"Most controversial herbicides and pesticides are banned in the E.U. and in spite of pressure from the bureaucrats in Brussels, genetically engineered seeds are still banned in most countries. Europeans are picky eaters. We're afraid of cancer or the transfer of antibiotic resistance through adulterated seeds. No, Fritjoe was on about something else."

"You talked with him?"

"Before your plane arrived."

Dinah didn't ask if it was Eftevang who alerted him to Mahler's presence rather than his instant recognition, but she thought it. "What did he tell you?"

"He hinted that he had a monster of a story. Something that would make headlines all over the world."

"He didn't say what it was?"

"He didn't have to. He'd just returned from Africa. There's a rumor circulating on the Internet that Tillcorp took advantage of the political upheaval in Myzandia. While the country was busy with the redistribution of land and fighting the spread of AIDS, Tillcorp's so-called agricultural advisers introduced a virulent cutworm that devastated the corn crop. Facing famine, the Myzandian dictator cut a deal for the purchase of Tillcorp's cutworm-resistant seeds."

"Tillcorp instigated a famine?"

"That's the rumor."

"But that's depraved."

"It's a journalist's dream. Fritjoe must have lucked into some witnesses, maybe even documentation. He said he had all the proof he needed."

If Dinah had her way, the laws regulating the food industry would be strengthened a hundredfold. She felt she had a right to know what weird or unnatural additives had been used to color and flavor the food she put in her mouth and she didn't trust companies that refused to divulge the whole enchilada on the label. But truth in labeling was picayune compared to this. If this rumor was true, if Tillcorp had precipitated a famine just to promote its products, it was an international outlaw of the highest order. "Maybe Eftevang exaggerated. Maybe he was tweaking your nose with talk of a monster story to make you jealous."

"Maybe," said Brander. "But if it's true, Senator Sheridan and Jake Mahler would rather see the story and the man who dared to tell it *drept*."

"Killed?"

Korrekt." He fished an unfiltered cigarette out of his pocket, lit it, and inhaled with tantalizing sensuality.

Dinah fought off a resurgent craving and turned her mind from Tillcorp's alleged crimes to Fritjoe Eftevang's intentions. "If he had proof of something that explosive, why didn't he just publish it? Why bust into the press conference, make some cryptic anti-American remarks, shoot the Norwegian minister in the eye with a laser, and get himself arrested? That just gives *you* a headline for *your* paper."

"Because he was first of all a crusader. He was a journalist only by accident and a second-rate one, at that."

Dinah raised an eyebrow. If Aagaard was an example of a first-rate journalist, the profession didn't have much to brag about. She wondered if Eftevang had had any contact with WikiLeaks, but she didn't want to kindle Aagaard's suspicions if he didn't know already. That really could get her in trouble. "Do you know where Eftevang was staying?"

"In a room over the pub. It's been padlocked by order of the police."

"How about the bartender? Did you interview him?"

"Yes. He recalls that Fritjoe was there last night, drinking beer and preaching about the evils of American biotechnology until shortly after ten. He seemed sober when he left."

"Did he leave alone?"

"The bartender couldn't be sure."

"Could he give you the names of any of the customers the man was preaching to?"

He grinned. "I've talked enough. It's your turn now."

"I'm sorry to tell you, Brander, but I don't know anything."

"You know whether Senator Sheridan and his Tillcorp cronies are, how do you say, circling the wagons."

"They are concerned about the possibility of unfavorable publicity."

"They should be. I'm going to pick up where Eftevang left off." He flicked his cigarette against the edge of the table, raining ashes onto the floor. "The murder took place sometime after ten o'clock. Has anyone got an alibi?"

"No one's accounted for his time to me."

"Inspektor Ramberg will demand it. My sources tell me he's persistent. Often at odds with the establishment, but effective. They say he's a Sami from over the border in Finland."

"Sami. Is that the same as a Laplander?"

"Lapp is no longer politically correct. The etymology of Lapp derives either from a word meaning 'dumb and lazy' or a patch of cloth used for mending. I've heard he got his job through Norway's affirmative action program. "

Dinah felt a knee-jerk defensiveness. Her Seminole ancestors had been despised and persecuted at a different latitude, but she felt an instinctive solidarity with anyone whose tribe was dissed by the dominant culture, even if the only member of the tribe she'd met had the personality of an iceberg. "Inspector Ramberg impressed me as a very competent investigator."

"I don't know. The Finns are a backward lot. Cold, stubborn, glum. But I'm told that Ramberg's no respecter of pomp or power. Your senators won't intimidate him." He took a long drag on his cigarette and exhaled with a smile of deep satisfaction. "Ramberg interrogated me at my hotel last night about the missing laser. Did he interrogate the senators?"

"I don't know. I think so."

"How did the female lawyer act? I'll bet she yowled like a wet cat."

"I wasn't present for any of the inspector's other interviews." Dinah didn't doubt that Val would have questioned Ramberg's authority to search the senators' rooms. Following news of the murder, her first instinct had been to claim diplomatic immunity. Even if she had yowled a bit, Keyes' inclination to cooperate had probably prevailed. In any case, the inspector had searched the Sheridans' room while Erika was present—just before she vanished like a mirage. Dinah wondered if she had told the truth about not having any friends in Norway. "Do you know anything about Fata Morgana?"

"Mrs. Sheridan's musical alma mater, you mean?"

"Yes. They were a few years before my time, but I've listened to some of their hits on golden oldie radio. They were good."

"They were a sensation despite the fact that they recorded only in English. Fata Morgana was the name of their first big hit and they took it for the band's name." He rested his cigarette in a saucer, closed his eyes, and erupted into song. "*That girl, whose kisses drive you to the brink,*" he drummed his fingers against the table, "*that girl spells danger and it's closer, closer, closer, yeah, it's closer than you think.*" He picked up the cigarette between his thumb and index finger and squinched his eyes. "Erika Olsen was the inspiration for that song. Fata's main songwriter was hung up on her. He wrote a lot of songs about mirages and distorted images and castles in the air."

Dinah said, "Fata Morgana seems an incongruous name for a Scandinavian band. I thought mirages only occurred on hot days in the desert."

"We see Fatas here in the Arctic, mostly on cold days when looking out over sheets of ice." He poured a couple of inches of Akevitt into his empty coffee cup. The peppery aromas of caraway and anise were almost stronger than the smell of his cigarette. He said, "I'd like to know if Erika Sheridan is as captivating as Erika Olsen."

If she were, thought Dinah, there'd be no intimation that her husband was philandering or that Erika had sneaked off for a secret assignation. But whoever Sheridan suspected her of meeting, it appeared not to have been Brander Aagaard. "Erika told me there were hard feelings when she left the band."

"They never made another album. Not that it would've been worth a crap without her." Aagaard sounded like a disappointed fan. "The thing I've never understood is what she saw in Sheridan."

Dinah was tempted to blurt out her fear that Sheridan was holding Erika prisoner, but she had to be wrong about that. Erika was a smart woman. If her husband abused her, she had the intelligence and the means to get away from him. It was easy to see Erika as fey and vulnerable, but she had demonstrated a bent for deception. It crossed her mind that the senator might be terrified that his wife had run amok and murdered Eftevang. "Did the bartender notice any strange women go in or out of the pub last night?"

"At last you've told me something."

"No, I haven't. What?"

"That Erika went out last night without her husband. Interesting."

"I didn't say that. There are lots of female tourists in town."

"The only two women you could have been referring to are Valerie Ives and Erika Sheridan." He stubbed out his cigarette, belted half his Akevitt, and squinched his eyes. "I can't see how Erika Sheridan would know Eftevang or why she would meet with him. But Mahler's lawyer knew him. Eftevang knew that Mahler would be on Sheridan's plane. He told me so. Maybe Mahler knew that Eftevang was here waiting for him. Maybe he sent the lawyer to meet with him. What do you think?"

"I don't know." And she didn't, but if she did, she wouldn't tell Aagaard. She had the sense that he was more interested in trashing Mahler and Tillcorp than discovering the truth. She should confide what she'd seen and heard to Thor Ramberg and let him suss things out. "Did you tell Inspector Ramberg what Eftevang told you about Tillcorp in Africa?"

"Yes. I asked Ramberg if he'd found documents or a computer disk in Eftevang's room. Without evidence to substantiate his allegations, it's all hearsay."

"And had the inspector found evidence?"

"He was a *musling*." Aagaard pinched his lips between his thumb and forefinger.

"Is that a clam?"

"He must keep to the rules."

"So he wouldn't tell you." Dinah gave Ramberg his due for professionalism.

"No. But if Eftevang tracked down the evidence, so can I. And I will be smarter than Eftevang. It's clear that Sheridan and Mahler will go to any lengths to squelch the story."

"Squelching a story is different from squelching a human being, if that's what you're implying. Senators and CEOs don't go around stabbing people with knives. They kill with words. Do we even know that the murderer used a knife? Did the police find the weapon?"

"You sound like a detective."

"I have detective acquaintances. Did they say what kind of weapon it was? Knife? Screwdriver? Icepick?"

"The inspector wouldn't answer that question either. But even if the murderer left it behind, it's unlikely there'll be fingerprints. Everyone wears gloves outdoors." He leaned across the table and leered. "So was it the insidious Ms. Ives or the intriguing Mrs. Sheridan who went out last night?"

"Neither reports her comings and goings to me, but why do you say Valerie Ives is insidious?"

"Isn't she?"

Dinah had grown wary of his contemptuousness and his aspersions. She didn't know if he had had a previous brush with Valerie or if he was just making up details as he went. She sensed a certain ethical flexibility in Brander Aagaard, a willingness to say and do whatever served his interests and fostered his career. She placed a mental asterisk next to everything he'd told her. "I should be going. Senator Frye may have errands for me."

"Give the senators my regards. Tell them to expect their names in tomorrow's edition of *Dagbladet* next to a picture of Fritjoe."

Dinah left him pouring another tot of Akevitt into his cup. She put on her balaclava, wrestled her arms into the parka, zipped it to her chin, and plunged out into the blizzard.

Damn it! Everyone wears gloves outdoors. She cursed herself as she fumbled in her pockets. She jerked one glove out of one pocket, but the other fell out onto the snow along with a crumpled envelope addressed to Erika Sheridan. She stuffed the envelope back in the pocket, jammed her stinging fingers into her gloves, and walked across the street toward the Beached Whale. A white car with the word POLITI blazoned on the side in big blue letters sat parked on the street in front.

Chapter Nine

The police car was empty and the Beached Whale was open for business, but, abruptly, she chickened out and kept walking. She had a hunch that Thor Ramberg would not welcome the inferences of an American busybody. And really, that's all she had. Inferences and a letter she could open if she were the sort of person who opened other people's letters. She continued down the street, one hand shielding her eyes from the blowing snow, the other fingering the corner of the letter in her pocket. It wasn't a business letter. The name on the envelope had been handwritten with sweeping, fluid letters. There was no street address and no postage. It had either been delivered in person or left for her at the hotel's front desk.

Dinah searched both sides of the street for the library or an Internet café. Her knowledge of African geography was woefully lacking, but she thought that Myzandia was somewhere in the center of the continent. The country made the news every few years, always as a result of some crisis or other—AIDS, civil war, malaria, malnutrition, internal corruption. If Tillcorp had sabotaged the country's corn crop, some astute blogger would have reported it. It wasn't plausible that something that egregious had occurred and the only proof that existed belonged to a lone, pudding-faced protester named Fritjoe Eftevang.

An expanse of black appeared in front of her. Adventifjorden. She'd reached the wharf and a triangular sign with a red border and a picture of a polar bear. *Gjelder hele Svalbard*. She didn't need a translation. If she was prudent about nothing else, she was prudent about bears. She turned around and headed back toward the hotel. As she passed the Beached Whale, two reindeer trotted around the police car on their way out of town. They didn't look like they'd make the cut to pull Santa's sleigh. Short legged and big-bodied, they reminded her of oversized corgis with antlers. Some peculiar subspecies, she supposed. They moseyed through the central business district of Longyearbyen as blasé as shoppers at the mall.

The cold penetrated Dinah's wool pants, her leggings, and the silk long johns under those. Her fingers ached and underneath the balaclava, her nose had gone numb. In the nick of time, she spotted the Longyearbyen Bibliotek and made a beeline for the front door. She hadn't cleared the threshold when a heavyset man with a Santa Claus beard and a New York Yankees baseball cap approached.

"*Kjære!*"

She pulled off her mask and stood with her back to the door, trying to rub some feeling back into her cheeks and nose.

He seemed startled. There probably weren't many patrons willing to brave this blizzard to go browsing in his library. "*God dag.*"

It took her a second to catch on that he wasn't swearing at her, but wishing her a good day.

"*God dag.* I've come to use your computer, if you have one."

"*Ja*, we have three, but the server is down and also the cell phone tower. It's like the old days. *Black become the sun's beams, weathers all treacherous, do you still seek to know?*" He smiled and waved her in.

"Is that from a poem?"

"The 'Poetic Edda,' circa the thirteenth century, 'though many of the poems date back much earlier. Back when Odin reigned and mortals endured the cold without complaint." He cocked his head to one side in a jaunty, Santa-ish way. "It wouldn't be Norse myths you're seeking to know, would it? I can show you a number of books."

"I'd love to see your mythology collection, but actually I'm looking for information about Africa, specifically Myzandia."

He held out his hands palms up in a gesture of regret. "*Dess-verre*, we have no books on Africa other than references in a world atlas and encyclopedia. And those are in Norwegian."

It was a letdown, but she felt a touch of relief that she wouldn't have to take off her boots. "I'll come back tomorrow."

"*Godt.* Maybe we will have connectivity restored."

She thanked him and resumed her slog through "weathers all treacherous" back to the Radisson and another cup of something hot. If their cell phones were inoperative, the senators would be foaming at the mouth. They depended on their ability to manage their lives and the lives of their underlings from wherever they happened to be. As she neared the hotel entrance, Herr Dybdahl stomped out the front door. He wore a black eye patch and a disgruntled frown and shouldered past her toward a waiting car. She wiped the snow out of her eyes and watched. He said something gruff to the driver, yanked open the passenger door, and the car took off.

In the entry way, she removed her boots, slid into a pair of clogs, and stopped at the front desk to ask if there were any messages. The weather had already convinced her there would be no tour of the seed vault today, but Senator Frye might have some pesky errand or question for her and, after all, she was his consultant. She halfway wished there would be a message from a certain marriage-minded Hawaiian, a message imploring her to reconsider his proposal and fly home at once. It was the kind of day that invited reconsiderations. But there was no message from anyone.

Shedding her outside clothes as she walked, she took the stairs to the second floor. The same bodyguard lolled in a chair outside Erika's door. He glanced up from his Lee Child thriller and gave Dinah the evil eye. Apparently, now wasn't a good time to return the parka or the letter. The housekeeping cart was parked outside her room and the door stood open. The maid who looked like Reese Witherspoon was poised over the bed about to change the sheets.

"Could you come back later?" It came out more brusquely than Dinah intended.

"*Ja, Greit.* Okay."

"*Tusen takk.*"

She beat it and Dinah threw her outside clothes on the bed. She unwrapped a package of kaffe and filled the coffee maker with water. Stranded. That's how she felt. Stranded physically and stranded mentally. There was no place to go, nobody to bandy ideas with, nothing to do but conjure up a mishmash of depressing scenarios and try to keep warm. She steeped a teabag in a cup of hot water and brooded. This endless night was disorienting. The hands on her watch showed high noon and it was still dark. Still snowing. Still cold as a frost giant's innards. Dinah didn't dispute the librarian's assessment of Norse courage and endurance, but she had her doubts that they never complained. This climate would drive the saints to complain.

She took her coffee and her book of mythology and installed herself in the armchair by the window. What kind of a theology had sustained the people who lived in such a harsh and inhospitable environment?

A bleak and fatalistic one, it seemed. The early Norsemen had a keen awareness of the transience of life, but they accepted the inevitability of death and strove to meet it heroically. They didn't expect their gods to deliver them from danger, or alleviate their hardships, or rectify the unfairness of life. Fate was fixed and implacable. Even the gods were fated to die in a flaming finale known as Ragnarok.

The only thing destined to survive Ragnarok was a gigantic ash tree called Yggdrasill, the roots of which linked the three tiers of the Norse cosmos and its nine worlds. The top tier was the lush and sunny home of the gods and goddesses, the resting place of the souls of fallen warriors, and the site of the Well of Urd from whence flowed the fate of all living things. The bottom tier was Hel, a prisonlike world of bitter cold and unending night, dwelling place of the dead where the wicked suffered a second death. Midgard, the middle tier, was shared by men, giants, dwarfs, dark elves, and a terrifying sea serpent named Jormungand who coiled around Midgard and bit its own tail. The tree nourished and sheltered the creatures that inhabited it, but it was subject to relentless predation. Deer and goats nibbled its leaves, snakes gnawed at its roots, and all day long a squirrel named Ratatosk skittered up and down its trunk relaying insults from a corpse-sucking dragon in Hel to a corpse-eating eagle flapping his wings on the topmost branch.

You'd think that would be enough excitement going on in one tree, but no. Odin, the king of the gods, hanged himself on Yggdrasill in a self-sacrificial death comparable to the crucifixion of Jesus Christ. He hung for nine days and nine nights while another man dangled above him. Odin was gouged with a spear, cried out in his anguish, died, and arose from the dead with new knowledge of magic songs and secret runes. Thereafter, the Vikings paid tribute to their "Gallows Lord" by regularly stringing up their enemies and anyone else who got in their way.

The early Norsemen were not a cheerful lot, decided Dinah. She closed the book and wondered what the Well of Urd held for Erika Sheridan. Was she destined to be the First Lady of the United States or a tragic figure in a murder case? Sitting and doing nothing heightened Dinah's temptation to read that letter. If it had nothing to do with the goings-on in Longyearbyen, it would be a base violation of Erika's privacy. But why was she cooped up and under guard? What were Colt Sheridan and Jake Mahler afraid of? Was it something she might say? Something she'd seen? Or something she'd done?

Dinah's eye fell on the phone. Cell phone towers might be down, land lines, too, for all she knew. But a room-to-room call should be doable. She picked up the phone and dialed Erika's room number. It rang five times. Someone picked up and she heard a click. Disconnected. Hell and damnation.

Well, she had done what she could. The house phones worked. If Erika needed help, she knew what to do. If she didn't communicate, it must mean that she was cloistered of her own free will. Whether she was or she wasn't, the problem was beyond Dinah's power to help and if she didn't stop agitating about it, she'd go as squirrely as Ratatosk. What she needed was a nice, relaxing lunch. She decided to go downstairs and try to forget about murder and the wheels of destiny for a while.

Without so much as a sideways glance at Erika's guard, she steamed down the hall, rode the elevator to the lobby, and walked into the Barentz Pub & Spiseri. A pert, blue-eyed hostess promptly showed her to a table, handed her a menu, and moved on.

Dinah surveyed the lunch crowd. Relieved to see that there were no senators or representatives of Tillcorp in the room, she perused the menu. Today's specials were smoked eel, mutton stew, American beef burger, and seal burger. The anthropologist in her wanted to order the seal burger, but she was hungry and somehow she didn't think she could choke down a lot of seal. When the waitress arrived to take her order, she inquired what came with the seal burger.

"Coleslaw, beets, and French fried potatoes."

"The seal burger, then. With all the trimmings. And a Bloody Mary, extra spicy."

While she was waiting, she studied her placemat, which showed a map of the Svalbard archipelago and Spitsbergen, the chain's largest island, along with snippets of geographical and historical data. Discovered by Willem Barents in 1596 in his quest for a northern route to the Orient, Svalbard's only inhabitants at the time were polar bears, Arctic foxes, and reindeer. The Russians began to drop by periodically during the seventeenth century, but the first people to show serious interest in the island were European whalers. The whaling business boomed for over a hundred years with English, French, and Norwegian ships competing for the most kills. The Dutch hold the record. They slaughtered some sixty thousand Greenland right whales, with the other nations racking up another sixty thousand among them, driving the species to the brink of extinction to make lamp oil and soap.

"You look engrossed."

Dinah looked up. Valerie Ives was staring down at her.

"Just waiting for my lunch, Valerie."

"I'll join you. We have a rather ticklish situation to discuss."

Chapter Ten

Valerie sat down and hooked the straps of her shoulder bag over the chair.

"I'm sure you've wondered about Mrs. Sheridan's, Erika's… seclusion."

"Looks more like imprisonment."

Valerie's steeply arched eyebrows arched more steeply. "Don't be ridiculous. As I said, it's a ticklish situation. Erika is a victim of her own weaknesses. Senator Sheridan is doing everything he can to protect her from herself."

"What weaknesses?"

Dinah's Bloody Mary came. She tasted it and sent silent kudos to the Barentz bartender.

Without looking at the menu or the waitress, Valerie ordered a cheese plate and a bottle of Perrier. When the waitress had gone, she said, "From what I understand, you're only an ad hoc aide to Senator Frye with no other connection to the Democratic party. Is that right?"

"I'm an independent."

"Someone like yourself probably hasn't the least interest in politics. We think we can rely on your discretion."

Dinah turned the "someone like yourself" remark over in her mind. What did this condescending bitch want from her? "What is it you want from me?"

"Inspector Ramberg was here this morning. We've agreed to cooperate fully, all of us, although there are certain matters,

matters not relevant to his investigation that we would like to keep private. Inspector Ramberg has pledged his discretion. Will you promise not to repeat what I'm about to tell you?"

"I don't make many promises. If you're worried, you'd better not tell me."

"Don't be coy. Erika says that she's told you already."

"She's told me many things."

"That being the case, I simply want to put the situation in context. I hope you'll keep our discussion confidential for her sake."

A waiter set a bottle of Perrier on the table and poured a glass. Valerie took a sip and stared at Dinah, as if waiting for her to raise her right hand and pledge.

"What specifically don't you want me to repeat, Valerie?"

"That Erika was a patient at the Nina Byrd Rehab Center in Virginia until a few weeks ago. That she is an alcoholic."

The alcohol part didn't surprise Dinah as much as the fact that Erika claimed to have confided in her. She waffled. "Alcoholism isn't as big a political liability as it once might have been. There are probably worse skeletons in the other candidates' closets."

"That may be true," said Valerie. "But you can be sure they'll keep the closet doors closed. Erika seems unwilling to do that. The only reason she came along on this trip is because Colt was afraid to leave her at home alone, afraid she'd start drinking again. And when she drinks, she tends to hallucinate things that never happened."

"What kind of things?" Valerie's proprietary hand on Sheridan's arm sprang to Dinah's mind, but she bit her tongue.

"It's enough that you are aware she's unstable and some of her tales are complete rubbish."

"Which tales in particular?"

Valerie's mouth tightened and she ticked her red fingernails against the table. "You tell me. You spent a lot of time with her on the flight over. What did she tell you?"

"That's the second time you've asked."

"Nine hours is a long time to talk about music."

"We played cards. Crazy Eights is her favorite game. She told me that it's called Mau-Mau in Germany, Tschausepp in Switzerland, and Pesten in the Netherlands. She likes the version where you have to tell the other player when you have only one card left to play. The only beverages I saw her drink were coffee and water."

Valerie attempted a more conciliatory approach. "Look, I don't mean to bug you or to put Erika down. She's a charming woman and we believe she has a lot to offer, eventually. All I'm trying to tell you is that, as of right now, she is mentally and emotionally fragile. The smallest thing upsets her."

"She saw somebody assaulted with a laser yesterday and this morning somebody was murdered. Not exactly small things."

"No, but if she overreacts to these events and starts babbling nonsense, if a mudslinger like Brander Aagaard were to hear some of her crazy talk and exploit her weakness, it could undermine Colt's candidacy. Colt's a gifted politician. Young, energetic, articulate. After his first term in the House, he quit and joined the Marines. He saw action in the Persian Gulf and when he returned, he was elected to the Senate in a landslide. He's at the top of the polls now and we're betting he can win the Republican nomination and defeat Obama in November. His Achilles heel is his wife. Jake and Whitney and I are doing all we can to make sure she doesn't wreck his chances."

"What are you going to do? Keep her locked up for twelve months?"

"Don't be flippant. Colt thinks she'll improve once they return to the States. If her problems are portrayed in the right way, they could generate more sympathy for Colt than criticism, although Whitney has advised Colt to check her into a clinic here in Norway for a few weeks to be safe. Visiting family in the old country would be a perfectly fine explanation of why she isn't with him on the campaign trail."

Their server returned to the table and offloaded the cheese plate and the seal burger. Dinah peaked under the bun, took a sip of her Bloody Mary, and bit into a French fry. "Is it possible that Erika knew the dead man? That would explain why she was so distressed by the news of his murder."

"Have you been listening to anything I've said? She's unbalanced."

Dinah's temper flared. "Eftevang's murder seems to have unbalanced everyone. Colt Sheridan, Whitney Keyes, your boss, you. You've been scuttling around like a passel of sprayed roaches."

"What a colorful expression." She pushed away her cheese plate, took her purse off the chair, and got up to leave. "Inspector Ramberg will be back this afternoon to question you. I trust you won't be quite so flippant." She stared at Dinah for several seconds, as if sizing up the aggravation she was dealing with here. She started to say something else, but apparently thought better and fumed out of the restaurant.

Dinah took a large bite of her seal burger and chewed over what had just happened. Valerie's speech was clearly designed to demolish Erika's credibility and invalidate whatever it was she might have said. Her "hallucination" must be a doozie for the Sheridan team to be in such a lather about it. Hallucination or fact? What could blow the leading Republican candidate's campaign out of the water? A drinking problem? A bimbo problem? A tax problem? Would Erika know anything about Tillcorp's misdeeds in Myzandia? If Sheridan knowingly accepted contributions from a company that had caused a famine and reaped a profit from it, that would cook his goose.

The texture of the seal was unctuous and the taste gamy. Dinah ate about half and chased it down with the dregs of her Bloody Mary. A knot of fear had begun to fill her stomach. Eftevang had known about the cutworms and now he was dead, his body waiting to be shipped south for burial, soon to become food for other worms. If Erika knew about Tillcorp's cutworm problem, she might also be in danger. And if they thought she had passed that knowledge on to Dinah…

Belatedly, it dawned on her that the letter in Erika's coat pocket could be a plea for help. Maybe she had scribbled it hurriedly while Lee wasn't looking and slipped it into her coat pocket before handing it to Dinah. The envelope could contain a clue to the whereabouts of those incriminating documents Eftevang claimed to have.

Dinah made up her mind. She couldn't care less what fate the Well of Urd held for Colt Sheridan or Jake Mahler or Valerie Ives. She was worried about her own fate and Erika's and the best way to keep them both safe was to make sure that Thor Ramberg knew everything. She could hardly wait for her interview.

Chapter Eleven

Erika,

*I helped you before when you were weak and couldn't
stand up to your husband. What you did was wrong
and you should beg God to forgive you. You ruined
Maks' life and now you would ruin Colt's. You chose.
You don't get to change your mind like Lofoten light. I
will pray for you, but I won't help you. It is the end.*

Inge

Dinah replaced the note in the envelope and peeled off her
gloves. Whatever additional questions the message may have
raised, it answered two. It had zilch to do with an infestation of
cutworms in Africa and Erika hadn't wanted Dinah to read it.

For lack of a better explanation, Dinah decided it must have
to do with sex. So much of life's Sturm und Drang revolved
around sex. Good sex, bad sex, too much sex, not enough sex,
sex with somebody whose heart you break, sex with somebody
who breaks yours. In Erika's case, sex with anybody other than
her husband would constitute a scandal. The way Dinah inter-
preted this Inge person's words, Erika had broken the heart of a
man named Maks and, if she changed her mind and went back
to him now, it would ruin Colt's life or his election prospects,
which probably amounted to the same thing. Maybe Erika had

Boston Public Library

Customer ID: ***********4191
Circulation system messages:
Patron status is ok.

Title: Bonereapers
ID: 39999077399671
Due: 02/12/2013 23:59:59
Circulation system messages:
Item checkout ok.

Total items: 1
1/22/2013 4:34 PM

Circulation system messages:
End Patron Session is successful

Thank you for using the
3M SelfCheck™ System.

gotten wind of a romance between Colt and a woman named Hannalore and that had ignited a yearning to return to Maks. Maybe Erika had lost track of Maks over the years and wrote to Inge asking where she could find him. It crossed Dinah's mind that Maks might have been the songwriter who'd been hung up on Erika back in the day.

It was hard to credit the unflattering portrait Valerie had painted of Erika, especially in light of Valerie's evident feelings for Colt. But Inge didn't paint a very flattering picture of Erika either. She sounded like a cold-blooded femme fatale. Dinah tried to picture her getting tanked in the Beached Whale, seducing Eftevang, and killing him at the end of the night. If she was disposed to alcoholic blackouts, she might not even remember what she'd done. The picture didn't gel. Alcohol could unleash all manner of demons, but Dinah couldn't see Erika driving a lethal weapon into a man's chest.

Feeling frustrated and ickily voyeuristic, she put the note back in the parka pocket and looked at her watch for the umpteenth time. It was already four-thirty. She wished Thor Ramberg would call and say that he was ready to re-interview her. More than anything, she hated waiting. To stave off a fit of the jimjams, she decided to break her number one birthday resolution and buy a pack of cigarettes. She didn't have to smoke them all, just one or two. These were extenuating circumstances. She would make a new and lasting New Year's resolution to quit.

She went to the small gift shop located in the lobby, bought a pack of Norwegian-made Petterøes, parked herself in front of the fireplace, and lit up. From here, she could monitor everyone's comings and goings. Tipton Teilhard III bustled through, running messages between the senators and Mahler, no doubt. He lobbed her a blameful look, as if she'd committed high crimes against the nation. Valerie must have advised him of her flippant attitude. The little toady. If he wasn't careful, he'd stick his nose too far up some politico's fundament and suffocate one of these days.

A man with a Bluetooth module in his ear and a stern look on his face bent over her and held out a saucer. "*Unnskyld, frøken.*"

"Excuse me?"

"Yes, yes. Excuse me. It is not permitted to smoke in the lobby."

"Can I smoke in the bar?"

"Not in the bar or in the restaurant. It is the law."

Grudgingly, Dinah crushed out her cigarette. Brander Aagaard was obviously a scofflaw and the Kaffe & Kantine a place where the law could knowingly be broken.

The elevator dinged and Jake Mahler and Thor Ramberg stepped out. Mahler held the door open with one hand and continued talking amiably and smiling. Ramberg didn't reciprocate the smile. Mahler patted him on the shoulder and held out his hand. The two shook, then Mahler got back in the elevator and the doors closed.

Dinah stood up. "Inspector Ramberg?"

He saw her and walked her way.

"Inspector, were you planning to interview me again? Because I have some information. Not about the missing laser. About Herr Eftevang. I don't know if it's important, but I'll feel a lot better after I've passed it on to you."

I've been talking all day, Miss Pelerin. Is it Miss or Miz?"

"Miz."

"I'm tired and my throat is dry. Perhaps…"

"No." She felt a pang of anxiety. Had Valerie said something to undercut her credibility, too? "I promise I won't talk your ear off and I'd really like to get some things off my chest as soon as possible."

He gave her an appraising look. "Will you have dinner with me? You can talk as much as you like as long as it's over a beer."

"Sure."

"It'll be my treat, a peace offering for invading your room last night. There's a *vertshus* that I like not far from here. I'll drive so you won't get too cold."

He seemed less arrogant and overbearing than he had during their first meeting, or maybe the American contingent had worn him down.

She said, "Give me five minutes and I'll get my coat."

In her room she grabbed her gloves and Erika's parka. She took the letter out of the pocket, put it in her purse, and started out again. A last minute glimpse of her face in the mirror stopped her. She tossed the parka on the bed, went into the bathroom and applied a touch of lipstick and a dot or two of perfume. Well, it was just sitting there in her cosmetic case wasting its sweetness in the Arctic air.

When she returned to the lobby, Inspector Ramberg was booted up and waiting for her at the front entrance. She removed the spent toe warmers from her boots and considered whether to insert replacements. "How far is your car?"

"Right in front. I'll turn on the heater for you."

She omitted the toe warmers and preceded him out the door. The wind had died down, but it was still snowing hard. She walked around to the passenger side, but he didn't follow to open the door for her. She reminded herself that this was a police interview, not a dinner date.

As soon as they sat down and buckled up, she said, "I know you spoke with Erika Sheridan the night you searched our rooms, but did Senator Sheridan make an excuse for her not to speak with you today?"

"I spoke with her."

It wasn't what Dinah had expected. "Did she seem frightened or under duress?"

"She was somewhat distant and evasive, but she didn't seem fearful."

"Did you speak with her alone?"

"Yes. Why do you think she's under duress?"

"Because she's been held captive with a guard posted outside her door ever since we heard about the murder this morning. The guard, acting on her husband's instructions, wouldn't let me talk with her. I'm surprised they didn't put you off with a story that she was indisposed or sedated or in a medically induced coma."

"I have a badge." He started the engine, turned on the heater full blast, and pulled out into the street.

Dinah started to doubt herself. If Erika were afraid or in trouble, she could have let Ramberg know her situation in her native tongue. Even if she hadn't spoken the language in decades, she must have retained a few basics, like "Help!" and "I'm being held prisoner!"

Ramberg said, "I will concede that my badge hasn't been as persuasive with the American senators as it usually is with people of lesser rank. It's frustrating to listen to so much talk and glean so little information."

"I hope tonight isn't similarly frustrating for you." She was wishing she'd kept her own counsel. He'd interviewed Erika and Aagaard and Mahler. She couldn't add anything to what he knew already. "Are there any dives in this burg where a person can smoke a cigarette without being arrested?"

"Only if you have immunity." He didn't say it as if he were kidding.

"Jerusalem."

He drove beyond the city center, past a polar bear warning sign, and past a large, brightly lit building with one or two cars and a flock of snowmobiles in every color parked all around.

"What's that?"

"Huset. Longyearbyen's finest restaurant, pub, and cinema. It has a Michelin star."

"I don't see anything beyond."

"Not a member of the Flat Earth Society, are you?"

"No."

"I'll show you Longyearbyen's seamier side. Where we're going they won't call the cops if you smoke."

"Call the cops. You sound like an American."

"Sounding American is a contagion."

"I take it you're not an admirer of American culture."

"I don't care much for American military swagger or its tendency to intervene in other countries' affairs, but I like American music and American slang. And I'm addicted to reruns of old American detective shows."

"You get American TV way up here?"

"How else could I have learned how to perform my job?"

She awarded him an inward smile. Maybe he wasn't as cold and arrogant as he'd first seemed.

After a couple of miles, they passed a ramshackle wreck of a building.

"What is that?"

"One of the old collieries. Coal mining was the main industry in Longyearbyen for a hundred years. It's still big business. Half the population works for Store Norske, which runs two mines. As the old mines have closed over the years, the buildings and equipment have been left standing as historical artifacts. They're handy as landmarks."

He turned left. There was no road sign or marker. He seemed to be driving off-road, across very rough terrain. The car whumped over a series of moguls and ground to a stop in front of what looked like the entrance to a mine. Lanterns mounted on a ledge over the door illuminated a crooked wooden sign: Løssluppen Hole.

A score of carelessly parked snowmobiles lay scattered about like discarded toys. "What *is* this place?"

"Used to be a rail spur for a mine. Løssluppen means abandoned. The mine was abandoned and now it's a pub." He killed the engine, doused the headlights, and got out.

Expecting no gentlemanly courtesies, she got out on her side. "You forgot your keys in the ignition."

"No car thieves in Longyearbyen." He opened the pub's door and motioned her inside. It was dark and dank and smelled vaguely of rotten eggs.

"We don't have to descend in a bucket, do we?"

"Nothing like that." He picked up two headlamps off a table. "Slip this on."

Feeling positively eerie, she put on her miner's head lamp and followed his back down a black tunnel. The ceiling was so low that he had to stoop and rail cart tracks stretched into the distance. Dinah felt the onset of claustrophobia. She began to have misgivings. Was he leading her into Hel, the realm of darkness and dwelling place of the dead? She imagined carbon monoxide and other noxious gases seeping out of the walls and filling her lungs. The Norwegians didn't mind eating in filthy underground mine shafts and they banned cigarettes?

Her guide pointed to a crude ladder affixed to a pillar. "This is where we climb up."

"I don't think so."

"At the top of the ladder is a bistro."

"Or a corpse-eating eagle."

"It's quite agreeable. Trust me."

An explosion of raucous laughter burst into the tunnel behind them. Dinah turned and saw a swarm of headlamps bounding toward them. They looked and sounded like college kids, jostling and hooting at each other. They reached the ladder and clambered up like a brigade of firefighters. When the last one disappeared up the hatch, somebody shouted, "Øl, øl, øl."

"Beer," translated Thor and started up the ladder after them.

What the hey. When in Rome. Dinah climbed up behind him and topped out in a rectangular room the size of a basketball court with a bar that ran the full length of the room. The glass shelves above it held the most comprehensive lineup of booze she'd ever seen. Thor gave her a hand and she scrambled out. The smell of garlic and fresh baked bread won her over immediately. There was a man sliding a pizza into a wood-fired oven so somehow this place was vented to the outside.

Thor hung their coats on an antique, multi-pronged coat hanger and led her back to the table farthest from the noise. "What would you like to drink?"

"Red wine, if they have it."

"They had over twenty thousand bottles at last count. Anything in particular?"

"Italian. Tuscan. Not too expensive."

"I'll ask Gunnar what he recommends."

He went to the bar and Dinah settled herself and looked around. The Løssluppen must have been dug out of the side of a mountain. The pine floor and bar had been polished to a golden sheen, but the walls were dark, rough-hewn rock studded with hand drills and sundry miners' tools. Porthole windows had been punched out of the rock and the lights of Longyearbyen shone in the distance. Above the bar hung a huge survey compass and at the far end of the room, an old-fashioned jukebox sat next to a wooden coal car filled with chunks of coal.

The inspector came back with a schooner of beer, an open bottle of Montalcino, and a wine glass.

She said, "I like this place."

He sat down and poured her a glass of wine. "Longyearbyen is riddled with abandoned mines like this one, some gypsum but mostly coal. Today there's only one operational coal mine. Some were destroyed by the Germans during World War II, some rebuilt and closed in the mid-nineties. But there are plenty of ghost shafts dating from the early years of the twentieth century covered by talus and ice and snow. Gunnar had the novel idea to turn this one into a restaurant."

Whether it was the wine or the laid-back atmosphere or the fact that Ramberg was an aboriginal like herself, she felt the stirrings of simpatico. She said, "It's bizarre to think of the Arctic as a former swamp with enough plants and trees and heat to decay and in a few hundred million years form coal."

"Our buried sunshine." He regarded her with another of his appraising looks. "I saw you in front of the Beached Whale this morning."

"It's on a public street, Inspector Ramberg."

"Call me Thor. This isn't an official interview. Dinah." He lifted his beer glass. "*Skål.*"

She touched her glass to his. "Is it true that toast comes from the Vikings' custom of drinking ale out of their enemies' skulls?"

"Behold the only skull, from which, unlike a living head, whatever flows is never dull."

She laughed. "Is that your own?"

"Lord Byron, probably in his cups."

"You Norsemen are more poetic than I expected. Brander Aagaard sang for me earlier today and the librarian quoted from 'The Poetic Edda.'"

He took a sip of his beer. "Tell me about your conversation with Aagaard."

She told him what Aagaard had said about Eftevang and the big scoop Eftevang claimed to have. "Mahler and Ives kept a low profile in the back of the audience during the press conference. Their visit was apparently intended to be sub rosa. Did Eftevang say anything about Mahler or Tillcorp when you interviewed him?"

"No. He said only that he was here to protest American greed and corruption and that he hadn't hurt anyone."

"That sounds so tame after his rant about Americans destroying God's creations. And if he had proof of some terrible crime against humanity, why wouldn't he go ahead and print it for all the world to see?" She had a brainstorm. "What if it was Eftevang who was greedy and corrupt? What if his words at the press conference were a veiled threat? A message to Mahler or Sheridan that he would blow the gaff if they didn't pay up."

"You mean blackmail?"

"Why not? If the rumor is true, they were on the spot. I don't know if Tillcorp's financial interests would be jeopardized by news of their shenanigans in Africa, but its reputation would take a hit. And Sheridan wants to keep his cozy relationship with the company on the down low. He can't afford to have his name appear in the same sentence with cutworms. Not this close to the Iowa caucus." She chided herself. "I ought to have paid more attention to what everybody on the plane was saying and how they were acting. My department head arranged for me to tag along on this trip to find out if the Svalbard Seed Vault is a safe depository for her heirloom seeds. I thought I could wait until we landed in Longyearbyen to start paying attention. I feel as if I've missed something that would make everything come clear."

"Why do you care about the murder of a man you don't know in a place where you will spend three days at most?"

"I don't know. Two years ago, while I was visiting my family in Australia, a man was murdered and until the truth came out, the police suspected all of us. It was horrible. At the time, I thought it was the worst thing that would ever happen to me. Then last summer in Hawaii, I was embroiled in another murder investigation." She made a wry face. "That probably makes you want to rush back to headquarters and run an Interpol check on me."

"What makes you think I haven't done that already?"

She looked for a sign that he was kidding and didn't see one. Maybe he just deadpanned really well. "Anyway, I hate murder, especially when the murderer seems to be getting away with it."

He said, "You didn't mention the possibility that Eftevang could have been sending a subtle message to Mrs. Sheridan. She has a rock-and-roll past and now she has to think about her husband's political ambitions."

"I suppose it's possible, but everything Eftevang said seemed to relate to pesticides and gene modification. Anyway, I like Erika. For some reason, call it intuition, I don't believe she's as loose and irresponsible as people say she is. I don't like Jake Mahler or his company's business ethics. And if Brander Aagaard is right and Colt Sheridan is using his office to further Tillcorp's rape of the earth, I don't like him either."

"What makes you trust Aagaard? He could have invented that story about Myzandia."

"I *don't* trust him. Or the dead man, either. You asked me before if Aagaard seemed to anticipate the laser. Is he a suspect in Eftevang's murder? Do you think the two of them were in cahoots?"

"He's what your American cops refer to as 'a person of interest.'"

She smiled. "What do the Norwegian cops call a person of interest?"

"I call him a *mistenkelig*. And there are too many, all of them, how do you say, pulling rank and pulling strings while pretending to help."

"Inspector…"

"Thor."

"Thor." Torr. No h. Torr as in torch. Torr as in torrid. She took a sip of wine and cautioned herself never to fall for another cop. "Thor, you haven't asked me for an alibi for the night of Eftevang's murder. Have you asked the others?"

"They all claim they were asleep in their hotel rooms. Isn't that what you'd say?"

"Yes." So Erika hadn't owned up to going walkabout last night. Was it because she'd met with Eftevang, or seen someone else meet with him? Dinah was torn. Of course she *should* tell Thor what she knew about Erika. She might be an eyewitness. She might be lying to protect someone or she might be lying to keep a guilty liaison quiet. But once again Dinah couldn't visualize Erika stabbing a man to death and she felt qualmish about ratting her out for a lesser offense.

Thor said, "Until I find a witness who saw somebody near the scene of the crime between the hours of ten o'clock and five a.m., I'll have to take their word for where they were."

She said, "Eftevang told Aagaard he had documents that would discredit Tillcorp. Suppose he got his information from WikiLeaks. From what I've read, WikiLeaks doesn't organize the material it collects. They pass their secrets on to journalists to analyze."

"That's an interesting possibility." He appeared to mull the idea. "If Eftevang tried to sell his big scoop to Aagaard, but Aagaard decided the price was too high or he didn't want to share the byline, he could have killed him and taken whatever documents or other proof that Eftevang had."

"But why would he freely admit to meeting with Eftevang or mention the existence of the documents in the first place? He could have kept quiet and published his scoop without anyone knowing where the information came from."

"Sometimes it's the people who talk the most who have the most to hide."

She felt her face grow hot. "People like me."

"Not at all. What you've said is very helpful. Of the senators, Whitney Keyes was the most talkative. He suggested that Herr Eftevang celebrated his release from custody with too much of the hard stuff, picked a fight with another drunk, and lost. 'Tragically,' the senator added, but not very convincingly."

She said, "Keyes seems very protective of Sheridan, but I sense bad blood between Keyes and Mahler. What was Mahler's theory of the murder?"

"He thinks that Eftevang was done in by one of his co-conspirators. He showed me some material Ms. Ives had gathered off the Internet about a cell of agri-terrorists. She gave me a list of their names and suggested I find out whether they were passengers on any of the flights or ships entering Longyearbyen in the last few months. That would keep me busy and out of their hair until their business here is finished."

"Did you talk to Tipton Teilhard?"

"As briefly as possible. What a *fanatiker.*"

"How old is Tipton?" asked Dinah.

"Twenty-eight by his passport, although he looks and acts much younger. He was mostly concerned about how the murder would play out in the media and the all-important need to deflect the spotlight away from Senator Sheridan. He didn't exactly come out and criticize Sheridan, but he did say that Sheridan had invited Mahler to Longyearbyen against Senator Keyes' advice. Tillcorp provokes controversy and controversy is poison to an American politician. Teilhard seems to believe that the only way to win an election is to 'spin' the story. Is that the guiding principle of American politics?"

"I hope not," said Dinah. "But Erika may think it is. Maybe that's the reason she doesn't want her husband to run for the presidency. Did she suggest any avenues of inquiry for you?"

"No. But she had the grace to ask if Eftevang had a wife and whether she had been notified."

Dinah reproached herself for not even thinking of that. "Did he?"

"Not that we've been able to find. We'll continue to inquire."

Dinah reckoned Thor to be in his mid-thirties. Too young to have listened to Fata Morgana, but she asked anyway. "You wouldn't by any chance know the names of her former band members, would you?"

"Norge doesn't have so many megastars that we can't name them all. Fata had three men and two women. Maks Jorgen, Piers Brokk, Bjorn Durin, Erika Olsen, and Gudlaug Bye."

So Maks *was* the songwriter. "Was there another woman associated with the group? Inge, perhaps?"

"I don't think so. Piers Brokk was ill and dropped out for a time. I can't recall the name of his replacement, but it wasn't Inge."

"Inge could be a man's name?"

"Male or female. Why? Did Mrs. Sheridan say something about an Inge?"

"No. I don't know where I heard the name." Dinah didn't know why she balked at showing Thor the note. She'd intended to tell him everything. But the more she thought about that note, the more it sounded like a scolding friend's response to Erika's decision to leave her husband, in no way relevant to the murder investigation. It sounded like what a friend might say to her about ruining Jon's life. It wasn't true and she felt reflexively defensive. "Did Valerie Ives warn you that Erika hallucinates things that never happened?"

"Senator Sheridan said that she is 'high-strung' and asked me to treat her gently. He said she was recently hospitalized for alcohol abuse and the laser attack and the murder had frightened her and exacerbated her desire for alcohol."

"It's exacerbated mine." Dinah poured herself another glass of wine. "At the risk of being overly talkative, I think Senator Sheridan and his team are trying to muzzle Erika. I don't know what they're afraid she'll say, or has already said, but I get the impression that both she and her husband are having affairs."

"Maybe she was having an affair with Eftevang," said Thor.

Dinah wrinkled her nose. "I wouldn't say that looks make *all* the difference, but …"

He completed her thought. "Fritjoe Eftevang looked like a troll."

"Let's just say he didn't strike me as Erika's type." Dinah had no doubt that Thor Ramberg was well aware of his own good looks. She tried not to notice. "Brander Aagaard said that you're of Sami descent. Tell me something about the Sami history."

"Sah-me."

She echoed his pronunciation. "Were they mostly nomads and reindeer herders?"

"Not all. There were a good many farmers and fishermen along the coast. The Russians, the Danes, the Swedes and the Norwegians vied for control of their lands and the Sami ended up paying taxes to all of them simultaneously. The Sami have always been regarded as outsiders. Before the Second World War, Norway invested big money in an effort to wipe out the Sami culture. Then the Germans came and burned down everything they saw that was Sami."

"Aagaard said that you're originally from Finland."

"Wrong. He's from Oslo. Some down south use the term 'Finn' to refer to the Sami." He finished his beer, fixed his eyes on her, and seemed to ponder. "Some cop shows these days use non-cops as observers and consultants. You're an observant woman. How would you like to be my eyes and ears, tell me what's really going on with the American *mistenkeligs*?"

"Are you kidding?"

"Think about it. I'm going to get another beer and order a pizza. Gunnar's special is pretty good. It's American style."

Chapter Twelve

The blizzard had abated overnight and the visit to the Doomsday Vault was back on the agenda. Norris Frye informed Dinah over *frokost* that the agriculture minister would be sending cars to pick everyone up for the grand tour at ten o'clock. Unfortunately, the senator's gout was such that he couldn't bear the pressure of a boot on his right foot. "This cold is brutal. Think I'd better stay inside and take care of myself. You go on in my place. Don't let that blowhard Sheridan bully you and be sure to prepare a thorough report. I'll…oh, good morning, Colt."

"Morning, Norris, Ms. Pelerin. Sorry about yesterday, Norris. Tensions got to me."

"That's big of you, Colt. And I apologize for my little taunt."

"Forget it. Are you going on the tour of the vault with us?"

"I'm under the weather today. Just going to put my feet up and try to keep warm. Dinah here will take the tour in my place."

"Not a problem. Should be an educational experience. Dybdahl's outfoxed the press so we won't be harassed."

Dinah asked him if Erika would be going on the tour.

"I think not. She didn't sleep well last night. I don't want her to overdo. Lee will stay with her in case she needs anything."

Dinah refrained from comment. She had unloaded her concerns to the local lawman and it was up to Erika to say whether she wanted or needed help.

After her muesli and *kaffe*, Dinah went back to her room to read for a while. She sorted through the various fact sheets Norris had given her about the facility.

Construction of the *Svalbard globale frøhvelv* cost approximately forty-five million Norwegian kroner, or about nine million U.S. dollars. The purpose of the vault is to preserve samples of native seeds from gene banks around the world in the event of catastrophic loss due to environmental disasters, wars, or nuclear holocaust. The underground cavern is built deep inside a sandstone mountain more than four hundred feet above sea level so that the site will remain dry even if the icecaps melt. The storage rooms are refrigerated to minus 0.4 degrees Farenheit and, even if electricity is lost, the surrounding permafrost will keep the rooms cold. At this low temperature and with limited oxygen, the seeds will not age as they normally would and will remain viable for hundreds, perhaps thousands of years.

The information sheets corroborated what Valerie had said: the depositors own the seeds they deposit in the bank. The contract they sign with the Norwegian government doesn't constitute a legal transfer of rights. But if the ownership issue was cut and dried, Dinah wondered how suspicion arose that the government was facilitating access to corporate breeders. And then she came to a line near the bottom of the last page.

The Norwegian Government makes all policy decisions regarding access in consultation with the Consultative Group on International Agricultural Research (CGIAR), a private entity funded by a number of different foundations and corporations.

It was a long name for any group and a cumbersome string of letters. It was the sort of name that cried out for a pronounceable acronym. CGIAR. C-jar? C-gar? Cigar. That rang a bell. Could CGIAR have been what the senators were talking about at the state dinner and not cigars? And how did that United Nations treaty that Aagaard talked about fit into the framework?

The phone rang.

"Hello."

"The cars are here. You'd better come down." Valerie's tone conveyed an unmistakable disrelish for Dinah's company.

Dinah rolled her eyes and resolved to make herself as much of a pain in Ms. High-and-Mighty's derrière as possible. "I'm on my way." She grabbed Erika's parka and reported to the lobby.

Herr Dybdahl waited by the door with his hands behind his back. His unpatched eye strafed the room like a sniper's scope and he rocked back and forth on his toes. The geneticist she'd talked with at the state dinner—Peder Halverson—nattered away in Dybdahl's ear, but the agriculture minister disdained to look at him and made no reply.

Dinah fiddled with her boot laces and pretended not to eavesdrop on the two men.

"Will your eye see again, Herr Dybdahl?"

Dybdahl grunted.

"Like Odin, eh? Did you receive wisdom in exchange for the eye?"

Dinah congratulated herself for getting the reference. Odin had given an eye to drink from the Well of Urd, which imparted wisdom and understanding.

Dybdahl's lone blue eye lighted on Halverson with a malevolent gleam. "I have not seen the foundation's grain tonnage report for the Sub-Saharan region. You are late."

"I am a geneticist, not a *sekretær*. The report is not my responsibility."

"Hurry up your *sekretær*, then. The Ministry of Foreign Affairs is after me for my input on the aid budget and the Agency for Development wants the numbers on the tonnage of mineral fertilizers you have shipped."

"Oh, hi!" Tipton scurried out of the elevator with a heavy briefcase in either hand. He wore a thick, whitish-gray cardigan knitted from an unusually hairy yarn and a look of cosmic urgency. "Where are the senators?"

"They haven't showed yet," said Dinah.

"Thank God, I didn't make them wait."

Dybdahl's eye gleamed with undisguised contempt.

Oblivious, Tipton set down the cases and flexed his fingers. "These are the logistics, everyone. We'll be traveling in separate cars. Colt and Whitney and I will be in the lead car with Herr Dybdahl. The videographer has his own car. He'll meet us there. Val and Jake will go in the car with Herr Halverson. I understand that Norris has begged off and you'll be going in his place, Dinah. Val said you could hitch a ride with them."

"Lucky me."

As if on cue, Valerie and Jake Mahler emerged from the dining room. They appeared to be having a difference of opinion. Mahler's characteristic dominance showed in his chesty posture and impatient eyes. Val seemed to be trying to convince him of something. She was talking with her hands and her eyebrows moved up and down like batwings. She led Mahler to the sofa in front of the fireplace and continued to argue.

"Housekeeping keeps shuffling the papers on the desk in Whitney's room," said Tipton. "It's maddening." He looked at his watch and hurried over to the front desk.

Dybdahl muttered something about Americans under his breath.

Halverson excused himself to go to the men's room.

Dinah sidled up to Herr Dybdahl. If he blamed his pain and suffering on the Americans, he probably felt a tinge of annoyance with all of them, herself included. She essayed a mollifying smile. "To have to coordinate so many ministries and agencies and foundations must be challenging."

"*Ja.*"

"You probably had to fly here from Oslo to host us Americans."

"*Ja*. And it is a holiday week."

"What happened to your eye is terrible. We owe you a tre-mendous debt of gratitude."

"It is my responsibility. I do not shirk."

"And you manage the seed vault, too?"

"*Ja*, along with the Global Crop Diversity Trust and the Nordic Genetic Resource Center. We will only accept samples that have not previously been deposited. No duplicates."

She smiled. "Like Noah took on board the minimum number needed to reproduce."

He defrosted slightly. "Svalbard is sometimes likened to Noah's ark. But copies of our seeds have to be stored in another gene bank somewhere else."

"What does CGIAR do?"

"It brings together scientists from all over the world. They engage in research and collaborate to maintain international gene banks."

"Where do they get the seeds for their research?"

"From the regional and national gene banks."

"Is a seed bank the same as a gene bank?"

"It's a type of gene bank. When those banks deposit samples with Svalbard, they must agree to make available samples from their own stocks."

Dinah did an auditory double-take. "So anyone who wants to experiment with a particular seed can simply request it from his local seed or gene bank?"

"*Ja*. Provided the local bank has deposited a sample with Svalbard. That is what the agreement says."

"Do the individual farmers and gardeners who entrust their seeds to the regional seed banks know that?"

His gaze turned glacial again. "What the local banks tell the farmers is outside my knowledge."

Dinah thought, you could drive a John Deere tractor through that loophole. It was tantamount to fraud. It *was* fraud if the depositor expected the DNA of his seeds to remain intact. The farmer gives stocks of his heirloom seeds to the local seed bank for safekeeping. The local seed bank gives a sample copy of those seeds to Svalbard to keep even safer for the next ten millennia. And then the local seed bank turns around and gives anyone who asks free access to whatever it wants.

The senators showed up, Sheridan in a heavy, khaki-colored anorak that filled Dinah with envy, and Herr Dybdahl waved them outside to his waiting car. Having chastised the clerk at the front desk, Tipton gathered up the briefcases and tagged after the senators like a puppy.

Halverson returned and he and Dinah waited for Jake Mahler and Val to wind up their confab. After five minutes or so, they appeared to call a truce. They sat in the foyer and put on their boots. They didn't speak. When they were ready to go, Mahler gave Halverson the nod and he conducted them toward a large black SUV.

Mahler said, "Sit up front with Peder, Dinah. Val and I haven't finished our discussion." He held open the front passenger door for her and the rear door for Valerie.

When they were all inside and buckled up, Halverson cranked the engine and turned on the headlights. They broadcast a brilliant, high-intensity blue light that seemed to compass the entire length and width of the town. The weather had cleared and in the nebulous distance, Dinah could make out the silhouette of a range of low, snow-covered mountains. The outline of a ship was visible at the wharf. She assumed it was frozen in the ice until spring, but she didn't break the interior ice to ask.

In the back seat, Val lowered her voice to a whisper. She sounded keyed up and angry. Dinah caught a word here and there, something about a note, or maybe a vote.

The SUV barreled past the polar bear warning sign, going too fast for the road conditions. In the refulgent blue lights, roadside mining artifacts littered the landscape. Halverson hit a clump of rock-hard snow and the undercarriage sounded as if it were being ripped apart.

Mahler's voice jumped. "Is he insane?"

"It was unavoidable!" exclaimed Halverson.

"I wasn't talking to you. Just drive." Mahler said something to Valerie in a hoarse whisper, "Don't buy it" or "deny it."

Halverson barreled on, his eyes focused on the rear view mirror instead of the road. His driving focused Dinah's mind on the perils of breaking down this far from town with a geneticist, a lawyer, and a CEO to get the car running again. The SUV bucked and slued, throwing its blue lights hither and thither across the barren hinterland. She gripped the grab handle and comforted herself that at least there were no trees to slam into.

There was more whispering in the back seat and then Valerie said, quite distinctly, "Somebody's playing us, Jake."

Dinah almost turned, but a shimmering greenish-turquoise fluorescence distracted her. The column of light soared three hundred feet into the sky. It was too geometrically perfect to be the northern lights.

"It's the vault," said Val.

"Damn it, slow down," growled Mahler.

Halverson slowed and they all inclined their heads for a good view. From their angle of approach, the vault appeared as a triangular wedge protruding out of the side of a mountain. Or the prow of a huge, iced-in ship.

Val said, "The roof and entrance are inlaid with steel mirrors and prisms and a mass of fiber-optic cables to reflect the polar light for miles around. The objective was to make it glow in the moonlight and sparkle in the midnight sun. If asteroids were to wipe out everyone who knows about the vault, it will stand out like a beacon and lure new people to investigate. It was designed by Dyveke Sanne. If it lasts as long as the Norwegians say it will, his name will go down with the Pharaohs who built the pyramids."

"Looks like Dr. No's bunker," said Mahler.

Chapter Thirteen

Halverson parked behind Herr Dybdahl's car. They donned their coats and gloves and plodded through deep snow to get to a partially shoveled concrete walkway that climbed toward the entrance.

Dinah didn't think she'd need the balaclava just walking between the car and the door, but the wind ripped off her hood and blasted her face. Her hair lashed around her eyes and she covered her ears with her hands. Mahler pulled the hood back onto her head.

"Thanks," she said through chattering teeth.

They were greeted at the entrance by an armed member of some branch or other of the Norwegian military. Herr Dybdahl, the videographer, and the senators, looking cold and crabby, were clearly tired of waiting. Only Tipton appeared bouncy and chipper.

"Let's get this show on the road," said Sheridan.

The guard unlocked the gate and motioned them through.

"Follow me." Dybdahl led the way. "This first section isn't completely sealed off from outside air and you must mind your step. As the permafrost walls thaw and refreeze, water drips onto the floor and it becomes slippery."

"The permafrost acts as a natural insulation," added Halverson.

Dybdahl rattled off facts and figures like a docent. "There are four steel-reinforced, air-locked doors in the tunnel before you reach the actual vaults. The walls are three meters thick and there is twenty-four hour video surveillance operated from Sweden. It is, how do you say in English…?"

"Impregnable," said Valerie, her breath escaping in a long white plume.

"Yes," said Dybdahl. "It is designed to function without any human intervention."

Valerie's boots skidded on the icy concrete and Mahler caught her before she went down.

Dybdahl unlocked the second door and they proceeded into a long metal tube. Dinah's face tautened from the cold. Her nostrils hurt and she fought down a nascent feeling of claustrophobia.

"How many seeds do you have at present?" asked Mahler.

"Approximately twenty million varieties. We have fifteen hundred varieties of Peruvian potatoes, alone." Dybdahl obviously knew the contents of his vault down to the last pip.

Some twenty yards ahead, a folding table had been set up with a photographer's screen behind it.

Dybdahl said, "We have chosen this place for the video. Peder Halverson will log in the seeds as you present them and Rolf will videotape each presentation."

"I'll help Rolf set things up," said Tipton. He removed the packets of American seeds from the briefcases and lined them up on the table.

Rolf adjusted his light meter and shouldered his camcorder. "Ready when you are."

"Go ahead and log in the Hawaiian stuff, Peder," said Valerie. "No need to film that."

"If it's not on film," said Keyes, "Norris will think we dumped his blue state's contribution on the side of the road." He looked back and saw Dinah. "Come on, Dinah. Say a few words into the camera about what it is you're depositing."

Dinah felt trapped, in more ways than one. She stepped forward, took the packet of seeds from Tipton, and looked into the camera. She would have delivered a caveat to the world's gardeners if she thought it would ever be seen or heard. But it wouldn't and, anyway, Norris was counting on her to act in a responsible way on his behalf. She said, "These are offshoots of the hapai banana donated by the Hawaiian Seed Savers Exchange. The hapai produces a sweet, ball-shaped banana. It was known as the "pregnant" banana because it grows inside the trunk of the tree and is ripe when the trunk becomes swollen. The hapai was one of the few varieties that women were allowed to eat during the period of Hawaiian history when kapu laws put many foods off limits to women. These offshoots should be stored in your cryopreservation chamber and kept extra cold." She handed the packet to Halverson and stood aside.

He transferred the packet into a thick silver envelope and labeled it with the name and provenance of the seed and the date of deposit. He then logged the entry into a laptop computer.

"I'll go next," said Keyes. "Mind if I place the seeds into the envelope, myself, Peder? American viewers like to see the do-it-yourself spirit at work."

"Brilliant," enthused Tipton.

Keyes took the packet Tipton handed him and smiled into the camera. "Everybody knows that the first Thanksgiving was celebrated in Plymouth, Massachusetts, in sixteen-twenty-one. Those early American pilgrims didn't have the opportunity to enjoy pumpkin pie at their first meal, but they soon learned that the land in which they had settled grows the finest pumpkins in the world. On behalf of the Great State of Massachusetts, I hereby donate these seeds so that future generations will never be deprived of this wonderful food." He inserted the seed packet into the vault's heavy-duty, silver envelope and folded over the self-sealing flap. In a seemingly heartfelt coda, he said, "Senator Sheridan and I would have preferred to store these American seeds in an American seed bank in Alaska, or there are some pretty cold places in Senator Sheridan's home state of Montana. But given the enormity of our national debt, that isn't feasible unless and until we embark on a domestic policy that makes use of America's God-given natural resources." He smiled like a Kennedy. "Until that time, Norway is our friend and ally and the Svalbard facility is a superb alternative. We support it wholeheartedly."

"Oh, that was beautiful," said Tipton.

Keyes passed the envelope to Halverson and clapped Sheridan on the back. "All right, Colt. You're on."

Sheridan picked up his seed packet and faced the camera. "Montana wheat is the plumpest, cleanest, highest…highest quality grain that…grain that…" he faltered and rubbed his forehead.

"Are you all right?" Keyes asked in a worried voice. "We can't bring a teleprompter in here. Did you memorize the speech Val gave you?"

"It doesn't have to be verbatim," said Valerie, giving Sheridan's arm an encouraging shake. "The object is to sound natural, Colt. If you make a mistake, you can do it again. Right, Tip?"

"Oh, right. It'll be edited and ultra-professional. We'll be using a clip on your website and in your campaign video. Whitney and I are assembling a collage of your most compelling TV moments."

"Take two," said Rolf.

Sheridan moved heavily, as if he weren't quite awake. "Montana wheat is the highest quality, most nutritional grain in the world. It is the pride…we take great pride in…"

"Our soil ecology and nutrient replacement programs," prompted Valerie.

"…our soil ecology and nutrient replacement programs and abundant harvests that permit us to export…we export…"

There was a long pause.

"Eighty percent," cued Tipton.

Valerie took charge like a protective stage mother. "He has a thousand things on his mind. Let's start all over again, Colt. Shall we? Let's take it from the top?"

"Thanks, Val." He smiled. "Montana wheat is the plumpest, highest quality, most nutritional…"

"Take three," said Rolf.

Dinah didn't know what was screwing up Sheridan's concentration, but she felt the walls of the tube closing in on her.

It wasn't that the space was too small or the ceiling too low. It was the thickness of the walls surrounding this tube, the ice that formed on the hinges of the airlocked doors, the feeling of containment. Her heart was pounding. Sheridan's words seemed to come from far away. She hugged her arms around her body. All she could think about was the cold and the fear of being buried alive in this cave for ten thousand years, like a living seed sealed up in an airtight, moisture-proof plastic envelope.

She couldn't stand another take, not another minute. She had to get out from under the weight of this mountain. She turned and bolted headlong down the corridor, skidding, catching herself, not stopping until she ran up against the door.

"Let me out! I can't breathe!"

Behind her, Sheridan exploded. "Christ! Does that mean I have to start all over again?"

"Somebody shut her up." Valerie's voice reverberated behind her. "Jake, get her out, will you? It's all right, Colt. Once more. You've got it down pat, now."

"Help! Please open the door."

After what felt like ten thousand years, the door opened and Dinah rushed into the first section. Another locked door lay ahead of her. The sterile, permafrost walls increased her panic. She bent double and took several deep breaths.

Mahler took hold of her arm. "Take it easy. I'll get you out."

She wasn't sure what he did, but the guard opened the first door and she stumbled out into the open and drew in a lung full of burning, icy air that made her wheeze.

"Are you okay?" Mahler sounded genuinely concerned.

"I will be." She pulled herself together. "I can usually control myself better. Sorry if I messed up the filming."

"They'll get it done. Come on. Let's go back to the car."

She hunched her shoulders against the wind and made a dash for it. Mahler was surprisingly fast for a stocky man. He beat her to the car and held open the front passenger door for her. She slid in and he ran around and jumped into the driver's seat.

Halverson had left the keys in the car and Mahler started the engine and turned up the heater. "Brrr. People who live in this godforsaken place have got to have antifreeze in their veins."

She said, "I feel as if my blood's congealed."

"It's hell for a man like me with no hair on his head." He laughed. "Mind if I smoke?"

"Go ahead."

He rolled down the window an inch, lit a Winston with a gold lighter, and leaned his head back on the headrest. "I can't wait to get back to civilization and that means at least thirty degrees above zero."

"You've been to Longyearbyen before, right?"

"Only once, in the summer. Val's been here a number of times since the vault opened in oh-eight. She speaks the language like a native. I've made our case to the agricultural ministries in most of the capitals of Europe, but Val's the face of Tillcorp in Norway."

"She seems more focused on Senator Sheridan's campaign than Tillcorp's business."

"If Colt makes it to the White House, it'll be a boon for companies like ours. He's a pragmatist. He doesn't put his head in the sand about climate change. It's here and it's already making a difference in what kinds of crops can be grown and where. Colt understands the potential of genetically modified foods to solve a lot of the world's problems. He has to tread carefully when he talks about it, but Val can help him make GM products more palatable to the folks in Peoria. Whit Keyes wants to drill off the Atlantic coast and she made that sound palatable even to the Massachusetts liberals."

"Was she his attorney or his campaign manager?"

"Both. She did a lot of what that Teilhard kid does now. But after a while, Whit was depending on her for everything."

"And you took her away from him." Dinah wondered how much Mahler depended on Val. Their communications seemed a bit bumpy. "Will Sheridan take her away from you?"

"Probably." He laughed. "She's a great wartime consigliere. She might be more of a loose cannon in peace time." He took a drag off his cigarette and blew the smoke out the window. "Val seems to think you pose a danger to our, how shall I say? To our aspirations in Norway."

Dinah's heart rate had returned to normal and she was beginning to warm up. But there was a suggestion of menace in his voice that chilled her all over again. "I don't see how I could pose a danger to a multi-national company like Tillcorp."

"Over the years I've learned that big trouble can come in small packages. And Val's a worrier. She's noticed that you're a little too chummy with people who may not have our best interests at heart. Brander Aagaard, Erika Sheridan, and word has it that you were socializing with Inspector Ramberg last night."

Her neck prickled. Who could have seen her with Aagaard at the Kaffe & Kantine, or with Thor at the Løssluppen? Erika said that Mahler and his guards spied on her. Were they spying on Dinah, too? She tried to sound blasé. "Senator Frye accused Senator Sheridan of being paranoid, but I think Valerie's the one who's paranoid."

"That's what I told her. You're smart enough to know what's what. You can't believe half the garbage these media types will tell you. They fabricate all kinds of wild stories to keep the lunatic fringe fired up."

Was he baiting her to find out if she'd heard the cutworm story? Would her knowing about it confirm Valerie's opinion that she posed a danger? She couldn't see Mahler's face in the dark, but she sensed a spring-loaded ferocity under the cordial exterior. She said, "I don't know anything about your aspirations in Norway. What is it you want from the Norwegians?"

"Not much. Norway is awash in petro dollars and a lot of those dollars are going to buy up farmland in third world countries. Depressed prices and desperate sellers make land a good investment for their Oil Fund. If I can persuade the Norwegians to teach the local peasants to plant our seeds, we can end hunger in the world within five years. We can eliminate those recurring African famines and never have to see another documentary of skin-and-bone children dying of starvation in their mothers' arms."

This high-minded speech didn't jibe with Aagaard's description of corporate greed and callousness. If Valerie thought she and Mahler were being "played," it went double for Dinah. But by whom? She said, "You sound as if you really mean that."

"I do mean it. My great-grandparents lived through the potato famine in Ireland and the Dust Bowl put my maternal grandfather out of the farming business in Kansas. Drought, soil erosion, the loss of a hundred million acres in the American heartland. Winds carried the topsoil from Oklahoma and Kansas and Colorado all the way to the East Coast where it rained into the Atlantic. Black blizzards, they called those winds. It was a preventable tragedy. Those bullheaded European immigrants believed that rain would follow their plows and the government encouraged them. They were wrong. Just like today's wheat farmers are wrong if they believe that fertilizers and crop rotation will keep them in business."

"But if all the wheat farmers used your seed, wouldn't that be bad for diversity?"

"Diversity is overrated. When bellies are empty, it's quantity and reliability that count." He took a last puff on his cigarette and pitched it out the window. "That's where back-to-Eden purists like Eftevang lose the high ground."

"But you make gene modification sound altruistic, when what you're really doing is converting other people's seeds into patented Tillcorp products to sell back to them at a profit."

"It's called intellectual property. If our scientists design a seed, we should be compensated for our invention like any other inventor."

"Year after year?"

Mahler must have heard it all before. He gave no sign that he'd taken offense. "Seventy-five percent of the earth's plant varieties have gone extinct in the last hundred years and today, sixty percent of the human diet comes from four foods—corn, rice, wheat, and potatoes, all of them susceptible to disease. We don't want to stamp out diversity or cram our products down the throats of people who don't want them. But incredible scientific advances are on the horizon—fruits that can produce vaccines against infectious diseases, fish that mature faster, cows that are resistant to mad cow disease. It's our obligation as leaders in the field of biotechnology and genetic engineering to devise new solutions, to take the knowledge embodied in disease-prone seeds and transform them into disease-resistant seeds. Already, our creations are an insurance against hunger in many parts of the world, improving both the yield and quality of the harvest."

She said, "It's convenient that the agreement between local gene banks and the Svalbard vault allow you to glom onto any seeds you like for experimentation."

"So what? The vast majority of the seeds aren't cultivated today. The Svalbard Vault is like a museum. Same with the local banks. If a seed can't grow a crop that will sustain a hungry population, what good is it? My company re-engineers the duds and makes them useful."

The senators and Valerie spilled out of the vault and into the blue-green light like Martians emerging from the mother ship. They walked toward the cars, slipping and sliding on the slick walkway.

Dinah said, "I don't know what's the right way to think about gene modification. I don't know why my talking to Brander Aagaard or Erika Sheridan worries Valerie. It seems to me that if anything poses a danger to your company's objectives in Norway, it's the murder of Fritjoe Eftevang."

"Did Aagaard tell you Eftevang was peddling a rumor that Tillcorp profited from the famine in Myzandia?" The timbre of menace in his voice was unmistakable.

She hesitated.

"Well, did he?"

"As a matter of fact, he did."

"Well, it's a crock. Eftevang had an ax to grind. He listened to the wrong people and cherry-picked his facts to support his opinions. Now Aagaard is angling to do the same."

"If the rumor is false, why are you so uptight about it?"

"Myzandia." The word came out in a hiss of disgust. "Every kind of scam and swindle under the sun spews out of that stinking pesthole." He opened the car door and the overhead light flashed on his face. It was congested with anger. He stood outside waiting for Valerie and Halverson, but after a few seconds he poked his head back inside. "You want to know why I'm uptight? I'll tell you why. Because even smart people will buy into a fairy tale if it pits the poor against rich SOBs like me." He smiled a sly, malign smile. "Ask Whit Keyes, why don't you? He can tell you what it's like doing business down there."

Chapter Fourteen

Mahler relinquished the driver's seat to Halverson and insisted, with notably diminished cordiality, that Dinah remain up front. He sat behind Halverson and Valerie sat behind Dinah. She could feel their hostility percolating through her headrest.

Valerie announced that the airport runways would be plowed and the tower opened by the next morning. Herr Dybdahl had reassured the senators that the Eftevang business wouldn't cause them any further inconvenience and they could leave tomorrow.

"What about Ramberg?" asked Mahler.

"His hands are tied. Dybdahl has the governor's ear. The governor of Svalbard is the de facto chief of police."

Halverson drove at a saner pace on the return and even tried to make chitchat. "At the turn of the last century, there were five hundred and seventy-eight varieties of beans in your country alone."

Dinah was abstracted, trying to work out whether Mahler was a devil or a misunderstood idealist. Whether Fritjoe Eftevang was a purveyor of dreck or an idealist murdered for the crimes he was about to expose.

"Guess." Halverson directed this imperative to Dinah. "Guess how many there are today."

"Beans? I don't know. Two hundred? Two-fifty?"

"We have just thirty varieties in the vault."

"Really?" She didn't like beans. Thirty sounded like plenty.

"Beans supply more protein and nutriments at a lower price than any other food plant."

"Who knew?"

"Thiamin, folate, niacin. Beans are a miracle food. And East Africa has the highest consumption of beans in the world."

"Good for them." She didn't like to think of herself as anti-science. Mahler's spiel was persuasive. The world was evolving. Animals and plants evolved to meet a changing environment. Maybe it wasn't so bad if science hurried evolution along and businessmen rewarded themselves for driving the process. There would always be those who resisted progress, but it was inexorable and, apart from the A-bomb, it generally improved people's lives and longevity.

Halverson lectured on. "Africa is always the worst case. Drought is a constant problem and beans are vulnerable to extremes of climate. Germination depends upon…"

Mahler inclined his head over the front seat. "Tell Dinah what Tillcorp did about the bean blight in Myzandia, Peder."

"There was root rot in the late nineties and it was hard to reach the small growers to inform them about newly developed, rot-resistant seeds. Tillcorp paid the people who sell soft drinks and snacks to disseminate the information at their kiosks. They also paid the workers at health clinics to spread the word."

Dinah frowned. How did Halverson know what Tillcorp had done in Myzandia? Had he worked for the company?

"Tell her what else we did," urged Mahler.

"Tillcorp distributed free bags of seeds. Famine was averted."

Mahler sat back, apparently feeling vindicated.

Dinah rolled over in her mind what he had said about Whitney Keyes and Myzandia. Ask Whit Keyes. Did his foundation have health clinics in Myzandia? Had Tillcorp's free, non-reproducing seeds been distributed by Keyes' clinics? Were they also the targets of false rumors and scams? Whatever happened in Africa, she thought how ironic it was that here—six hundred miles from the North Pole—the continent with the hottest recorded temperatures on earth should be so much on everyone's mind.

◇◇◇

Back at the hotel, Dinah went straight to her room and turned up the thermostat. She brewed herself a cup of hot tea and phoned Norris Frye's room. Either he wasn't there or he wasn't answering. She left him a message that the hapai banana shoots had been duly delivered, cataloged, and locked away in the Svalbard Vault for the next ten thousand years, or until such time as they might be wanted to re-vegetate a tropical island or to supply a corporate breeder with genetic material for experimentation.

She placed a call to Eleanor without knowing exactly where to begin the conversation. Local seed banks acquired the seeds from growers and collectors and, in turn, they consigned samples of the seeds to the Svalbard Vault. The samples on deposit in Svalbard couldn't be touched except upon request of the donor. But the contracting donor was the local seed bank, not the individual grower, and there was no guarantee that the local seed bank wouldn't allow the seeds to be removed and re-engineered into a miracle food or a Frankenstein by Tillcorp or anyone else who asked.

Eleanor didn't answer her phone. Dinah hung up and worked out the time difference. Longyearbyen was twelve hours ahead of Hilo, which would make it two o'clock in the morning Eleanor's time. Lucky thing Eleanor hadn't picked up. Dinah was already imagining a very edgy conversation.

The person she most wanted to talk to was Thor. She needed to warn him that Dybdahl had short-circuited his investigation and his American *mistenkeligs* would slip the net tomorrow. But Thor didn't answer either. It was a trifecta of frustration. She wouldn't be surprised if Dybdahl had sent Thor on a wild goose chase until the senators had made their getaway. She might never see him or talk with him again, although she wasn't sure what she would say to him. She had no idea if anything she'd learned from Mahler or Peder Halverson bore on Eftevang's murder. So far, Africa seemed to be the only connection between the dead man and the Americans.

If Valerie had her way, she might never have the chance to talk with Erika again either. Sheridan would probably keep her locked up in his suite on the return flight. Dinah felt stymied. And then she thought of Brander Aagaard. Valerie couldn't keep her from talking to him. She would be very interested to hear his rejoinder to Mahler's side of the story about Myzandia. She didn't know where he was staying, but it would have to be a place where smoking was tolerated.

A drop of sweat dribbled out of her hair and she realized that the room was sweltering. Fire or ice, there was no in-between in this town. She lowered the thermostat, washed her face and, on the spur of the moment, decided to return to the Kaffe & Kantine. With luck, Aagaard would be there drinking *kaffe* and Akevitt and, if he wasn't, she would stick around for a late lunch. Maybe on her walk there or back, she would spot Thor riding around in his patrol car and flag him down. When her body temperature had returned to normal, she re-dressed for the opposite extreme.

The lobby was filling up with rosy-cheeked tourists who'd apparently returned from their outings. They milled about in front of the big fireplace with drinks in their hands, telling stories of dogsled rides and snøscooter safaris, asking each other when the aurora borealis might again become visible, and gossiping about the murder. A flame-haired woman with a Texas accent introduced herself as a psychic and held forth on the disposition to murder by birth sign. "I have a strong feeling that the murderer is a Cancer," she said. "But don't take my word for it. FBI statistics show that Cancer is the most dangerous sign of the zodiac."

Dinah finished lacing up her boots, pulled on her balaclava and Erika's parka, and headed out into the darkness. There were more people on the street this afternoon, almost all of them wearing ski masks and more than a few toting rifles. In most places, the citizens would freak out at the sight of so many armed and masked individuals. In Longyearbyen, nobody batted an eye.

In spite of the ski mask, the cold paralyzed her face. She quickened her steps, but by the time she reached the Kaffe & Kantine, she was half-frozen again. Erika was right. Too much warmth made the cold feel all the colder.

When she stepped inside the Kantine, her face felt too stiff to speak.

"*God dag*," said the man behind the counter. He was the same man who'd brought Aagaard his Akevitt. Lars, Aagaard had called him. He had a lean and wiry frame, but the skin on his face sagged like the dewlaps on a bloodhound.

She peeled off her balaclava and looked around. Except for Lars, the place was deserted.

"*Komme* in. *Komme* in." He walked around the counter with a bottle of clear liquid. "*Sider? Glögg?*"

"No, thanks. I was hoping I'd find the gentleman I met here yesterday morning. Herr Aagaard?"

He shook his head, which caused the skin around his mouth to jiggle.

Aagaard had spoken to him in English. She tried again. "Wild hair, high-pitched voice. He smoked and drank a good deal of Akevitt."

"*Ja, ja*. He was in for *frokost*."

"Do you think he'll come back later?"

"I don't know."

"Did he say where he was going when he left?"

"*Ja*. It was *merkelig*."

"Is that a business in town? If you could give me the address…"

"*Merkelig?* No. *Merkelig* is odd. What he said was odd."

"Odd in what way?"

"He is not someone I would expect to go to the *kirke*."

"What is that, sir?"

"The house of *Gud*."

Dinah's astonishment must have showed.

He expounded. "Where you go to pray. Red steeple. You can see it from here."

She couldn't picture Aagaard in a church. Had he gone to meet someone? *Frokost* was hours ago. He'd be long gone by now. "Do you serve lunch?

"*Nei.*"

"Well, thanks anyway. *Takk.*" She turned to go, then turned back. "How late are you open?"

"Midnight. Maybe your friend will come back."

"Maybe." She replaced her balaclava. "Well, good-bye."

"*Adjø.*"

"Right."

She left and made her way toward the library. The server should be back up and running by now and she could at least see what rumors and conspiracy theories about Myzandia were circulating in cyberspace.

Snowmobiles scooted up and down the street and there were lots of people out walking and speaking in a medley of languages—German, French, Spanish, English. Tourists or students from the university, she guessed.

Today the library was lit up like a Las Vegas casino. A person with a satchel of books over his shoulder and a white skull face mask over his head was leaving as Dinah entered. She took off her balaclava and looked around for the librarian. A young man sat at a table and pored over a large, oppressive-looking tome. She went and stood beside the information desk.

After a couple of minutes, she cleared her throat. "Excuse me. Is the librarian here?"

The young man looked up from his tome. "Sorry, I didn't hear you come in. I'm the librarian." He got up and came around to the desk. "How may I help you?"

"Isn't there another librarian? An older, heavyset gentleman with a white beard?"

"No. I'm the only one who works here weekdays and the Saturday fill-in is a woman."

Dinah's confidence crumbled. When was she going to quit jumping to conclusions? She should have known that librarians don't wear baseball caps on the job or act shocked when a patron walks in the door. Come to think of it, she had been wearing a mask and Erika's parka. The fat man had looked startled when he saw her face. He must have been expecting Erika.

"Is there something in particular you were looking for?"

"I came to use your computer yesterday, but the gentleman told me your server was down."

"The server is up, but our computers have been taken away to be repaired and upgraded."

"I don't suppose you'd have a personal computer that I could use for a few minutes?"

"No. I'm sorry."

Thwarted at every turn. Well, this was God's way of telling her to go home and leave Longyearbyen's Sami constable to grapple with Eftevang's murder and its African ramifications. She thanked the librarian, jerked on her face mask, and shoved off.

The absence of sunlight was taking a toll on her ability to think, constructively or otherwise. She felt despondent, alien, lonely, at loose ends. On an impulse, she decided to go to the church. Not to play sleuth, although she did wonder what had possessed Aagaard to visit a house of worship. But she wondered a lot of things and the way events were shaping up, she would die wondering. She had accomplished her mission for Eleanor and from this point, it hardly mattered what she did with her last few hours in Longyearbyen. Church seemed like a good place to sit for a while and meditate.

A sign at the cross street pointed her up the hill toward the *kirke*. As it happened, she wasn't the only one going in that direction. A pair of reindeer trotted along just ahead of her, snuffling and snorting. She couldn't keep up with them, but stayed in their tracks and the walking seemed easier. The widely-spaced street lamps showed the odd human boot track, too. She climbed above the houses and at the top of the hill, her four-legged companions diverged and started downhill again. She read the sign in front of the church, printed in several languages, "Lutheran State Church. Northernmost Church in the World." The wind had blown the snow off the steeple's conical roof in places and she saw that it was black atop the red tower. Another sign outside the door read, "No Guns in Sanctuary." The gun rack held one rifle. Presumably, there was no fear of a polar bear following an unarmed worshiper into the sanctuary.

In the vestibule, Dinah took off her boots and lined them up in a rack next to four other pairs. No inside slippers were provided. A wooden table held a large coffee urn, several plates of cookies, and picture postcards describing the church, which apparently never closed. Brochures in every language were displayed on graduated shelves and a motley collection of souvenirs had been laid out for purchase on the honor system. Pens, mugs, socks, and cutesy stuffed polar bears with button eyes. Dinah's eye was drawn to a pair of red, fleece-lined mittens with "Longyearbyen" embroidered on the cuffs. She took off her gloves and tried them on. They were a perfect fit and much warmer than what she had. Like everything else in Norway, the mittens cost three times what they would have cost anywhere else. But when the chill factor dipped below zero, any additional warmth seemed a bargain at twice the price. There were also a few chemical hand warmers which she dropped into her bag. She happily overpaid for her merchandise and padded into the sanctuary in her sock feet.

She sat down in a pew near the back to soak in the ambience. Colorful frescoes adorned the walls, ornate murals decorated the ceiling, and an aura of warm light bathed the altar and chancel. It was beautiful, except for a pervasive cheesy odor, suggestive of the many sock feet that had tramped across the carpet.

Three female tourists ambled around taking photographs in a hushed, reverent way, and an elderly man knelt in front of the altar. Dinah took off her coat and gazed around at the kindly faces of the plaster saints. After a while, her spirits began to lift. Maybe she should start going to church more often. The denomination didn't matter. Her love of mythology had turned her into something of a pagan. There had been so many interesting gods over the course of human history and so many of their biographies read the same. Jesus hung on the cross for three days and was pierced with a spear. Odin hung on that big ash tree for nine nights and was pierced with a spear. Both died voluntarily. Both arose from the dead. To his credit, only Jesus spoke of forgiveness.

Dinah pulled Inge's note out of her purse and smoothed it out on her lap. *You ruined Maks' life and now you would ruin Colt's. You chose. You don't get to change your mind like Lofoten light.* Lofoten light. Alliterative. Poetic. Like the faux librarian. Could he be Inge? Or perhaps Maks, the Fata Morgana songwriter? She folded the note and put it back in her purse. For what it was worth, she would leave it for Thor. She thought about his quirky line about imitating American TV cops and smiled. She wished she'd had more time to get to know him, but such was life. She would give him her e-mail address and ask him to let her know if he ever solved the murder of Fritjoe Eftevang.

The elderly man finished his prayers and doddered down the aisle past her. He looked frail and mopey. Perhaps he was here to prepare his mind for that final journey south. She hadn't noticed when the tourists left, but they were gone. She checked her watch. Four o'clock. Maybe Thor had gone back to his office. If she went back to the hotel, she could phone him and tell him about Inge's note and the senators' plans to sky off home to D.C. tomorrow, although he probably had been informed already. Maybe he'd suggest they have a last supper together. If he was still unreachable, she'd write him a short letter and leave it with the front desk.

She snuggled into Erika's coat and returned to the vestibule to put on her boots. As an afterthought, she helped herself to a chocolate chip cookie, and sashayed out into the darkness.

The first shot confused her. The second tore through her right arm. She tasted blood and chocolate and hit the snow in a heap.

Chapter Fifteen

Jesus, Joseph, and Mary. What was happening? She slithered across the snow on her belly, scrambling for her life toward a snow bank, maybe twenty feet away. She didn't know, but she thought the shots had come from somewhere down below, from one of the barracks-style houses. She reached the bank, turned, and flattened her back against its highest point. She didn't have the nerve to peek over the top. She ran her tongue around her mouth and spit out a gob of bloody cookie crumbs. In her terror, she had bitten the inside of her cheek and a painful, bloody ridge had formed.

Her thoughts were churning. She had seen the action heroes and heroines in the movies do this scene a hundred times. What did they do after they reached cover? They drew their guns. Terrific. She hadn't noticed if the rifle was still in the church's gun rack, but the elderly man had probably taken it. He'd left only a minute ahead of her. Was he the shooter? The target? Had a drunken hunter mistaken her for a polar bear?

She drew her body up into a hunker, being careful to keep her head below the rim of the snow bank, and assessed the damage to her left arm. The sleeve of the parka had been shredded and so had the flesh of her upper arm. Blood oozed toward her elbow. She stifled a gag and shuddered. On the bright side, at this temperature, she would freeze to death before she bled out.

Without a gun, all she could do was cower and pray until help arrived or else make a run for it. People in the movies were always "making a run for it," but where was her "it" and could she get there without being shot again?

Why wasn't a crowd forming? Was the sound of gunfire so routine on a Thursday afternoon in Longyearbyen that nobody bothered to check out the source? The sound of a siren would be music to her ears. Her arm felt as if it were being flayed by a thousand whips.

She duck-walked to the end of the snow bank nearest to the street she'd taken up the hill and peeked over the top. She didn't see any movement, but there weren't many streetlights up here and the shooter could still be out there in the dark, waiting for her to show herself.

Footsteps sounded in the snow behind her. She twisted her head around so fast she nearly lost her balance. A man and a woman were walking toward the church from another direction. The man had an old-timey camera with a telephoto lens slung over his shoulder. The woman was shining a flashlight on a map. Not assassins. Ordinary tourists.

"Help! I've been shot!"

"*Hva?*" The man wheeled around as if he'd heard God speak to him out of a burning bush.

"Police! Call the *politi,* p-p-please." She began to feel light-headed. She pushed herself to her feet and held out her arm to the woman.

The woman shone her light on the bloody sleeve and screwed up her face in horror. "*Ekkel! Blødende!*"

"I think I'm going to be sick," said Dinah, but she fainted instead.

The nurse at the hospital was cool and matter-of-fact. She finished stitching Dinah's wound and began to bandage it. "It is not grave. A bit of torn flesh is all."

"A bit of *my* torn flesh."

"Who did this was a bad shot. Not from Longyearbyen, I think." Her name was Vanya and she radiated the warmth and compassion of a mackerel. She busied herself at a tray table across the room and returned with a loaded syringe. "This is for tetanus." She jabbed the needle into Dinah's other arm.

"Ouch."

"And this is an antibiotic." She handed Dinah a bottle of pills. "Take one twice a day for seven days and have your doctor change the bandage when you return home."

"What about pain pills?"

"You can buy ibuprofen at the *apotek*."

"Thanks for the TLC."

"What?"

"Nevermind." Dinah hopped off the examination table, grabbed her shirt, and tried to ease her painful left arm through the sleeve.

Nurse Vanya came up behind her and guided the arm. "You will be sore for a few days."

"I will be sore until the creep who did this to me is behind bars," she said and stalked out of the room.

Thor got up from his seat. "The nurse said…"

"Don't tell me that I'm lucky or that the damage was minor or say anything whatsoever to minimize my suffering, do you hear?"

"I hear." He was holding a clear plastic bag with Erika's parka inside and a folded blanket. "Lean on me." He offered her his arm. "If your suffering has eased by the time we get back to your hotel, I'll buy you dinner and a bottle of wine."

She hooked her unhurt right arm in his left. He was wearing a neatly pressed flannel shirt and gave off a light, woodsy scent. Had he spruced up and dabbed on aftershave for her benefit?

He said, "I'll call my friend from the Radisson and postpone our date until tomorrow."

So much for vanity. "No need to do that. I can tell you everything I know in the car in three Longyearbyen blocks."

His car was parked just two feet from the door. He let go of her and handed her the blanket. "You can wrap this around your shoulders if you like."

"I can survive two feet, but haven't the Norwegians ever heard of underground parking?"

"Not practical on Spitsbergen. Most buildings are built on pilings. Otherwise, the heat of the building would melt the permafrost and it would sink."

Tonight, he opened the passenger door for her and tucked her inside like a true gentleman. He tossed the blanket and the bag with Erika's parka into the trunk and took his place behind the wheel. Dinah pulled down the shoulder harness with her right hand, but when she tried to use her left hand to snap the tab into the holder, a feeling like hot pincers bit into her biceps and she let go of the belt. "If there's a seat belt law in Norway, I'm breaking it. If there's a fine, give the bill to Senator Frye."

"Do you always require immunity from the local laws?"

There was a hint of a smile in his voice and, in spite of her pain she felt a tingle of triumph. All it took to warm him up was getting herself shot. She said, "Laws are getting pettier all the time. In America, there's a new batch of anti-bullying legislation aimed at keeping people from being mean to each other, but it's legal to carry loaded guns. I thought Norway was more civilized than that."

"Svalbard is a special case. We are on the frontier of the wilderness. The gun laws here are more relaxed than they are in the rest of the country."

"And you Europeans call Americans gun-happy."

He drove through a maze of parked snowmobiles and out onto the main street. She rested her head on the headrest, closed her eyes, and thought about Nurse Vanya's opinion of her assailant's skill. Was he a bad shot or a very good one? In her mind's eye, she placed a rifle in Mahler's hands and pictured what he could do with it. Even when he waxed benevolent about saving the world, he transmitted a menacing vibe. She imagined the gun in Valerie's hands. She might have the temperament for murder, but she was small in stature and the recoil of a rifle would have knocked her down. Rod and Lee, on the other hand, were more than capable. They probably had to demonstrate their prowess with a gun to get hired as bodyguards.

Dinah dismissed Norris Frye out of hand. Even if he weren't crippled by gout, he had no motive and anyway, he'd probably fall down and cover his head if somebody showed him a loaded gun. She had no trouble picturing Whitney Keyes holding a rifle. He probably went duck hunting in the Berkshires with the president of the National Rifle Association. And what about Colt Sheridan, whose first name was synonymous with a firearm? He had grown up in Montana where hunting was practically de rigueur and he had served in the military.

Thor said, "I've been asking myself who would attack the Norwegian agriculture minister with a laser and stab a journalist with a hotel carving knife. Now I must add to this *skurk's* rap sheet a gun attack on a visiting banana expert."

She laughed, which seemed to have been his intention. "Sounds like three very different crimes. Or three different *skurks*."

"I don't know, Dinah. Maybe one or two of these crimes are red herrings."

"Why would Eftevang's murderer think that shooting me was worth his while?"

"It depends on whether he, or she, intended to kill you or merely wound you. Perhaps, the purpose was to divert attention from the original murder." He drove into the Radisson's parking lot and parked. He helped her out of the car and squired her into the foyer. He unlaced her boots for her and said, "Go ahead into the restaurant, the fancy one, not the pub. I'll call my friend and join you in a few minutes."

Her arm panged. "I forgot to buy Ibuprofen at the pharmacy. Could you scare me up a bottle from the gift shop?" She reached for her purse.

"Please, no. The governor of Svalbard owes you dinner and a bottle of painkillers."

"Well, then. *Tusen takk*." She proceeded through the lobby and into the Brasserie Nansen where the state dinner had been held. "There'll be two of us," she told the hostess.

"This way, please." The woman picked up two menus and showed her to a table next to a window bordered by winking

Christmas lights. Dinah situated herself in a cushy chair and scanned the room for familiar faces. Apparently, the Americans were dining elsewhere tonight, probably at the place with the Michelin star. It was just as well. She wasn't sure how she would respond to seeing any of them just now and the thought of being trapped in a jet plane six miles over the Arctic Ocean with the person or persons who may have shot her gave her the heebie-jeebies. Maybe she should ask the governor of Svalbard to grant her asylum in addition to the painkillers.

A blue-eyed blonde who could have been Erika twenty years ago brought a pitcher of ice water to the table. Dinah shivered and asked for a hot buttered rum. While she waited, she stared out the window into the unrelieved gloom and racked her brain for a motive that would connect the three disparate crimes. Bio-technology? Politics? Financial corruption? Atrocities in Africa? Sex, drugs, rock-and-roll? It was a regular *koldtbord* of red herrings. And weapons. Had Thor intended to tell her that Eftevang was stabbed with a hotel knife or had it just slipped out when he was trying to be funny? If someone filched a carving knife from the chef's cutlery set, wouldn't he notice? Of course, a rifle could have been swiped from a gun rack anywhere in town and returned without attracting attention. Even if someone noticed, everyone wore ski masks.

Thor returned to the table and sat down just as her hot buttered rum arrived. He ordered a beer and when they were alone, he gave her the ibuprofen and appraised her with his inquisitive brown eyes. "You married or have a boyfriend?"

It wasn't what she'd expected. "The latter."

"Don't you want to call him and tell him what happened? Prepare him not to hug you too tightly when he sees you again?"

She shook two pills out of the bottle, popped them into her mouth, and swigged them down with a slug of warm rum. "We've agreed to suspend physical expressions of affection for the time being." She declined to ask him about his girlfriend. She took Inge's letter out of her purse with her napkin and laid it on the table. "This was in the pocket of Mrs. Sheridan's parka."

He took the note out of the envelope and gave it a once-over. "Inge. The name you asked me about before. You said you didn't know where you'd heard it."

"It didn't seem relevant at the time. I tried to respect Erika's privacy."

"There is no immunity for withholding information from the police."

"Arrest me. I'd feel a lot safer. Anyhow, I've been careful not to smudge the fingerprints, if there are any. At first, I guessed that it had to do with an affair Erika was having. Now I don't know. Maybe Erika told Inge that she was going to pass ruinous information about her husband to the media. Maybe she tipped off Aagaard or Eftevang that Mahler would be on the senators' plane. I suppose she could have met with one or both of them the night she sneaked away from the hotel. I neglected to tell you one other thing."

"What's that?" He did not look amused.

She steeled herself for a lambasting. "Erika left the hotel on the night of the murder. She was out for hours."

"Anything else you haven't regarded as relevant until now?"

"No."

He made a sour mouth and reread the note. "Lofoten light. That's a pretty way to express what seems to be a rather cruel rebuke."

"Is Lofoten the Arles of Norway?"

"It is, actually. It's a chain of islands in the Norwegian Sea with sheltered bays and picturesque fishing villages. A number of artists live there."

Dinah told him about the man she'd met in the library. "I think it may have been Maks Jorgen or, perhaps, Inge—if Inge is a man. I was wearing Erika's coat and before he saw my face, he said something in Norwegian. *Kir* or *kar*."

"*Kar* means a guy, or a chap. Could it have been *kjære*?"

"Maybe. What does that mean?"

"It's an endearment. Darling."

"Someone who loves her then. Is there any way you can trace him?"

"If he's Norwegian and has ever applied for a passport, his fingerprints and biometric identifiers will be on file." He removed a plastic bag from his jacket pocket and slid the note inside. "Too bad the information can't be obtained while you're still here."

"Can't you seize my passport and detain me for questioning?"

"I don't know. Herr Dybdahl is rather anxious to get rid of his American guests. Let's order some dinner and wine and discuss it."

Neither of them wasted much time over the menu. Thor beckoned a nearby waiter. Feeling the need for protein to compensate for her blood loss, Dinah ordered a beefsteak. Thor ordered smoked lamb and a bottle of Sangiovese.

When the waiter had gone, he said, "If you decide to stay for a while, perhaps I'll take you across the tundra by dogsled."

"Aren't you afraid of polar bears?"

"I have a pair of Karelian bear dogs. Crockett and Tubbs."

She couldn't hold back a guffaw. "The old TV show cops?"

He accorded her a sheepish half-smile. "I've always had a yen to visit Miami. It looks so lush and tropical. Do the men still wear t-shirts under pink and white Italian blazers and loafers with no socks?"

"I don't think so, Thor."

"Anyway, the Karelian dogs are bred and trained to drive off the *isbjørn*."

"Is that Norwegian for bear?"

"Ice bear. It's against the law to shoot a bear unless it attacks. The Karelians help to remind the *isbjørn* that his territory ends at the city limits." Another sheepish smile. "But to be safe, we erected a fence around the kindergarten."

She laughed. "I wouldn't want to meet one of your *isbjørns*, but I'd love to see the northern lights."

"In the Sami language, they're called *Guovssahas*, the lights that can be heard."

"Do they actually make sound?"

"Scientific instruments haven't detected them, but I've heard them and so have a lot of other people. But it's the colors and the movement that dazzle you. The Sami believed *Guovssahas* would punish those who failed to appreciate their beauty."

"Tell me about the Sami gods."

"It was mostly ancestor worship and animal spirits. White animals carried special importance. There was a sky god, Horagalles, who was a precursor of Thor, the Viking god of thunder."

"Does Horagalles have a lot of namesakes in Norway?"

A full smile. "Not so many as Thor, although they had roughly the same job—thunder, lightning, the weather, the oceans, and nailing the bad guys. Like Thor, Horagalles carried a hammer which he used to bash out the brains of evildoing trolls and giants."

"Did the Sami pray to Horagalles?"

"All communication with the gods went through their shamans, called *noaidi*. They drummed and chanted and played the flute until they fell into a trance and abracadabra, enlightenment came."

Their wine came. The waiter poured a taste. Thor gave the glass to Dinah. She swished it about pronounced it fine. The waiter poured and withdrew.

She held up her glass. "*Skäl.*"

"Cheers." He took a sip and furrowed his brow. "I missed something. A man is dead because of it and you've been hurt. I should have held Eftevang until his enemies had left the country. If I had more time and the support of the governor, I could nail Mahler and his bodyguards."

"You think it was Mahler?"

"He would be my prime suspect if I were allowed to investigate the murder properly."

She fingered the bandage on her arm. She felt as if it were shrinking and cutting off circulation. "Why do you think Herr Dybdahl is so anxious to get rid of us?"

"I've asked myself that question."

"And what was your answer?"

"I think he is what the American TV cops would say, 'on the take' from Tillcorp. Maybe he thinks that the longer I investigate, the more likely it is that his own corruption will be exposed."

"Do you have cause to believe Dybdahl's dirty or is it more of a gut feeling?"

"He lives exceptionally well on a minister's salary. I've seen photographs of his home on Oslofjord."

"His grandmother didn't die and leave him the house and a chest full of kroner?"

"It's possible."

"Do you know of any special privilege or dispensation that he or the Norwegian government has granted to Tillcorp?"

"No."

"Then I'd classify your suspicion as more of a gut feeling. But if Eftevang had documents that could implicate him in a bribery scandal, that would give him a motive to commit murder. But why would Eftevang or his accomplice, if he had one, shoot the agriculture minister in the eye with a laser?"

Thor stared into his wine glass and seemed to contemplate. "Maybe Dybdahl staged the attack on himself."

"Why would he do that?"

"Perhaps to prevent the media from learning that he knew in advance that Mahler would be on that plane and that he expected to do business with him. Dybdahl seldom visits Svalbard or personally entertains foreign dignitaries. But if he came to get a payoff from Mahler, that would explain it."

Dinah was skeptical. "A, nobody but you suspected him of being on the take. B, Eftevang hated Tillcorp. He wouldn't be conniving with Dybdahl if Dybdahl was in league with the company. And C, Dybdahl wouldn't sacrifice an eye when he could simply deny any accusation that he was on the take."

"Odin sacrificed an eye."

"You're the second person who's mentioned Odin's eye today. But Odin was a god. If he'd wanted to, he could've conjured up a brand new eyeball. Dybdahl's eye is irreplaceable."

"Okay, I take your point. We'll know more when we examine the laser for fingerprints."

"You found it?"

"The postman found it. It had been dropped into a mail slot at the airport."

She couldn't fit the pieces together. "I can accept the proposition that Jake Mahler or Valerie Ives tried to bribe Dybdahl. I can accept the proposition that Eftevang knew something damaging about Tillcorp or possibly Whitney Keyes' health foundations. And I've been warned against talking to people who don't have Tillcorp's best interests at heart, including you. But why would anyone want to kill *me*? It couldn't be a case of mistaken identity. I've been wearing Erika's coat for two days."

"I don't know who or why, Dinah. All I know is that Dybdahl's going out of his way to obstruct my investigation." One side of his mouth slanted up. "If I knew who shot you, I'd put a *nid* on him."

"What's a *nid*?"

"A Viking curse. You stick a horse's skull on top of a pole called a nidstang and point it toward the house of your enemy. The destructive forces of Hel, the goddess of death, are channeled up the pole and out through the horse's skull."

"I thought Hel was a region. Like hell, only icy cold instead of hot."

"That's right. Hel was the fortress of Niflheim. But Hel was also a goddess, one of the children of Loki, who was the Father of Lies, and Angrboda, an evil giantess. The lower half of Hel's body was greenish-black and decayed and she was always in a foul mood."

"Not hard to see why."

Their dinner arrived. The waiter laid a steak knife beside Dinah's plate, replenished her wine, and retired.

She picked up the knife. "Was it a Radisson knife that killed Eftevang?"

"Yes. The logo was engraved on the handle."

"No prints?"

"No."

"Did the medical examiner find anything noteworthy?"

"We don't have a medical examiner in Svalbard. Nobody dies here."

"Because it's against the law?"

"Against public policy anyway. The body was flown to Tromsø. I'll have to wait for a report from the examiner there. He's on holiday until after the New Year."

"Isn't there a backup?"

"Also on holiday." He cut into his lamb. "Have you heard Mahler say anything about Eftevang?"

"Nothing except…"

"Except?"

"Eftevang may have been in Myzandia and Mahler seems to think Myzandia is the root of all evil. He said I should ask Whitney Keyes what happened there." Dinah didn't think she'd get an answer, but why not ask? "Aagaard said you wouldn't tell him what you found in Eftevang's room. Will you tell me?"

"I didn't tell Aagaard because he is a pain in the *rumpeballe*. But there's no point in secrecy. There was nothing there."

"No documents of any kind?"

"Not a scrap, not a cell phone, or a computer, or a digital device of any kind."

Dinah perked up. "You could search everyone's rooms again tonight. Whoever has Eftevang's PDA is the murderer. Case solved."

"I wouldn't know what I'd be looking for. Anyway, thanks to Dybdahl and the influence of the senators, the governor has blocked my authority to search or detain any of you Americans."

"And the shooting of an American citizen won't alter his decision?"

"Not so long as you're able to walk onto that plane tomorrow."

Dinah touched her tongue to the sore spot where she'd bitten the inside of her cheek and cradled her sore arm. She was glad her injuries didn't disable her from walking. Her life might have been changed forever if the bullet had found a vital organ or her head. But when it came to being shot, there was no such thing as a minor injury. She was unnerved by her close call and it would be nice if somebody babied her just a little. "Will you cut my steak for me?"

He cut the steak into small bites. She watched his hands as he worked and wondered if the attraction was mutual. He slid her plate back across the table. "There you go."

"*Tusen takk.*"

Conversation tapered off. She chewed her steak as delicately as she could and tried to conceal her thoughts, which were inappropriate in the extreme. Thor quaffed his wine and looked at everyone and everything in the restaurant but her. Perhaps he was attracted, but had a girlfriend and the decency not to cheat on her with a one-night stand. Dinah wasn't feeling as decent as she ought. If he were to suggest…

He stood up and waved. "Senator Sheridan, a word please."

Dinah stiffened. Sheridan was walking into the dining room with Mahler and Valerie. Sheridan broke away and came over to their table. "Good evening, Dinah, Inspector Ramberg. Any progress to report on the investigation?"

"I'm afraid not. I must tell you there's been an attempt on Ms. Pelerin's life."

"An attempt on…Are you serious?"

"As a bullet hole." Thor's face was inscrutable. "We don't know if she was the target. She was wearing your wife's coat. Do you know anyone who might want to harm Mrs. Sheridan?"

"Jesus, no." Sheridan blanched beneath his tan. His eyes fastened on Dinah's bandage. "Are you all right?"

"My arm hurts."

"But who…?" Sheridan appeared at a loss.

Thor said, "With the death of Herr Eftevang, it is unlikely that any other resident of Norway would have a reason to attack a member of your entourage."

Sheridan heard the innuendo and brought himself back to a brusque, authoritative mode. "I'll make sure that both Dinah and my wife receive protection until we leave for the U.S. tomorrow,

Inspector. And if you need anything further following our departure, feel free to contact my Washington office or Senator Keyes' office. We'll be happy to provide written statements or... or whatever you need."

"On behalf of the governor of Svalbard, we appreciate your cooperation."

"Certainly." Sheridan nodded summarily and rejoined Mahler and Valerie. The three of them spoke excitedly and left in a hurry.

Thor said, "Sheridan's a worried man."

Dinah didn't doubt that the senator was worried, but his problems seemed too gnarly and convoluted to think about at the moment, maybe ever. She was beginning to reconcile herself to the idea that she might never know anything more than she knew right now. In twelve hours, she'd be out of Longyearbyen and on her way to Washington and she wouldn't tarry there longer than it took to get a flight to Honolulu. That was as far as she could see into the future.

Thor paid for the meal and walked her to her room.

At the door, she said, "Will you keep in touch? Let me know what you find out about Inge and...and anything else?"

"You may learn a bit more before take-off. If the runways haven't been graded because the work crew was called away on an emergency, there's not much anyone can do."

"Inspector Ramberg, you *are* devious."

"It's only a holding action. When Dybdahl finds out, he'll see to it that the governor sends a fresh crew and an official reprimand for me."

"Then I guess we'd better say good-bye tonight. How do you say good-bye in Norwegian?"

"Like this," he said, and kissed her in a way that made jouncing over the tundra in a dogsled seem considerably more desirable than she had previously imagined.

Chapter Sixteen

It was ten p.m. in Longyearbyen, therefore ten a.m. in Hilo. Eleanor would have had her usual two cups of mamaki tea, which lowered her blood pressure, and she would have finished her traditional morning hula, which always put her in a tolerant, spiritual frame of mind. She would be as mellow right now as Dinah was ever likely to find her. All Dinah really needed to tell her was that her hapai banana shoots were safe in Svalbard, but pursuant to international treaty, they were up for grabs from the seed bank back home. There was no pressing need to communicate this fact. The deposit had been made and the die was cast. But somehow, she felt the need to speak with Eleanor.

Without going all introspective and psychoanalytical, she supposed this need had something to do with her guilt feelings. Not that she had any reason to feel guilty. It wasn't as if she owed Jon a duty not to kiss another man and she certainly didn't owe his Aunt Eleanor an explanation for her extracurricular kissing. But as she had learned to her sorrow, whenever she had to try and rationalize her actions in order to feel good about herself, she was already pretty well launched on a guilt trip. She reached for the phone.

Somebody knocked on her door. Fate.

Dinah accepted it. She unhooked the chain and peeped out.

Valerie smiled solicitously. "Colt told me that you'd been wounded. Is there anything I can do?"

"No. Thank you for your concern."

"Please, Dinah, may I come in?"

"I'm all right, Valerie. Don't trouble yourself."

"Please?"

Sensing an ulterior motive and in no mood to be pushed around, Dinah nevertheless relented and opened the door.

Valerie looked hard at her bandaged arm and then at her face. "Someone really shot you?"

"What do you want, Valerie? A surgeon's report?"

"No, of course not." She walked around to the armchair by the window and sat down, uninvited. "Don't take this the wrong way, but it does seem to be a very slight injury."

"This is a test, right? If I haul off and punch you in the mouth, that will prove that my arm is fine and I wasn't shot?" It was amazing how fast this woman could bring her to a simmer.

Valerie didn't seem to notice. "But why would anyone want to kill *you*?"

"Gosh, Val. You make it sound as though I'm not worth wasting a bullet on."

"That's not what I meant." She stood up and bit her lower lip. "Look, Dinah, I know we started off on the wrong foot. But it's my job to look out for Senator Sheridan and my employer and some very strange things have been going on."

"You think, Val?"

She ignored the sarcasm. "Since you were wearing Erika's coat, we don't know whether the target was you or her."

"That's true," said Dinah. "But Erika's coat is pretty distinctive. Erika and Lee and everyone who went on the seed vault tour knew that I was wearing it."

"I expect this will infuriate you, but until we know who is doing these things, I would appreciate it—Senator Sheridan and Jake Mahler, all of us would appreciate it—if you didn't speak to the press when we get back to D.C. It's difficult enough to have a Norwegian with some connection to us murdered. But to have an American, a member of the senators' entourage shot, you can imagine. It would cause a feeding frenzy. Can we count on your discretion, Dinah?" She humbled herself. "Please?"

"I don't expect to be mobbed by reporters in D.C. and I don't plan to call a press conference."

"Thank you." She bounced up to leave. "And I really am sorry you were hurt."

Chapter Seventeen

Overstimulated on multiple levels, Dinah changed into her nightshirt, performed her nightly regimen, and tried to calm her nerves by reading something boring. She browsed her book of myths for a benign, soporific story, but Norse mythology, like the climate in which it was conceived, offered no respite from the grim reality of Fate. The main thrust was that everyone dies and, according to the page she ended up on, the Valkyries got to choose who died in battle.

The Valkyries were a squadron of winged female death angels with names like Shrieking, Raging, Axe-Wielder, and Wrecker of Plans. This fearsome ensemble circled above the battlefields, meting out death or deliverance as they saw fit, and bearing away the fallen heroes to Valhalla, Odin's celestial hall of the dead. The queen of the Valkyries was Freyja, a golden-haired, blue-eyed beauty who divided her time between accommodating lovers and accumulating corpses. Her husband Od must have known she was a corpse goddess when he married her, but he may have objected to the free and easy way she bestowed her sexual favors. Giants, dwarfs, goats—she serviced them all. Od didn't cite his grounds, but one day he walked out and didn't come back. Freyja never stopped weeping for him.

"Er-i-ka!"

Dinah tensed. Sheridan reminded her of Stanley Kowalski bellowing for his Stella.

A riot of angry shouts went up outside her door. "I don't know, Senator. She was here a minute ago."

"Don't give me that. Where the hell is she now? Er-i-ka!"

Dinah sighed and closed her book. Shrieking and Raging hovered over the battlefield of the Sheridans' marriage, seemingly without letup.

"Weren't you watching?"

"…to the toilet and…"

"The hell with you. Er-i-ka!"

If Sheridan's frantic tone was any indication, Wrecker of Plans had entered the fray.

Someone hammered on Dinah's door.

"Are you in there, Erika? Open up."

Dinah threw on her Radisson-issue robe and cracked the door to the length of the chain. "Is she in there?" Sheridan was yelling.

Lee, Erika's guard, stood behind him. He looked flummoxed, nothing like the tough guy who'd guarded Erika's door. Whitney Keyes, Tipton, and Valerie had gathered behind Lee.

"I'm alone," said Dinah. "I haven't seen Erika since yesterday morning."

"We'll see about that. Let me in." Sheridan jerked the chain, but it held.

Valerie detached from her huddle with Keyes and Tipton and stepped in front of him. She was dressed in her robe, but her make-up was flawless. "Is she in there, Dinah? Are you hiding her?"

"No."

"I don't believe you," said Sheridan. "Let us in."

"She's not here, Senator."

"If you don't open this door, I'll break it down," said Sheridan.

"Colt, please." Valerie put a hand on his sleeve, but he threw it off. She said, "Dinah, if you will let him satisfy himself that she's not there, we will leave you in peace."

Dinah took off the chain and opened the door. Sheridan and Lee charged inside. The senator looked inside the bathroom. Lee searched the closet.

Sheridan raked his fingers through his hair. "Christ. Now what?"

Without coming inside, Keyes began to issue orders. "Lee, you go ask the people at the front desk if anyone saw her leave and notify Rod that we'll need his help. Tip, you'd better let Jake know there's a problem. Colt, you've seen she's not here. Let's take the problem elsewhere."

Lee hurried out of the room. Tip beetled off toward the elevator. Sheridan stood frozen.

"Come on, Colt," said Valerie. "Let's have some coffee and talk. She can't have gone far."

Keyes moved Valerie politely aside. "Valerie, if you would check the women's room off the lobby and the ladies dressing room in the fitness center, that would be helpful. And see what we can find out from the night staff."

She was obviously reluctant, but yielded to necessity. "Try to keep calm, Colt. I'll be back in a few minutes."

Keyes walked into the room. "We, all of us, owe you an apology, Dinah. You've been through an ordeal of your own today. Thinking that his wife may have been the target of that bullet has knocked Colt off his hinges."

Sheridan unfroze and spoke up in a controlled voice. "If you'll excuse us, Whitney, I'd like to speak to Dinah privately."

"Come to my room when you're through," said Keyes.

Sheridan closed the door behind him and turned back to Dinah. "Did Erika say anything, anything at all about where she was going?"

"No."

"This isn't a game, Dinah. If you know where she is or who she's with…please, I'm begging you. Tell me now."

"Don't talk to me about games, senator. A man was murdered and, in case Inspector Ramberg's words didn't sink in, somebody tried to murder me." She held out her bandaged arm, which had begun to throb.

"It could have been Erika." When he spoke her name, his voice went husky.

Dinah was unmoved. "I don't know where Erika has gone or what she's thinking, but if she's playing hide-and-seek, maybe it's because you've had her penned up like a prisoner."

"You don't understand. Erika is a recovering alcoholic. She has delusions."

"Valerie gave me the party line. Alcohol, hallucinations. But I have to wonder if keeping Erika locked up has more to do with your concern that she'll spill the beans about some hanky-panky of your own. Maybe something that would lose you the election."

"Erika has no interest in politics. She wouldn't say or do anything to embarrass me publicly."

Inge's note contradicted that rosy view. "You accused Erika of tipping off Eftevang that Jake Mahler was on your plane."

"She had no idea who Eftevang was until after his death."

"You accused her of tipping off somebody. Was it Aagaard?"

"No." He plopped into the chair beside the window and rubbed his eyes. "I thought she'd communicated with Maks Jorgen. Years ago they were lovers."

"And you think *he* sicced the press on you? Why? Is he an activist of some kind?"

"I don't know. I don't know who she talks to or what she's thinking anymore." He put his head in his hands. "I just don't know."

"Maybe she's run away with Maks to get back at you for being unfaithful to her."

"In twenty-seven years of marriage, I've never once been unfaithful to Erika."

"She seems to think you have."

"What do you mean? With whom? Did she tell you I was unfaithful? Did she say that?"

The fact that the candidate would broach the subject of his wife's former lover or ask such a personal question told Dinah that his veneer was cracking. She said, "I heard you arguing about someone named Hannalore. Who is she?"

He rubbed his forehead and pressed his thumbs against his eyelids. "There is no Hannalore."

"She's one of Erika's delusions?"

"Yes." He teared up.

Jerusalem. Was this guy for real? She kicked herself for being a smart ass in the midst of what was apparently a real crisis. The thing she didn't know was whether those tears were for Erika or for the complications Erika added to his campaign. Either way, she diagnosed the need for a bracer. She went to the mini-bar, took out a bottle of vodka and a can of tomato juice, and mixed him a drink.

His cell phone rang. He dived into his breast pocket and put the phone to his ear. "Nothing? And her boots are still there? Then she has to be in the hotel somewhere. Yes. Yes, I will." He put the phone back in his pocket and stared out the window, perhaps thinking what to say to Erika or do with her once they had her corralled.

Dinah pushed a strong Bloody Mary into his hand. "Drink this. It'll steady your nerves."

"Thanks." He put away half of it in a single gulp.

"Valerie seems very fond of you. Maybe Erika misunderstands your relationship with her."

"That's absurd."

"Your close working relationship with someone as attractive as Valerie would make a wife wonder."

"Val's a political advisor. That's all. She was Whitney's go-to person for years until she moved on to Tillcorp. Ever since Jake decided to underwrite my campaign, she's been my right-hand man and a trusted confidante. She likes Erika and Erika likes her." He stopped, seemingly aghast. "Erika can't think that Valerie and I...?"

His look of sheer, gobsmacked innocence confounded Dinah. Was it possible he didn't see that Valerie was in love with him? That they *weren't* having an affair? She scrolled through the long list of politicians who lied their heads off about their extramarital frolics even when they were caught on Twitpic with their pants down. And yet it appeared that Colt Sheridan was telling the truth. "If it's not another woman, what it is that has Erika so wrought up, senator."

"She's probably told you already."

"Most of it." Why keep on denying it if no one believed her? "But I'd like to hear your version."

"We'd been married for a few years when Erica found out… we found out that we couldn't have children. We talked about adopting, but we were back and forth on the idea and it never happened. We went on. Everything was normal. Then a year ago, Erika began to exhibit signs of depression. She began to drink, more and more heavily as time passed. She…she dreamed up a child we didn't have. A daughter. She calls her Hannalore."

Dinah hadn't expected that, but Erika's remark that what she wanted didn't matter to Colt now made sense. And if she was running around telling everyone there was a little Sheridan out there somewhere and her husband didn't care enough to help find her, the tabloids would have a field day. "Does Erika see this imaginary daughter? Talk to her?"

"No. I don't think so. But she's got it in her head that she actually gave birth and the infant was kidnapped from the hospital. She's obsessed with finding this phantom."

"Here in Norway?"

"A figment isn't confined to a single country."

"So your solution is to confine Erika?"

He looked up, eyes glazed. He will never be president, thought Dinah. His skin's too thin and his wife wielded not just the power to cripple his candidacy. She wielded the power to cut him to the quick. "Do you think she's gone to find this make-believe daughter now?"

"Not without her coat or her boots." He passed a hand across his eyes and lumbered to his feet. "I know Val's asked you not to speak about this. I'm the one who should be asking. Plenty of people, people in both parties, would love nothing better than to use this to ruin me."

"I'm not one of them."

"Thank you."

"Who is Inge?"

He couldn't have looked more stunned if she'd slapped him.

"Is Inge a man or a woman?"

"Erika's sister is named Inge. Did she tell you she was going to find Inge?"

Jake Mahler burst in the door without knocking, followed by Whitney Keyes and Tipton.

"We beg your pardon," said Keyes. "Sorry to intrude, but…"

Mahler talked over him. "I've called Dybdahl. He says we've got to find her tonight or report the situation to Ramberg. I say call him tonight. He has the authority to search all the rooms. If she's holed up here in the hotel, it would save us time and effort."

"Dybdahl doesn't like him," said Keyes, "but the policeman has no incentive to cause us any trouble."

Mahler sneered. "He's got no incentive not to, but your wife has given us no choice but to bring him in."

Keyes addressed himself only to Sheridan. "I've been on the phone to D.C. and given your campaign chairman a script. Delayed due to high level talks on modifications to the Svalbard Treaty and increased U.S. naval activity in Norwegian waters. That should hold off the media for one or two cycles."

Sheridan turned to Dinah. "If she calls you, tell her I'll do whatever she wants if she'll just come back."

"Depends what she wants," said Mahler. "Or so I'd guess."

Sheridan belted the rest of his drink and set the glass down on the window sill. His eyes hardened and the veneer of presidential decisiveness returned. "While you're thinking about incentives, Jake, have you questioned your man, Lee? She couldn't have gotten past him unless he let her." He shoved past Mahler and Keyes, pushed Tipton out of his way, and walked out.

Mahler scratched his face and tugged at his chin. "Just two things could derail Colt Sheridan."

"What are they?" asked Dinah.

"Both of them are women."

Chapter Eighteen

There was nothing to be done but wait. Dinah tried to relieve the tension by reading a myth. She opened her book to the story of Idun, the Norse goddess of youth and rebirth. Idun had an orchard in Asgard, the home of the gods, where she grew the apples of immortality. An apple a day kept the gods young and full of vim and vitality. Thiazi was an evil, shape-shifting giant who coveted Idun's magic apples. One day in the shape of an eagle, Thiazi captured Loki, the trickster god. After torturing him for a while, Thiazi exacted a promise from Loki to lure Idun and her basket of apples across the rainbow bridge from forever-young Asgard into Midgard, the world where mortal men squabbled and made war and suffered and died. The next time that Loki saw Idun, he made up a story about a fabulous tree he'd found in the forest, a tree that bore golden fruit that might also contain the gene for unending youth. Trusting as a child, Idun hung a basket of her marvelous apples over her arm and went with Loki to have a look at this new variety. But as soon as she crossed the bridge into Midgard, Thiazi swooped down and nabbed her. He whisked her away to his aerie in the land of the giants where he vowed to live forever while the gods back in Asgard withered and aged.

Sometime in the wee hours, Dinah dozed off and didn't wake up until her travel alarm clock blatted. Seven o'clock. It would be morning if there were such a thing as morning in this neck of the woods. There weren't even any woods. She shut off the alarm and listened in vain for sounds of combat coming from the room next door, hopeful that Erika had returned during the night. Maybe she had had a change of heart and called her husband. Maybe they had both swallowed some camels and the two of them were reunited and canoodling quietly—she vowing to abstain from alcohol forever after, he vowing to forsake dreams of the White House. If she had returned, the American delegation would be preparing to leave Longyearbyen bright and… well, early anyway. As soon as a crew could be rounded up to clear a runway.

Dinah shambled to the window and looked out. It was as black as she remembered. Black with those aggravating little blue Christmas lights that automatically set off a melancholy reprise of "Have Yourself a Merry Little Christmas" inside her head. Small wonder Erika had fallen off the wagon. The statistics for alcoholism in the Arctic in winter must be staggering. Suicide, too. She thought, if I woke up to this scene every morning, I'd kill myself. She hummed a few bars of "Here Comes the Sun," but it did nothing to lighten her mood.

Thor's POLITI car was nowhere in sight. She wasn't sure if that boded good news or bad for Erika's return. She had fallen asleep before she learned whether Idun made it back to Asgard. In the end things usually worked out well for gods and goddesses. She hoped things worked out well for Erika. As for the senator, she wasn't sure what to hope for him or what to make of his emoting. His tears had touched her, but she couldn't overlook the fact that he was using his office to pull strings for Tillcorp with a foreign government and lying about it, or if not actually lying, he was keeping his efforts on Tillcorp's behalf under wraps. What's more, if Tillcorp was bribing Dybdahl as Thor suspected, Sheridan probably knew and condoned it.

Her arm hurt worse this morning than it did yesterday. She dragged into the bathroom, swallowed two Ibuprofens, and turned on the shower. On second thought, she probably shouldn't get her bandages wet. She gave herself a sponge bath with some of the Radisson's citron, honey, and goat milk body wash and studied her reflection in the mirror. She felt as if she'd aged ten years in the last forty-eight hours. There were dark circles under her eyes and, was it her imagination or had she begun to lose color? She was part Indian, for crying out loud. She held a warm washcloth over her eyes for a long time. When she was through, she moisturized with the Radisson's Thermo-Active moisturizer and began to feel a little less Asgardian and shriveled with age.

Back in the bedroom, she plugged in the coffee maker and turned on the TV. The English language station that she found carried no news about Erika Sheridan. It carried no news about Svalbard at all. There was a great deal of talk about the European debt crisis and turmoil in the Euro zone. A Norwegian commentator couldn't help but be smug that Norway had its own currency. She considered calling Sheridan's room to ask him about Erika, but decided that would be too presumptuous. When she was completely awake and caffeinated, she would seek out Valerie or Tipton. They would have stayed tuned to the Sheridan drama all night without rest. One or the other of them could fill her in on what had transpired while she slept.

Valerie had exacted a promise not to talk to the press about being shot and Sheridan had exacted a promise not to talk about Erika's make-believe daughter. But the more she thought about all this secrecy and high emotion, the more suspicious she became. She hadn't seen Erika since she handed her the white parka day before yesterday. Erika might be laboring under the delusion that her daughter had been kidnapped, but what if Erika herself had been kidnapped? She could have been smuggled out of the hotel before last night and all of this angst and high emotion was just play-acting, part of an elaborate cover-up. From Valerie's perspective, Erika was the number one impediment to Colt Sheridan's coronation. With her gone—

Oh, for heaven's sakes, Dinah. You're turning into one of those conspiracy nuts.

The phone rang and she flinched. What were the odds this was good news calling? She held her hand over the receiver, hesitating. But what if it was Thor? Or Erika? She took a sip of coffee and picked up.

"Hello?"

"Looks like this trip's turned into a game changer." Norris Frye chortled. "Golden Boy's lost his better half and his team's in an uproar. I'm waiting for a call-back from the White House. Leaked to the right people, this could send Colt Sheridan into a tailspin and throw the rest of the Republican field into disarray. I saw Keyes and Mahler come out of your room around midnight. What dirt can you give me?"

"No dirt. Everyone's worried is all."

"You can say that again. I just came up from the lobby. Valerie Ives demanded to look at the hotel register and what she saw got her all excited. She bugged off to find Sheridan and I asked 'em at the desk what was the name that grabbed her. Maks Jorgen. Ever hear of him?"

"It's hard to say."

"Checked in yesterday afternoon and paid in cash. I rang his room and he's not answering. Could be he and Erika ran off together. If she's in there with him, Sheridan will kick in the door. Say, did you bring a camera?"

"No."

"Well, I've got one on my cell phone. It'll do in a pinch."

Dinah couldn't believe it. "Are you going to stake out his room?"

"Right now I'm watching Sheridan's war room. He and the others went behind closed doors not five minutes ago. If you learn anything juicy, get back to me ASAP."

She dropped the handset as if it were a live skunk. Had politics always been this vicious? The tone could be no uglier if senators were plucked at random out of state prisons and party affiliation broke down along the lines of gang membership. At least Norris had put her mind at ease about one thing. The fact that Maks

Jorgen was registered in the hotel put paid to the notion that Erika had been abducted.

She drank another cup of coffee, got dressed, and called the number Thor had given her. A computerized voice told her to leave a message. She had no help to offer and hung up. Maybe he'd already been rousted out of bed to search for Erika. Maybe he'd been searching for her all night. The fact that Erika and Maks Jorgen were lovers didn't change the fact that she would have to be found. If she didn't come forward and verify that she had left of her own free will, people with more authority than Thor would have to become involved. Erika would know that. She might want to fade away like a mirage, but the wife of a prominent U.S. senator couldn't vanish in a foreign country, not even if it was her homeland, without causing an international incident.

Dinah headed off to the dining room for *frokost*. As she passed the Sheridans' room, she saw that the door was ajar. She halted, looked up and down the hall, and walked back.

"Hello? Senator? Anybody?"

She threw a stealthy glance over her shoulder and pushed the door open. Nobody at home. She slipped inside and did a slow turn around the room. The bed was unmade. Erika had lain in it last night plotting her escape while her husband did his thing with Keyes and Mahler and Valerie. Maks could have been watching Lee and waiting for him to take a break. He could have phoned Erika from his room and told her the coast was clear and she slunk out and flitted off to his room. Escaping to another room in the hotel didn't seem like much of an escape. Maybe Maks had brought her another coat. She could have dressed in his room and the two of them stolen away into the night. When Lee returned, he wouldn't have realized that he was guarding an empty room.

Dinah looked in the closet for the khaki colored anorak she'd seen Colt wear to the vault yesterday morning. It wasn't there. Two long white Radisson robes hung to one side next to a lavender velvet evening gown and matching long cape. Erika must have brought it to wear it to the state dinner she skipped out on. Dinah swooshed the hangers with the dress and robes aside, stepped into the closet, slid everything back into place, and crouched down behind them in the corner. She was pretty sure she was invisible except for her shoes. If Colt didn't rummage through the closet looking for Erika, and why would he, she might have been hiding in here when he came in. And when he left in a tizzy, she could have skulked away down the hall while he and Lee searched Dinah's room.

Lee looked like a guy who knew which side his bread was buttered on. He wouldn't be swayed by the pleas of a damsel in distress. Erika and Maks might have bought him off. But if they had, he would have hatted up and hit the road long before Sheridan got around to questioning him. Erika might be an alcoholic. She might be delusional and she might be a loose cannon, but she was no dummy. She could have pulled off an escape without anyone's help.

Dinah climbed out of the closet, tidied the garments, and hurried out of the room, closing the door behind her. She took the elevator down to the lobby. The doors dinged opened and she walked out into the middle of several arguments.

Colt stood toe to toe with Thor. "Don't patronize me, Ramberg. I want every rock in this town turned over until you find her, do you understand?"

Thor remained stolid. "If you have reason to believe that the lady did not leave of her own free will, you should call in your American F.B.I."

"I don't want the American FBI. I want the Norwegian police to do their job and do it in a hurry."

"Be careful what you ask for, Senator."

"I'm in Norway," shrilled Tipton, "and I don't care what time it is in Iowa." He paced about the lobby with his cell phone wedged between his cheek and his shoulder, riffling a sheaf of papers. "You'll have to wake him up. Senator Sheridan wants the caucus put off for a week." The hand holding the papers made an arc of sweeping frustration. "It's not impossible if you want to see a Republican in the White House."

Valerie was arguing with Lee. Her voice was too low to hear what she was saying, but she seemed peeved in the extreme.

Lee said, "Lady, you're barking up the wrong tree."

Dinah exchanged a quick look with Thor and went into the dining room.

Mahler and Keyes were standing at the buffet.

"I thought he was made of sterner stuff," said Mahler. "He's good on the stump and good at the negotiating table, but he's acting like a wimp over that blond baggage. She's a Norwegian. Can't we leave her here and get on with our business? Val can trump up a story about the absent wife that passes muster. I'm counting on Colt to kill that bill requiring labels on GMO foods."

"Keep your voice down, Jake." Keyes cast a look around the dining room. "This is a public place. You never know who's listening or shooting a video from behind a potted plant."

Mahler spotted Dinah at the end of the buffet and mock saluted. "The only one listening is Dinah and she already knows more than's good for any of us. Isn't that right, Dinah?"

She might have taken it as a joke if it weren't for the stitches in her arm. She put a piece of bread and few cold cuts on her plate and removed herself to the farthest corner of the dining room.

To her surprise, Keyes brought his plate and followed her to her table. "May I?"

"Sure."

He pulled out a chair and sat down across from her. "Jake's angry. We're all on edge and he doesn't appreciate the way Colt's going after Lee." He turned over his coffee cup and looked around for a server.

Dinah stared at the slab of dark, smoked eel sprawled across his plate. She tried not to think what the creature must have looked like fresh out of the water.

"How are you holding up, Dinah?"

"Fine. Thanks for asking."

Greta breezed by with a pot of coffee. She filled both of their cups and breezed off again before Dinah could say *takk*.

Keyes blew on his coffee and set it down to cool. "When we get back to the States, I want you to see my doctor, no cost to you. He's the best there is. Anything you need, therapy, whatever you need it."

"Thanks." She could only guess what promises he would try to exact.

"I don't know what Colt told you last night. Not enough, I expect. He's overwhelmed."

Keyes affected a rueful smile. "Erika is an enchanting woman. I think it's her reticence. She mostly listens and lets others talk. I've known her for years, but I have to confess—lately I've wondered if she may have some sort of a dissociative disorder. Multiple personalities. One day serene and composed, the next day dissolving in tears at the death of a stranger and flying off in the middle of the night with her old band mate."

With so many warnings about her alcoholism and hallucinations and an imaginary daughter fantasy, a charge of multiple personalities seemed like piling on. She said, "I guess her departure can't help but damage her husband's campaign."

"To think she might be the First Lady of the United States and she'd throw it all away to go slumming with a has-been musician. The French have a phrase, nostalgia for the mud." Keyes loaded a forkful of eel into his mouth.

Dinah nibbled on a piece of rye bread. He was taking his sweet time to get around to saying what he wanted from her. While his mouth was full of eel, she veered off topic. "I think the motive for Eftevang's murder originated in Myzandia."

For a split second, he seemed nonplussed. He reached for his coffee cup and took a long, slow sip. "Why do you say that?"

"Eftevang hated Tillcorp because of something it did over there. Have you heard a rumor about the company taking advantage of a crop failure, or causing it?"

"There are always rumors. The country has dozens of warring factions and no reputable institutions. It's a hotbed of misinformation and distrust." He flicked a look toward Mahler, whose face was hidden behind a newspaper. Once again, Dinah thought she saw a flash of malice in Keyes' eyes.

"Mr. Mahler told me that you've also had difficulties doing business in the country."

"Suspicion and superstitions are a given in that part of Africa. My clinics try to serve as large a section of the population as we can with the widest range of care and medicines we can procure. It's a challenge, but we hope that the people will eventually trust us enough to let us vaccinate their children against measles and polio."

"Do your health clinics also distribute Tillcorp's seeds or information about them?"

"If they do, I'm not aware of it. The clinics are managed by doctors hired by a consortium of international philanthropists, including my wife and a group of Norwegian contributors." He removed his little half-moon glasses and polished one lens with his napkin. "Norwegians have a penchant for philanthropy. They need to assuage their guilt, I expect."

"What do Norwegians have to feel guilty about?"

"Nothing more nefarious than capitalism. Norway has substantial commercial interests in Africa. They've acquired large tracts of timber and a number of disused and underdeveloped plantations to grow corn and sugar beets for biofuels."

He set his glasses back on his nose. "Back to Erika. Of course, we hope her little exploit doesn't torpedo Colt's presidential chances."

"Senator Sheridan doesn't think she's motivated by politics."

"He may be right. He doesn't want to believe she would hurt him deliberately and neither do I. Actually, we think she was influenced by someone else, someone who is working for one of Colt's rivals." His voice became cunning. "I'm sure you've heard about the dirty tricks that go on during a political campaign. Colt's rivals are constantly on the lookout for gotcha moments they can use against him and, while we'd like to remain above such gamesmanship, it's not possible to be both noble and victorious. Politics is war."

"It's supposed to be war without bloodshed," she said, "and yet Mr. Eftevang's murder appears to have been motivated by politics."

His forehead pleated. "I doubt that very much. But Valerie thinks that Erika was manipulated by someone with a political motive."

"Who?"

"You."

It was Dinah's turn to be nonplussed.

"A pretty young woman in a low-level position would pass under our radar without raising anyone's suspicion. Playing cards with Erika, talking to her about music, coaxing her into revealing confidential secrets. Someone with knowledge of our excursion to Longyearbyen, someone who knew that Mahler would be traveling with us contacted this Eftevang person. Val has learned that he was in France only a few days ago and yet he showed up here, knowing that she and Jake were aboard our plane. How could he know that? You can see that the timing is suspicious."

A pain streaked down Dinah's arm and she winced. "I didn't know the man existed until he yelled 'death gene' in the Svalbard Airport and I certainly didn't contact him. Valerie was right when she pegged me as apolitical. I have no desire to meddle in Senator Sheridan's campaign or his marriage."

Keyes drank a bit of coffee and pushed the smoked eel aside. "If that is so, if it's only a matter of money, the Sheridan campaign can find a way to match or better what you're being paid. We could find a place for you on Colt's staff. In exchange, we would naturally want to know which campaign is behind the mischief and the full extent of what has been disclosed. And of course we'll need to know where Erika and Jorgen have gone."

"Senator Keyes, I'm employed by the University of Hawaii and no one else. I don't know where Valerie came up with this idea that I'm some kind of mole. I admit that I've been asked by my department head to determine whether the Svalbard Vault can be relied on to safeguard her seeds and keep them out of the hands of people who want to alter them, but that is all. If there's a mole inside your campaign, it's somebody else." Dinah thought about Valerie's backbiting and her conspicuous crush on Erika's husband and her temper boiled over. "Frankly, I wouldn't put it past Valerie herself to spoil the Sheridan show. You know what they say about a woman scorned. Maybe she arranged to have Erika spirited away by Maks Jorgen. Maybe her way of making herself seem essential to you and Mahler and Sheridan is to create moles and spies that only she can recognize."

Keyes responded more in sadness than in anger. "I've known Valerie for years. She's a scrupulous and loyal attorney, honest as the day is long. So is Colt. He doesn't deserve to have his political future destroyed by something like this."

"Erika is the one who needs to be persuaded, Senator Keyes. And for the last time, I have no idea where she's disappeared to or how to get in touch with her."

"I'm afraid it's more than that. Inspector Ramberg searched Jorgen's room this morning. He found a document that was stolen from Valerie's files."

Dinah studied his face. "You think I stole it?"

"Someone did and passed it on to Erika. Don't misunderstand me, Dinah. This isn't a threat. But you're playing with fire. You'd better tell us what you know before it's too late."

Chapter Nineteen

Dinah blazed out of the dining room into the lobby looking for Thor. No such luck. The lobby was empty except for the man behind the front desk.

"Would you happen to know where Inspector Ramberg went or when he'll be back?"

"He didn't say. But he did leave a message for you, Ms. Pelerin." He handed her an envelope with the Radisson logo.

She opened it and read, "*The murder is solved. Dinner?*"

He should be flogged for teasing her that way. What kind of document had he found in Jorgen's room? At least, it didn't sound as if he suspected her of stealing it. She tucked the note in her pocket. "When the inspector returns, would you tell him that Dinah Pelerin needs to speak with him urgently?"

"*Ja*, sure."

"What is Valerie Ives' room number?"

"Room three-thirty-eight, next door to the presidential suite."

"Who's in the presidential suite?"

"Mr. Mahler."

Why did I have to ask, she thought.

"Shall I ring Ms. Ives' room?"

"No, thanks. I'd rather surprise her."

Dinah headed for the elevators. Honest as the day is long. What the hell did that mean in a place where it was always night? Something was rotten in the Kingdom of Norway. Valerie didn't whisper with Mahler and keep Tillcorp's wheeling and dealing a secret because she was honest, and Keyes' talk about political dirty tricks sounded fishy as smoked eel. How better to garner sympathy for Sheridan than to spin Erika's disappearance as a political plot by one of his rivals and "trump up a story" about a mole inside his campaign? That would be the ultimate dirty trick. She couldn't see Erika's former lover going along with the plot, but then it struck her that Sheridan could have hired somebody off the street to impersonate Maks. The impersonator could have lured Erika to his room, drugged her, and carted her off to a sanitarium where she could be held until after election day. Until Doomsday if it suited Sheridan's or Valerie's purposes.

The elevator doors opened on the second floor and Tipton stepped inside. As always, he was breathless from the weight and urgency of his mission. "It's a political fiasco. I can see the headlines now. *Candidate's Wife Goes Off Rocker, Runs Off With Rocker.*"

"Let's hope that's the true story."

"What do you mean?" His cowlick sprouted from his crown like corn stubble and there was a downy growth on his chin. He looked as if he hadn't slept all night. He re-punched the button for the third floor.

"I'm not so sure she eloped with Jorgen. I'm on my way to Valerie's room to get a few straight answers."

"Jake's looking for her, too. He's called a meeting in his suite, but Valerie's gone AWOL." The elevator door opened on three and Tipton stepped out.

Dinah stepped out, too. "Any idea where she is?"

"The last time I saw her she was coming out of Colt's room. She's been trying to calm him down. He and the inspector got into quite a tiff this morning."

"About what?"

"Oh, some document he found in Jorgen's room, I think. Colt went ballistic and Val hustled him away all mother-hennish for a one-on-one. Jake says it's bad."

Dinah batted the elevator door, which kept trying to close. "Do you know what it is?"

"Only that it was something Valerie shouldn't have let anyone see." Tipton looked at his watch. "Jake wants Whitney at the meeting. I've been trying to get him on his cell. Have you seen him?"

"As a matter of fact, he and I have just had a serious talk."

"Why would he want to talk with *you*?"

"My superior grasp of the situation. What else?"

He laughed. "You're funny. It's good to inject a little humor. When Whitney has finished his breakfast, he and I are going to strategize. If anyone can see a way through this mess, it's Whitney."

Dinah got back in the elevator and rode it down to the second floor. She rapped on Sheridan's door and waited. "Senator Sheridan, it's Dinah. I need to speak with you." She rapped again. "It's important."

No answer.

"I've heard from Erika."

The door opened. His face, haggard and unshaven, stared out at her like a defeated warrior feeling the flutter and rush of Valkyrie wings overhead. He looked like a man who knew already that he'd been singled out by Axe-Wielder and Wrecker-of-Plans. "Is she all right?"

His undeniable misery brought Dinah up short. He wasn't acting. If there was a plot, he wasn't in on it. "May I come in?"

He searched her eyes. "She didn't call you."

"No."

He turned and walked back into the room. Dinah followed him. His suitcase was open on the bed. He went back to taking his clothes out of an open dresser drawer and folding them in the suitcase.

"What do you want?"

"I'd like her to call, Senator. I'd like to know that she's all right, too."

"It's too late. Everything's ruined now."

"Why is it too late?"

"She thinks I killed that man. Eftevang." He went to the mini-bar, pulled out a beer, and twisted off the cap. He expelled a bitter laugh. "Soon, everyone will think I killed him."

Dinah glanced back at the door, which was still open. "Did you kill him?"

"No."

"Why would Erika think that you did?"

"Haven't you swapped the latest developments with your inspector friend this morning?"

"No."

"He found a printout of an e-mail from me to Valerie telling her not to worry, that I'd be meeting with Eftevang and I'd make sure he didn't give us any more trouble. I don't think the inspector believed me when I said my account had been hacked." The senator gave a self-deprecating laugh. "Who would?"

Dinah would and did. She couldn't believe that anyone in his right mind, let alone a senator and a scholar, would write an e-mail announcing a murder he planned to commit. "Was this e-mail what the inspector found in Jorgen's room?"

"Erika must have left it there, 'though how she got hold of it is a mystery." He took a drink of beer, set the bottle on the dresser, and continued his packing. "I don't know if I'm packing for a return flight to the States and a perp walk across the Washington Mall or a stint in a Norwegian jail."

"You didn't write the e-mail? Not even as a joke?"

"No. It's completely bogus." He let out another bark of bitter laughter. "Maybe Val wrote the note to herself and gave it to Erika to turn her against me. Maybe Val wanted to punish me for not falling in love with her."

So he did know that Val fancied him. Dinah could understand Valerie trying to get Erika out of the way by hook or by crook, but surely it defeated her purpose to frame Sheridan for murder. "Did Valerie have your password?"

"Probably." He raked his fingers through his hair. "I didn't mean what I said about Val. She's on my side no matter what. She showed me the damn e-mail as soon as she saw it. It must have been sent before the Internet went down and stayed in her inbox. She didn't receive it until the morning of the vault tour and immediately suspected that I'd been hacked."

Dinah could imagine the consternation that e-mail must have caused. No wonder Sheridan muffed his lines during the video.

He flumped into one of the armchairs in front of the window and hiked his cowboy boots up on the hassock. "Valerie and Tipton have been trying to figure out how the hacker got through our firewall. However it was done, and whatever the police make of it, it'll go viral and my career will be water over the dam."

"Did Erika know your password?"

"I don't know. She may have. Maybe *she* wanted to punish me. Eftevang's not the only death she blames me for."

"What do you mean?"

"I don't suppose it matters now that I'm out of the running and no longer have to lie my head off to get elected." He took a long pull of beer and fell silent.

She prodded him. "What other death does she blame you for, Senator?"

"I asked her to terminate a pregnancy. We'd only been married a few months. I said I didn't want the distraction of a newborn during my first big campaign. I don't know. Maybe I didn't want to share her with a baby. Anyhow, I sent her back to Norway to…" he made air quotes, "'to visit her folks.' My conservative constituents would never know that my right-to-life rhetoric was pure hypocrisy. Later, when Erika and I were ready to start a family, she couldn't get pregnant."

"Is the abortion what you were afraid Erika would talk about?"

"It was a risk. Since I moved us from Montana to Washington, she's been lonely, more regretful and obsessive. She talked as if the child might actually exist."

"Maybe she does, Senator. Did it ever occur to you that she didn't go through with the abortion?"

His eyes widened. "Did she tell you…?"

"Colt!" Whitney Keyes stormed through the open door with his hand raised. "I advise you not to say anything more until you've spoken to Valerie. I advise you specifically not to say anything more to Dinah."

Sheridan frowned and his eyes remained glued on Dinah.

"I'm not the mole," she said. "How could I have hacked into your e-mail?"

"With Erika's help," said Keyes.

Sheridan's face went slack and old, Asgard to Midgard in a split second. All it would take to drive him over the edge was another Valkyrie circling overhead. Nothing Dinah could say would help him now. She turned on her heels and left as Keyes began to lay out Valerie's theory of Dinah's treachery.

She took the elevator back to the third floor and banged on Valerie's door. It was time she heard the theory from the horse's mouth.

Mahler answered. "She's not here."

"Do you know where she is?"

"In hiding if she knows what's good for her. She's dropped a bomb on Sheridan, me, the whole damn enterprise."

His emanation of menace took the steam out of Dinah's anger. She took a step back. "How?"

"She's succeeded in getting Sheridan accused of murder, that's how. Not just any murder, but the murder of one of Tillcorp's most vocal critics, which makes me look like a co-conspirator. She's succeeded in setting back all our efforts, not just in Norway but all over the world. The media will be crawling over this like ants at a picnic. If you track her down, tell her she's fired and she can find herself alternative transportation back to the States." He ran a hand across his bald head and his eyes bulged with anger. "No. You tell her to stay in Norway. If I see her Judas face again on the other side of the Atlantic, I'll wring her neck."

Before he closed the door in her face, Dinah caught a glimpse of Lee and Rod. One of them was working at a laptop. The other was sorting through a stack of loose papers that had been strewn across Valerie's bed.

Chapter Twenty

Dinah was pretty sure there was a Valkyrie maiden named Cloud or Fog. Evil Fog, Noxious Fog, Fog of War. Something stealthy and pernicious. The Radisson Blu Polar seemed to be enveloped in a pernicious fog and there was nothing she could do but wait for Thor to return and tell her about this e-bombshell that had shattered everybody's plans.

Mahler's anger seemed to be centered on Valerie, which must mean that he blamed her for the fact that she had allowed Sheridan's incriminating e-mail to be stolen. She obviously hadn't gotten around to telling him that Dinah was the spy who stole it and the chaos was all her fault. Dinah was grateful for that. Mahler scared her. He was a man she could as easily picture in a maximum security prison cell as a boardroom. Before discovering that e-mail, Thor had considered Mahler his prime suspect and with good reason. Eftevang hated Tillcorp, he had hounded Mahler across Europe, and he had told Aagaard he had a dynamite story and the documents to prove it. That was motive aplenty. And was Mahler just a little too quick to accept Sheridan's guilt? Maybe that hasty acceptance and his anger at Valerie were contrived to cover his own guilt.

Someone had hacked into Sheridan's computer, sent Valerie an e-mail, then stolen it and printed it, and left it in Maks Jorgen's room—presumably with the intention that the police would find it. It would take a computer forensics expert to say whether the e-mail had been sent to a printer by Sheridan's computer or Valerie's. Maybe Valerie herself had printed it. There was only her word that it had been stolen. But it went against logic that she would frame Sheridan for murder. She was too professionally and romantically invested in him.

Only two things can derail him. Both of them are women.

Mahler's words resounded in Dinah's ears. She still couldn't picture Erika as a murderess, but she no longer thought of her as a helpless victim. Her disappearance had hurt her husband already. Would she go so far as to frame him for murder? A late-life revenge for domestic crimes, real or imagined? If the scandal of a runaway wife didn't nip his political ambitions in the bud, a charge of murder in the first certainly would.

Both of them are women. Erika Sheridan and Valerie Ives— either one of them could be Sheridan's Valkyrie angel of destruction.

Waiting for anything or anyone was worse than tedious for Dinah. It was an affliction, and today the waiting was unbearable. She had to do something to burn off her mental fog. The hotel had a fitness center and a sauna. She would have to be careful because of her arm, but she could run on the treadmill or ride a stationary bike. She needed to move or she'd go berserk and it would feel good to work up a sweat inside a nice, warm building.

The elevator doors opened and Dinah stared straight into the eyes of a giant painted polar bear on the facing wall. This obsession with bears was beginning to seem overdone, although she supposed it was only to be expected on an island with twice as many polar bears as people.

At the far end of the hall, a blond girl in a maid's uniform was vacuuming. She had earbuds in her ears and didn't look up. There was a faint smell of chlorine embedded in the carpet and a suggestion of mold spores kicked up by the vacuum. Dinah followed the signs to the fitness center, passing murals of the less fearsome Arctic fauna—snow-colored foxes, caribou, and a rather sad-eyed walrus with enormous tusks.

There were a few doors en route marked *ANSATTE,* which she assumed meant Employees Only. Double doors at the end of the hall proclaimed *SVØMMEBASSENG og BADSTUE* and below that in English, POOL and SAUNA. She didn't know the proper pronunciation of *Badstue,* but bad stew sounded appropriate to the circumstances. She pushed on through and, with the aid of the standard male-female figures on the locker room doors, she went into the women's room and stripped down to her zebra striped bra and panties, which would have to double as a bathing suit as she hadn't planned on any Arctic swimming when she packed her bag.

A sign in several languages instructed her to shower before entering the pool. She rinsed off, careful to keep her bandage dry, took a towel from a rack beside the door and went into the pool area. It was a small pool, but she didn't intend to swim, just wade around a bit and loosen up. It was empty so no need to feel self-conscious about her underwear. She stepped into the shallow end and jumped out clutching her heart.

Holy moly! The pool must be fed by a glacier. She shivered. Oh, well. This would make a good story to tell them back in Hawaii. She sucked in her breath and waded in up to her waist. She did a few leg lifts, but she had chill bumps all over and her teeth were clicking together like castanets.

She got out of the water and toweled off. There were murals in this room, too—on one wall, a mother *isbjørn* and two cubs meandering across the tundra against a backdrop of white, pointy mountains. On the facing wall, a rampant bear. It appeared to be snarling at her.

The emptiness felt creepy. It was early in the day, but there ought to be a few fitness fanatics taking the polar bear plunge with her. She had started back into the locker room when she noticed a sign on the far side of the pool. "If booze, tar, or the sauna won't help, the illness is fatal. Suits Required." The sauna. She didn't know if it had cured Norris' gout, but it would warm her icy bones.

She edged around the pool, dodging a set of dumbbells somebody had left in the middle of the floor, and peeked inside the cedar plank sauna. It seemed to be more like a steam room than a dry heat sauna. The touch-pad controls mounted on the outside wall showed the temperature was already set to the maximum. Excellent. She pulled open the door. A billowing cloud of warm steam engulfed her. She let the door shut behind her and groped through the fog to a low wooden bench on the right. She sat down, drew her knees up against her chest, closed her eyes, and rested her head against the wall.

Now this was heaven. A hundred percent humidity. It felt like July in South Georgia, only without the mosquitoes. The steam permeated her pores, diffusing warmth throughout her body. She thought about Thor mushing across the icy tundra in a dogsled. Did he really fantasize about visiting Miami? She pictured him in a tight t-shirt and cut-offs. And then without.

Sweat began to trickle out of her hair, into her eyes and down her neck. A little of this heat was restorative, but a full five minutes and she'd cook. She uncurled, wiped the sweat out of her eyes, and looked up. Good grief! There was someone on the upper bench across from her. Someone in a long-sleeved green turtleneck and dark ski pants.

She must be seeing things. Hallucinating like…

She stood up. It wasn't a figment.

"Hello!"

No response.

Jerusalem! What was she doing in here with her clothes on? Dinah leapt up and bumped the door open with one hip to let out some steam so she could see through the mist. She shook the woman's shoulder. A tendril of wet blond hair fell across her hand. "Hey, you've been in here too long. Come out!"

One thin green arm fell off the bench and dangled, limp as a vine. Her bright red fingernails looked like blossoms.

"Valerie!"

Dinah held open the door with one hand and turned off the steam.

"Val, wake up!" She reached in and shook her again. No movement. She was unconscious.

The door wanted to fly shut. Dinah looked around desperately for something to prop it open. Her eyes lit on the dumbbells. She let go of the door and ran to get them. She grabbed up the ten pounder. A fiery pain shot up her left arm and she remembered that she'd been shot. She hefted the five pounder in her left hand and the ten pounder in her right hand and carried them back to the steam room. She pulled the door open wide and tried to prop it open with the dumbbells, but it continued to slide.

Skitt! She went back for the twenty-pound weight. She carried it in her right hand and another five-pounder in her left and stacked them in front of the door. This time it stayed open. She shook Val again and felt for a pulse. She couldn't tell if what she was feeling was Valerie's pulse or her own trembling. She thought, if I try to lift her off that bench one-armed, I'll drop her and she'll break her neck if she isn't dead already.

"Hang on, Val. I'm going for help."

She raced back through the locker room, jerked on her pants and shirt, and ran into the hall. The girl who'd been vacuuming was gone and the elevators weren't there. She took the stairs two at a time and tore barefoot into the lobby, dripping wet, shirt unbuttoned, and yelling for help.

Thor turned from his conversation with the woman at the front desk. They both stared as if she'd gone stark mad.

She pushed her wet hair out of her eyes. "I think Valerie's been murdered."

Chapter Twenty-one

Separate the witnesses. That was Cop 101 back in the States. Apparently, things were different in Norway or else Thor had missed the episode of *Law and Order* where that dictum was delivered.

Two hours after the discovery of Valerie's body, Dinah sat at a long conference table in the Radisson business center with Whitney Keyes, Colt Sheridan, Norris Frye, Jake Mahler, Lee Keany, and Rodney Craig. Tipton had been picked to be the first interviewee and ushered down the hall to a different room. Watching over the remaining seven were two uniformed policemen. Legs apart, eyes aloft, side arms at the ready, they stood inside the room blocking the door. Matters had reached a point where the Norwegian police felt obliged to strap on pistols to keep the peace in the wake of the American crime wave. The faces around the table were solemn, if not exactly grief-stricken. Dinah couldn't judge the emotional impact of Valerie's murder on anyone else. She hadn't absorbed the impact yet, herself. Her thoughts kept returning to the scene of the crime, to the moment when Thor lifted Valerie out of the steam bath and they saw that she had been bludgeoned.

Dinah had been allowed to shower and make herself decent, but her alliance with Thor was kaput. It ended when Sergeant Lyby, the policewoman who'd given Dinah a hard time at the airport, noticed blood on one of the five-pound dumbbells that Dinah had used to prop open the steam-room door. When she also noticed blood on Dinah's hands, the jig was up.

"Dybdahl oughta be here," said Mahler. "He was here this morning to renege on clearing us to leave. He came to my suite to tell me it was out of his hands until Erika shows up. Then he and Val got into some kind of a rhubarb."

"About what?" asked Keyes.

"Damned if I know. Two words in, they lapsed into Norwegian and Val left."

"You didn't ask Dybdahl what she was upset about?"

"I didn't have to. She was upset because of that note she let Erika get hold of. She was upset that she was the one who shot her boyfriend out of the saddle."

Sheridan pounded his fist on the table. "I was not her boyfriend."

"You would've been," said Mahler. "Val wouldn't have cared who you killed. I still can't believe she was dumb enough to keep that note. I told her to burn it, but no-oh. She had a bee in her bonnet that you'd been hacked and thought she could trace the e-mail back to who sent it. In her mind, it was never going to be you."

"Thanks for the vote of confidence, Jake, but I didn't kill Eftevang and if I was going to, I wouldn't have written a note announcing my intention." Sheridan had rallied since Dinah last saw him. He had shaved and put on a fresh shirt. And he seemed more in control, more willing to defend himself.

"It doesn't matter to me who you killed or why," said Mahler. "My investment's down the tubes. Your wife's humiliated you, your girlfriend's been clubbed to death, and the Norwegian police have evidence that links you to a murder. Guilty or innocent, you're done in politics. Luckily, I always hedge my bets."

"Meaning what?" asked Keyes.

Sheridan hooted. "Can't you guess? He's been secretly supporting another candidate. Is it Zeb Warren?"

Thor appeared at the door and tapped. The policemen stood aside and he put his head inside. "We're ready to interview Senator Sheridan now. Please follow me, sir."

"You'd better hope they don't let me cast a vote on that GMO food labeling bill, Jake." Sheridan stood up and marched out past the policemen without a backward glance.

And then there were six, thought Dinah. The policemen closed the door and resumed their soldierly stance and disinterested gaze. She wondered if they were wired and everything that everyone said was being recorded. Could they do that in Norway without telling you?

Her hands were still quaking. She clasped them together in her lap, tried not to dwell on the vision of Valerie's blood staining her hand. How could she have failed to see the blood on that dumbbell? How could she not have felt it? She felt it now. She'd scrubbed her hands until they were chapped.

Keyes took out his half-moon eyeglasses and placed them on his nose. "Is that true, Jake? Have you been secretly funding Zeb Warren?"

"Don't act so shocked, Whitney. Val's told me how you operate. She worked for you for ten years. She ought to know. You've got your eye to the main chance twenty-four, seven. Your wife's late husband wasn't cold before you swept in with the flowers and candy and look at you now, a billionaire philanthropist. If you haven't put out feelers to Warren's people, I'll eat my hat."

This time, the look of malice on Keyes' face was flagrant. "A man with your vulnerabilities shouldn't go out of his way to be offensive. You never know what repercussions will follow."

"Is that a threat?"

"It's a fact."

Mahler's mouth crimped in a malign smile. "If Valerie were alive right now, she'd advise the both of us to keep our mouths shut."

Valerie's posthumous advice put the quietus on everyone. Ten minutes of silence passed before Thor tapped on the door again. The policemen stood aside and he looked in at the rancorous faces around the table. His own face revealed nothing. Dinah tried to make eye contact with him, but he wouldn't meet her eyes. "Mr. Mahler, if you will come with me, please?"

Mahler pushed himself up from the table so forcefully that he knocked over his chair. He held Keyes eyes for a tense few seconds and went out without a word.

And then there were five.

Lee righted the overturned chair and motioned to Rod with his eyes. The two got up and moved into the corner to powwow. Lee wore a worried look. Whatever he was saying to Rod brought a worried look to his face, too. Dinah wished she could hear what they were mumbling about.

Sheridan's interview hadn't taken long. Maybe he'd invoked his right to counsel, if there was such a right in Norway. And what questions was Thor asking? He must be trying to pinpoint the last time Valerie had been seen alive and by whom. How long had she been lying in that steam room? Dinah knew nothing of forensics except for the wizardry she saw on *CSI*. Could real medical examiners ascertain the time of Valerie's death after even a few minutes in a steam room?

The clash between Keyes and Mahler confirmed her suspicion of bad blood between the two. What vulnerabilities was Keyes referring to? Was this the specter of WikiLeaks again? Or Myzandia? It seemed pretty clear that Valerie and Mahler had been arguing about the authorship and legitimacy of Sheridan's e-mail, but what had she argued with Dybdahl about? So far, there was only Mahler's word that Val and the agriculture minister had argued at all. Dinah hoped that Thor would have the authority to question Dybdahl. If Mahler killed Val—and he gave the impression that he was plenty angry enough to have done it—he would want to put her in as many arguments as he could.

Norris Frye poured himself a glass of water and shook his head. "It's a tragedy, Whitney. A sad day for us all. Of course, I didn't know Valerie well, but I understand she was a great asset to you. Same for Jake. And she was doing a bang-up job molding Colt's image. You have to wonder, what was he thinking? Must've had it in his mind that Tillcorp's troubles would come around to bite him and he couldn't handle the pressure. Like he said, his life was under a microscope, false insinuations. The first murder, he probably just snapped. Didn't know what he was doing. But killing Valerie, now, that was insane. The GOP will be better off with Zeb Warren. The charisma of a block of wood, but predictable."

"I don't believe that Colt murdered either one of them," said Keyes. "And can the holier-than-thou shit, Norris. You'll get the third degree same as the rest of us."

Norris' smugness grated on Dinah, too. He seemed to presume that he was the least likely suspect.

Norris shrugged off Keyes' put-down. "You may be right that Colt's innocent. Erika is the one with the drinking problem and I believe she was out on the town the night Eftevang was murdered. She and her Norwegian boyfriend could have knifed him. They may even have killed poor Valerie before they disappeared. Whether Erika had a hand in Valerie's murder or not, it really was all her fault."

"How do you figure that?" asked Dinah.

"If she hadn't pulled her disappearing stunt, we'd be home by now. Valerie would be alive and maybe Colt's candidacy, too."

"Don't get too far ahead of yourself, Norris." Keyes' normally refined manners had turned nasty. "You could wind up with a libel suit or better still, your wife could wind up with a keepsake photo of you in the sack with Dybdahl's pretty little assistant."

Thor returned with a tall, very thin policeman and the blond policewoman. "We will do our best to speed up this process. Senator Keyes, I will interview you. Sergeant Lyby will interview Senator Frye, and Sergeant Tjølhelm will interview Mr. Rodney Craig."

Four little, three little, two little Indians. Dinah watched the parade move off down the hall and proffered her fellow non-selectee an uneasy smile. "Well, Lee, it looks like they're saving us for last."

He came back to the table and sat down. "Do you know anything about the system over here? Can they keep us from leaving?"

"They can't hold the senators for long without starting a war. I'm not sure how they'll treat a low-level technical assistant and a pair of company bodyguards."

"Yeah. I've been thinking about that. With Sheridan raising hell about me losing his wife, like I was in on kidnapping her or something, things could get sticky. The Norwegians may try to hold me 'til she's found.'"

Once again, Dinah wondered if the guards had recording devices in their pockets or the room was bugged. If it was and if she could get Lee talking, she could maybe fill in some of the blanks inThor's investigation. "Jake Mahler has clout with the Norwegian government. He'll make certain that you and Rod leave when he leaves."

"He has clout with the ag minister, that Dybdahl clown. I figure he's got no say in a missing person case."

"Did you and Erika talk at all while you were guarding her?"

"Not really. She was all the time asking about her husband. Was he still in the hotel, when would he be back, that kind of thing."

"Did she seem afraid of him?"

"No. It was more like she was champing at the bit to tell him something and he was avoiding her."

"And she didn't say anything to suggest where she might have gone?"

"If she had, I wouldn't be keeping it a secret. The airport's closed. There's no trains, no buses. She could've skied or dogsledded or snowmobiled to that Russian town, Barentsburg. If not, she's still somewhere in Longyearbyen. If she'd call the police and tell them she was safe in the arms of her boyfriend, I'd be off the hook."

Dinah tried not to sound accusatory. "There *is* the problem of Valerie Ives' murder."

"That's nothing to do with me."

"Even so, the police will probably ask what you and she were arguing about in the lobby this morning."

"She was ragging on me about the e-mail Ramberg found in Jorgen's room. She said it had been slipped into one of her files and then stolen. I told her I didn't know anything about it."

"Did she say when it was stolen?"

"No."

Dinah reconstructed the timeline. The e-mail had showed up in Valerie's e-mail on the day of the vault tour. She had shown it to Sheridan and probably to Mahler. That was obviously the "note" she and Mahler were whispering about on the drive back from the vault. Mahler had said he didn't buy it and Valerie had replied that somebody was playing them. She must have finally deduced that it wasn't Dinah and when she confronted the real culprit, he killed her.

Dinah tried again not to sound accusatory. "What were you and Rod looking for in Valerie's room this morning?"

"All I know, Mahler had us looking for anything with the words Africa or Myzandia."

Sergeant Lyby appeared at the door and called Dinah's name. So Thor had recused himself. Fear mingled with disappointment. She got up, squared her shoulders, and followed her interrogator down the hall. Sergeant Lyby had her hand on the door when Thor came loping down the hall.

"They've found her. Adjourn the interviews. Let's go."

Sergeant Lyby gave Dinah a narrow-eyed, just-you-wait look and loped off after him. In Longyearbyen, it wasn't necessary to warn the suspects not to leave town.

Chapter Twenty-two

The lobby was jammed. A knot of people stood in a ragged line in front of the reception desk, waiting to check in. They were laughing and gabbing with one another and futzing with their hotel-issue clogs. Their suitcases and duffel bags lay scattered carelessly across the floor, making walking a hazard. Dinah asked a woman in a fur hat near the back of the line where they'd come from.

"London. We've flown in for New Year's Eve."

"The airport is open?"

"I should jolly well hope so by now. We thought we'd have to camp out in Heathrow through the holiday and lose our hotel deposit, but it's all come right. The party's already begun."

This was evidenced by a well-irrigated gentleman in a Dickens top hat and green felt vest passing up and down the line pouring gin into outstretched plastic cups.

Dinah maneuvered her way through the crowd to the elevators and pushed the up button. The relief in Thor's voice when he said, "They've found her" could mean only one thing. They'd found Erika and she was alive. Maybe she'd tried to book a commercial flight at the airport or, as Lee suggested, gone overland by dogsled to Barentsburg. Dinah hoped that Norris Frye was wrong about Erika being a murderess, although at this point she wouldn't bet on the innocence of anyone.

"I hear you're the one who found the lawyer's body."

She jumped. "Brander, you frightened me."

"Stabbed? Strangled? What was she wearing?"

"I'm not going to give you that information."

"I didn't really think you would, but I've got another story. Get your coat and I'll show you something."

"I'm not going anywhere. You shouldn't either. They've found Erika." She put on the brakes. "Did you know…?"

"Everybody knows. I've already wired the story to *Dagbladet*."

"Well, then, you should lurk about here in the lobby until they bring her back. Maybe she'll give you an exclusive."

Brander grinned. "They only think they've found her." The elevator door opened. He propelled Dinah inside, walked in behind her, and pushed the button for the second floor.

"What do you mean they only think they've found her?"

"Somebody gave them a, what do you Americans call it? A bum steer."

"How do you know that?"

"As I told you once before, it's my business to know things."

"Did you call in a phony tip?"

He winked a naughty-boy wink.

"Thor Ramberg will nail your hide to the jailhouse wall."

"He doesn't know where the tip came from and he won't unless you tell him."

The elevator stopped. They got out and he propelled her toward her room. "You're in two-eighteen, right?"

"Why," she asked, "would you do something so perverse? And illegal?"

"I needed to pry you loose for a while."

"Well, you can't. I'm going to lock myself in my room until the police call me to be interviewed."

"They've gone to Barentsburg. They'll be gone for hours. Let's go in your room and I'll explain."

"You're not setting a foot inside my room." She noticed that he hadn't removed his boots. "Anything you have to say to me, you can say it right here in the hall."

"I think I know where Erika is. All I want is a chance to speak with her before the police and her husband get to her and she's never seen or heard from again."

"How could you know where she is?"

"I don't *know*. I *think* I know. Fata Morgana once put on a Christmas concert in Longyearbyen. It was televised—lots of glitz and glamor with the northern lights as a backdrop. The group stayed at an old Victorian hotel on the peninsula by Adventifjorden, not far from the airport. The coal baron John Longyear and his cronies used to host parties there during the summer. The hotel is dilapidated now, but maybe Erika holds fond memories. It's worth a try."

"Brander, if you think that's where she is, why don't you go and speak to her by yourself? Why do you need me?"

"She might open the door to you."

Dinah weighed the pros and cons. In the pro column, she could verify that Erika was safe and had eloped of her own free will. On the con side, Thor and everybody else would assume she'd known where Erika was from the get-go and had lied about it. She could be jailed for obstructing a police investigation or worse, participating in Erika's kidnapping. But on the pro side, Erika could solve the mystery of the stolen note left in Maks' room and perhaps shed light on Eftevang's murder. A major con, Erika and Maks could turn out to be the murderers and they wouldn't take kindly to being tracked to their lair by a sleazy journalist and the Nosy Parker who'd ruined her parka and read her mail.

Aagaard frisked himself, apparently searching for his cigarettes. "Will you come?"

"How do I know you didn't kill Eftevang and Valerie, too? How do I know you didn't shoot me and now you're trying to entice me out of the hotel to finish the job?"

He looked at her bandaged arm as if it had suddenly dropped out of the sky. "When did that happen?"

"Yesterday." In fact, she hardly knew what time it was any more. It had been one long, continuous night since the moment she landed at Svalbard. "I take it that's your denial?"

"I didn't shoot you. I didn't kill anybody." He found a cigarette and lit up in defiance of hotel rules, city ordinance, and national policy. "I won't say a homicide doesn't make great copy because it does and, save for that monster who slaughtered all those teenage children of the Labor Party last year, there are damn few homicides in Norway to write about. But I like to skewer my victims alive. In forty point bold."

He was insufferable, but plausible. And no one had ever accused her of an excess of caution. She said, "I'll get my coat."

She left him in the hallway and went into her room. Erika's parka was still in Thor's trunk or being analyzed in a lab somewhere, so it was the flimsy wool pea jacket or nothing. She swaddled herself in every piece of clothing she had and topped it with the pea jacket. In a nod to prudence, she dashed off a note to Thor. "Have gone to the old hotel on Adventifjorden with Aagaard. He thinks Erika may be hiding out there. Dinah."

Thor's refusal to face her and talk to her rankled. It didn't matter that it was the professional thing to do or that she would do the same thing if she were the one wearing the badge. She had handled the dumbbell that brained Valerie and it was perfectly rational to chuck her into the pool of suspects. But Dinah didn't feel especially rational. A kiss like the one the detective inspector had laid on her made rationality moot. She tore up the note and tossed it in the waste basket.

Aagaard was waiting for her, stinking up the hall with his cigarette smoke. She stared at the torn pieces of the note as if she could divine her fortune from the pattern of the pieces. Whatever the immediate future spelled, it was lame to let punctured vanity keep her from taking a simple precaution. She rewrote the note and propped it on the dresser.

She and Aagaard rode the elevator down to the lobby and threaded their way through the festive crowd. In the foyer, she pulled on her boots, snugged her cap down tight, put on her mittens, and followed Aagaard into the wild black yonder. The temperature had dropped since her last outing and the wind had picked up. The tassels on her ski cap thrashed about her face like angry snakes and she had to hold them out of her eyes. "How far is the car?" she asked.

"What?"

"The car. How far?"

Aagaard turned down a dark side street and pulled a flashlight out of his jacket. The wind changed, now hitting her in the face. Her eyes felt gelid and her nose began to run, wetting the balaclava. She began to obsess about frostbite—the ice crystals forming inside her tissues, the cells dying, her nose turning black, the doctor breaking the news he'd have to amputate.

"Is the car on this street?"

Aagaard stopped and the flashlight beam homed in on a two-man snowmobile. "Climb in the back."

"Are you out of your mind?"

"It's only a mile beyond the airport."

"We're two blocks from the hotel and I'm already numb."

"You can rest your head against my back to break the wind. We'll be there in five minutes. There won't be any hikers or skiers tonight. We'll take the Burma Road."

"Burma Road?"

"Nordic humor." He pulled two pairs of goggles out of the glovebox, strapped one around his head, and handed the other to her. "You'll need these."

Like an utter idiot, like the ditzy heroine in some had-I-but-known melodrama, she put on the goggles and climbed into the back seat. Who was it who said that bad decisions make good stories? Somebody whose bad decision hadn't included a snowmobile ride over the Burma Road on a sub-zero evening in December with a man she didn't trust. Somebody who lived to tell.

"Do you know how to operate one of these contraptions?"

"Is the Pope Catholic?"

Aagaard folded his lanky legs into the front seat, turned the ignition, and off they roared. Dinah huddled low and buried her face in the fabric of his coat. It stank of stale smoke, but it shielded her from the wind and the worst of the exhaust fumes. A mini-blizzard kicked up by the sled's track threw snow onto her back and the noise of the engine cut through her senses like a band saw. Every now and then she raised her head and tried to get her bearings, but there was nothing to see except for the twin headlights of the snowmobile hurtling into a black, featureless infinity.

Her butt bumped up and down like a paddle ball and she clenched her teeth to keep from yelping. Her goggles fogged up. Perspiration? How could she possibly be perspiring? And if she were perspiring, the next thing would be hypothermia.

Aagaard leaned hard to the left, swerved off the road, and jumped the machine across what must have been a drift. Dinah flew up in the air and landed hard on her butt. The engine sputtered and coughed. What if this machine broke down out here? How long could she last in this cold, in this pea jacket with its chichi red buttons? She saw her fate flash before her eyes. She saw her brother, laughing uproariously at her stupidity. She saw her mother placing a wreath atop her headstone. *Here lies Dinah Pelerin. She should have stayed in South Georgia.*

The engine and the lights of the airport tower came into view. Aagaard made a wide arc to the left of the airport and continued into the darkness. The snow deepened. Somewhere off to her right, hungry polar bears foraged for meat on the ice floes of Adventifjorden.

She shouted, "I thought you said we'd be there in five minutes."

"What?"

The wind whipped her tassels across her face and she lowered her head and pressed her face into his coat again. It had been longer than five minutes. Way longer. She counted off another sixty seconds. If Aagaard didn't stop in another minute, she would have to assume the worst. Having a Plan B would be oh-so-comforting at a time like this. She scoured her brain pan for options. Flight across this snow-covered waste wasn't one of them. If her left arm didn't hurt so much, she could yank Aagaard's goggles down around his neck and garrote him with the straps. She could take off her ski cap and garrote him with the tassels. She could try to cold-cock him with one of her boots, but it wouldn't be likely to achieve the desired result. A blow to the driver's head at this speed and this snow buggy would flip and kill them both. She thought how she would explain her bad decision to Sergeant Lyby in the event she survived. If she weren't so cold and so scared, she would have laughed.

Aagaard cruised to a juddering stop. "That's it."

Dinah took off the goggles and, in the harsh beam of the headlights, beheld the decaying hulk of an old, three-story hotel worthy of a Halloween horror flick. Its lopsided contours were in monochrome, slate gray to battleship gray to oyster gray. Even the snow leading up to it looked gray. She saw no tracks, but there had been intermittent, blowing snow during the day. The windows had been boarded up, but a sliver of light showed under the front door. Somebody was at home. Dinah couldn't see the pampered wife of a U.S. senator in such a place. It seemed more likely that some down-and-out squatters had moved in.

Aagaard pulled something out a dark bag and unwrapped it. His camera.

Dinah felt a wave of revulsion. "You're going to ambush her?"

"What did you think I'd do? She's not going to pose for me now, is she?"

"Maybe Maks Jorgen will open the door and sock you in the nose. Anyway, I thought you wanted a story. You snap a picture and that's it. You won't get anything else and you know it."

"*Skitt.*" He took off his goggles, turned around in his seat, and lifted his ski mask. "What do *you* want from her?"

"I'm not sure. Maybe all I want is to give her my blessing. What I won't do is help you embarrass her, or her husband."

Aagaard hopped out of the sled into hip-high snow. "I'll forget about the photo. We have plenty of those on file at the paper. But I want to know why she's here with Jorgen and what she knows about Fritjoe Eftevang's murder. She'll have to tell Ramberg sooner or later and anything I write about the murder will have to be cleared with him before it goes to print. This isn't an ambush, it's a rehearsal. Anyway, Erika's no babe in the woods.

She's been grist for the media mill in Europe since before you were born." He cut the engine. The headlights went off and he turned on his flashlight. "I'll plow a path to the door. You can follow and I'll let you ring the bell."

Chapter Twenty-three

The porch had disintegrated into a pile of rotten wood covered in snow. There were no steps leading up to the door, but someone had stacked a few cinder blocks in stair steps alongside the rubble and they had been swept clean of snow. Aagaard climbed up and held his hand out to give Dinah a boost, shining his light on each step. The substitute cinder-block stoop was small and she balanced on the edge to keep from touching Aagaard.

If there had ever been a bell, it had long since ceased to function and there was no knocker. Dinah thumped her mittened hand against the door, knowing it wasn't necessary. You can't sneak up on somebody in a snowmobile. Whoever was inside knew they had company.

Aagaard held his light on the door and they waited.

She said, "What if they don't answer? We can't make them."

"They know we can send somebody who can."

The door screaked open and the white-bearded man from the library loomed over them. Dinah had forgotten how large he was. Tonight he didn't look so much startled as resentful.

"What do you want?"

"You're Maks Jorgen," said Aagaard. "I recognize you."

"You're not welcome," said Maks. The 'you' was clearly a plural.

Dinah feigned an audacity she didn't feel. "My name is Dinah Pelerin. I'd like to speak with Erika if she's here."

"She's not."

Erika called from inside. "Let them in, Maks." Her voice sounded resigned. "It was only a matter of time."

Maks cast a look behind him and returned surly eyes to Aagaard. "Both?"

"Of course. They must be numb to the knees. They'll want the fire and a cup of hot tea."

Maks moved aside and Dinah and Aagaard entered the ruined hall of what must have been the finest hostelry in the Arctic once upon a time.

"This way," said Maks.

He walked ahead of them across a sloping floor into a large room, thick with the oily smell of coal smoke. Heat from an old-timey pot-bellied coal stove poured into the room and the light from a pair of lanterns on either end of the mantel imparted a spectral haze.

"Is that thing safe?" asked Aagaard, inspecting the flue.

Maks and Erika ignored him. Erika sat cross-legged on the floor next to a portable CD player. A bottle and a half-full glass of red wine sat within easy reach. Her hair hid her face and she bobbed her head in time to an old Joni Mitchell song about love's illusions.

"There are no chairs," said Maks.

Dinah sat down on the floor beside Erika and hugged her knees. "I'd like to help you, Erika. Senator Sher...Colt opened up to me about your..." she glanced up at Aagaard..."your troubles."

Erika wasn't so into her cups she didn't take the hint. "Maks, dear, why don't you take Dinah's friend into the kitchen and give him a warm schnapps."

"No thanks," said Aagaard, sitting on the floor next to Dinah. "I'll stay."

Erika shook her hair out of her face and studied him. "Weren't you the reporter who questioned my husband at the press conference?"

"That's right. Brander Aagaard."

"I've seen you somewhere else."

"Years ago. At a concert maybe. Today I've come to ask you about your husband's relationship with Tillcorp and Valerie Ives. With her murder…"

"Valerie murdered?" She looked at Dinah.

"I found her body this morning, Erika. She'd been bludgeoned and her body hidden away in the sauna."

Erika put a hand to her mouth.

Aagaard pounced. "The police found a printout of an e-mail your husband wrote to her in Jorgen's room. Did you leave it there on purpose? Did you see Sheridan with Eftevang the night he was killed?"

Erika pushed herself to her feet and backed away from him.

"*Tosk.*" Maks spat out the word and dragged Aagaard to his feet.

"No, please." Erika combed her hair out of her face and seemed to gather herself. "Maks, would you take Mr. Aagaard into the kitchen and show him that box of our old album covers you found? He was one of our fans. I'm sure it will bring back memories."

Maks gripped Aagaard's arm, hoisted him to his feet, and shoved him toward the hall. "Don't give me an excuse to hurt you."

Irrepressible, Aagaard continued to reel off questions. "Will she file for divorce? How long have the two of you been planning this? What has she told you about Sheridan and…?"

"Shut up!"

Their voices receded down the hallway and Erika bent and picked up her glass of wine. "Would you care for wine? I'll have Maks bring another glass."

"No thanks."

She gestured toward a kettle on the stove. "There's hot water. I'm afraid you'll have to go to the kitchen for teabags."

"A cup of hot water would be appreciated."

"A cup of…" She threw a cursory glance around the floor. "It appears a cup will also require a trip to the kitchen."

"Nevermind, Erika. The warmth from the stove is all I want."

"I expect Colt will be bereft without Valerie. She was his mainstay." She leaned one shoulder against the peeling wall and assumed an air of casual aplomb, as if this were just another gossipy Washington cocktail party.

"He didn't requite Valerie's affections, Erika. He seems to be more bereft without you."

"What did he tell you about me?"

"He's afraid you think he murdered Fritjoe Eftevang."

"Why on earth would he think that?"

"Because of the e-mail Valerie showed you, the one Aagaard was talking about. Either Colt or someone pretending to be Colt sent a message to Valerie saying he meant to take care of the Eftevang problem."

"I've never seen it. I don't know what you're talking about."

Dinah tried to reconcile the testimony. If Sheridan was telling the truth, somebody else had written the e-mail. If Valerie had told the truth, somebody had stolen it from her files. And if Erika was telling the truth, she didn't write it, steal it, or plant it. "Is that the truth, Erika?"

"Largely." She tossed her hair. "As much as you or anyone else is entitled to."

Dinah didn't like being talked down to. She stood up and locked eyes with her. "We're talking about two murders, Erika, and your husband has become the number one suspect."

She dropped her chin and her hair closed around her face like a curtain.

Dinah said, "Tell me when and how you left the hotel."

"I met Maks at the cinema the night that man was stabbed. Maks told me the number of the room he'd rented at the Radisson. The next night, he kept watch and when Lee left his post, Maks came and told me and I sneaked out and went to his room. We were there just long enough for me to change into outside clothes. He had bought me another pair of boots so Colt wouldn't notice that mine were missing from the rack in the foyer. I borrowed Colt's anorak."

"Did you let anyone into that room or leave the door open when you left?"

"No." She took a defiant sip of wine. "I suppose Colt told you that I'm an alcoholic."

"Valerie did. She said you'd been in rehab. Senator…Colt said that you began drinking because you were grieving for a child you lost. A child he asked you to abort."

"My goodness! He *is* morose if he's told you that."

"He says that you blame him."

"I did blame him. I don't anymore."

The music segued into a rock number with a driving beat. "*You can go your own way.*" Erika turned up the volume.

Her elusiveness might charm the daylights out of her male admirers, but Dinah wasn't having any. She turned off the CD. "I don't think you went through with the abortion. I think you had the baby and you're here in Norway to look for a living daughter named Hannalore. I think you called upon your old friend Maks to help you find her."

"That's perceptive of you. Unfortunately, any child of Colt's, whether living or dead, would be a setback to his political… what? His political persona." She sank the last of her wine and poured another glass.

"I don't think he's proud of what he asked you to do. Or of his hypocrisy. He seems genuinely remorseful."

She wobbled slightly, held onto the wall to keep from falling, and flipped her hair out of her face. "We are all remorseful. We are all sick with remorse." Her tone was caustic. If she had swallowed the camel once, it had become indigestible.

"Is giving up your baby the reason Inge told you to pray for forgiveness?"

"How do you…?" She smiled. "Ah. You found her letter."

"Did you give Hannalore to Inge?"

"She didn't let me hold the baby when she was born. No touching. No bonding. No naming. I'd made up my mind. Colt came first. I was to leave the baby with her and go back to him. She would put the baby up for adoption after I went back to the States."

"And did she?"

"Yes. I begged her to give me the names, the place, anything at all. But she won't tell me. Maks went to see her and she gave him that note for me. He's contacted the hospital, all the agencies, but the records are sealed. I don't even know if my daughter is in Norway." She slid down the wall until her backside bumped the floor. "I loved Colt. I wanted to do what he wanted. I made a decision. But I don't know. If I'd held her, I might have changed my mind."

Dinah knelt down beside her and squeezed her hand. Bad decisions made interesting stories, but not many happy endings. "You must have stayed in Norway longer than Colt expected. What did you tell him?"

"Medical complications, a slow recovery. Colt has always thought of me as fragile." She gave an acrid laugh. "It's too funny."

"Didn't he fly over to make sure you were all right?"

"He offered, of course. But I could hear the reluctance in his voice. He was campaigning for a seat in the Montana House, shaking the hand of every person in the state, kissing all of their babies. I told him not to come, that I was recuperating at my grandmother's farm."

There weren't many times when the subject of murder was less painful than the alternative, but Dinah deemed this to be one of them. "Erika, what do you know about Fritjoe Eftevang? You seemed so upset when you first heard about the murder. Did you see something that frightened you?"

"I saw the corruption of my husband's soul."

"What do you mean? Did Colt kill him?"

"Not directly. I don't think he knew what was in store for the poor man, but he would have done nothing to stop it if he had. You see, Colt belongs to Jake Mahler now. Like Whitney. Like Val. They dance to Mahler's tune. I knew the instant I heard what had happened that Mahler was behind it. He's like a cancer." She bowed her head and covered her face with both hands. "I tried to get through to Colt. I wanted him understand why I had to get away. He wouldn't listen. He shut me away in that room and he wouldn't talk to me. Once again, politics took precedence over everything. Over his wife. Over his conscience, too."

Dinah wasn't entitled to an answer, but she couldn't resist asking. "Aagaard said that Maks was in love with you. Will you go back to him now?"

"Why not? If you believe Inge, I've already ruined his life. Inge would call herself an objective moralist, but she's the worst kind of romantic. She's always looking for a villain to blame. She underestimates the hero's willingness to ruin his own life, often for something that was never real." She laughed. "Of course the same is true for the heroine."

Maks reappeared in the doorway. "Rika? What do you want me to do? That *tosk* is threatening to have us arrested for false imprisonment. I can't keep him shut up in the pantry for much longer."

Dinah said, "Inspector Ramberg has gone to Barentsburg to search for you, Erika. Even if you don't go back to the States with Colt and the others, you'll have to talk to the police."

"You're quite right." She stood up and dusted herself off. Her voice was suddenly cool and assured, the voice of a senator's wife, unfazed by wine. She wrapped a thick rag around her hand, lifted the lid on the stove by its cast-iron handle, and added a few chunks of coal from a metal bucket. "Invite Mr. Aagaard to come in and join us by the fire, Maks. He must have a cell phone. He can call the police for us and we can sing a few of our golden oldies for him while we wait for them to arrive. I'm sure that Dinah would rather return to town in a police car than a snøscooter."

Chapter Twenty-four

Thor and Sergeant Lyby manifested anger in different ways. Whereas Thor maintained an icy and forbidding façade, Sergeant Lyby showed a more volatile side. Her questions to Dinah came barbed and freighted with prejudice. Dinah would have liked to believe that her prejudice stemmed, in part, from sexual jealousy. Her baby-blues kept drifting behind her to Thor, who stood stock-still and silent, as if staring out through a block of ice. He hadn't exuded this much chill even when he learned that Brander Aagaard had duped him into making a pointless trip to Barentsburg to search for Erika. Dinah, who didn't think she'd done anything illegal or wrong, repaid his coldness and Lyby's prejudice, with the insolence they deserved.

"I can't cut a piece of meat, let alone whack somebody in the head with a five-pound dumbbell." She pointed to her bandaged arm.

"The bullet only grazed your arm," said Sergeant Lyby. "The nurse at the hospital says it is a very minor injury."

"Nurse Vanya doesn't have much empathy for other people's pain. But I expect that even she would acknowledge that lifting over a hundred-pound woman onto the top bench of that sauna would rip out the stitches she so gently sewed."

Dinah gazed around the comfy and commodious Radisson conference room and took heart. At least she wasn't undergoing questioning in some poorly-heated, depressing jail. In fact, there was so little crime in Longyearbyen that it had no jail. Only Aagaard had been formally arrested on a charge of interfering with police business. He was being held temporarily in Thor's office. The rest of the "*mistenkeligs*" remained at large, somewhere in the hotel.

Lyby's pupils constricted. "Valerie Ives was not the only victim. Herr Eftevang was stabbed before you were injured."

"Eftevang had to be at least five-seven or eight," retorted Dinah. "I'll bet you've already concluded that the person who stabbed him was at least as tall, if not taller. I'm five-four and Erika's maybe an inch taller. The killer had to have been a man."

Thor didn't bat an eye.

Lyby's pupils constricted to pinholes. "Inspector Ramberg has informed me that you withheld important information regarding Mrs. Sheridan when he questioned you earlier. Are you withholding information now?"

"No, I am not. But Mrs. Sheridan is available for you to question when you get tired of haranguing me."

"Norwegians do not tire easily, Ms. Pelerin. Now, will you tell us once more what Mrs. Sheridan told you?"

It was up to Erika whether to divulge her quest for her long-lost daughter, but Dinah saw no reason to withhold anything else. "Mrs. Sheridan thinks that Jake Mahler murdered Eftevang."

"And did she say why?"

"Other than her personal dislike, she gave no reason."

"Do *you* think Mahler killed Eftevang?" Thor's voice made her jump.

"I don't know. But before I discovered Valerie's body this morning, he and his bodyguards were searching Valerie's room looking for documents relating to Myzandia. Mahler was angry. He blamed her for losing the e-mail from Sheridan saying that he planned to take care of the Eftevang problem, or words to that effect."

"How do you know what that e-mail says?" piped Lyby.

"Colt Sheridan told me. Inspector Ramberg must have showed it to him."

"And how," asked Lyby, "did Mr. Mahler know about it?"

"I don't know. But Valerie knew about it before it turned up in Jorgen's room. She showed it to Sheridan and I overheard her telling Mahler about it the day we toured the seed vault."

"What did Mahler say about it when you spoke with him this morning?"

Dinah thought back to Mahler's words with a surge of disgust. "He said if he saw her Judas face again, he'd wring her neck. He seemed less bothered that Sheridan may have murdered a man than that Valerie had let the evidence out of her keeping."

Lyby consulted her notes. "Senator Keyes says that Ms. Ives suspected you of secretly working for one of Sheridan's rivals and perpetrating dirty tricks against Sheridan's campaign. Is it true?"

"No."

"You didn't lure Herr Eftevang to Longyearbyen to protest Tillcorp?"

"No."

With a hesitant glance back to Thor, the sergeant terminated the questioning. The two of them conferred briefly and Lyby advised Dinah not to leave the hotel again without permission.

"From whom?" asked Dinah, just to smart off.

Thor gave her an unreadable look and left without deigning to answer. Dinah sidestepped Lyby and followed him out the door. "Inspector Ramberg. A moment of your time, please."

He stopped and turned around.

"Why are you treating me like a suspect, Thor? You know I didn't murder either of those people."

"I know it."

"Then why? And why the cold shoulder?"

"By socializing with you, I've compromised the investigation. Compromised my job, perhaps. Senator Keyes has spoken to the governor. Sergeant Lyby is now the lead investigator. It's a cliché in the TV cop shows. The cop gets in trouble for becoming personally involved with a civilian." His mouth quirked up on one side as if he were enjoying a mordant joke at his own expense. "You'd already guessed that I've never worked on a murder case before, hadn't you?"

She hadn't. Her face must have showed her surprise.

He laughed. "The only killer I've ever brought down was a polar bear."

The lobby was packed with the British tourists who'd arrived that morning. They all had drinks in hand and their revelry seemed to be building toward a drunken Saturnalia. Dinah had one of those "time out of joint" sensations. Had it been only twelve hours ago that she found Valerie's body? It seemed ages ago. And tonight people would be swilling cocktails and wishing one another a happy New Year one floor above where Valerie had been bludgeoned. Dinah couldn't blame the Radisson for keeping the news of an in-house murder quiet, but it seemed heartless nevertheless.

She weaved her way through the crowd to the Barentz Pub, hoping to find an empty table. It was past eight o'clock and she hadn't eaten anything since her boiled egg and toast at *frokost*. She felt hollow as a gourd. A live band played soft rock in the corner of the room, the music barely audible above the hubbub, and every table in the restaurant appeared to be taken.

It was the same story next door in the hotel's elegant Nansen Brasserie. To her amazement, a smiling Herr Dybdahl—his eye patch gone—was yukking it up at a large table with Jake Mahler and a stout woman with a tight blond bun. Mrs. Dybdahl, Dinah assumed. If there had been animosity between the two men, as Thor had thought, it seemed to be bygones now. From the semblance of bonhomie, Dinah could only surmise that those peasant farmers working on or near Norwegian plantations in Africa would soon be getting a "nudge" as to what seeds to plant next season. Evidently, Sheridan's troubles hadn't been as great a setback to Tillcorp's plans as Mahler had feared and Valerie's murder seemed not to have dimmed anyone's spirits.

Dinah's stomach growled. If all of the merrymakers in the lobby were waiting for a table, she'd never get anything to eat.

And the kitchen was probably too busy to bother with room service. She wished Thor had asked her to join him for New Year's Eve at Løssluppen Hole or somewhere away from the madding crowd. But he obviously felt the need to distance himself from her and rightly so. She faulted herself for the spot he was in. She shouldn't have let anyone see them together. She definitely shouldn't have let him kiss her, although an encore would be highly enjoyable tonight around midnight. Again, she felt a twinge of guilt about Jon. It wasn't cricket to switch one's feelings from one man to another this abruptly. It was a character flaw, the upshot of her fickle genes.

Her stomach growled more insistently. Where was she going to get something to eat? Lyby had ordered her not to leave the hotel, but what could she do about it? It wasn't as if she could throw her in the pokey and her absence for a couple of hours wouldn't be noticed with all this carousing going on. The thought of venturing outside again was discouraging. The pea jacket wouldn't keep her warm over many blocks, but she might make it as far as the Beached Whale without freezing. The Whale served soups, hot sandwiches and cheese plates. She'd seen a menu posted in the window. And in spite of the recent reminder of the dangers of alcohol, she needed a drink. Valerie's dead face and blood-matted hair came back to her every time she closed her eyes. She thought about what Thor had said about Erika. She had the grace to ask if Eftevang had a wife. Dinah hadn't had the grace to think about Valerie's family or the people who would mourn for her until now.

Back in her room, she bundled herself into all the usual outdoor accoutrement. She was getting the hang of "taking the air" in Longyearbyen. She returned to the foyer, booted up, and ducked out of the hotel into a howling wind and a horizontal snow. Passing through doors in this part of the world was like inhaling fire. She cupped her hands over her nose, took one moist, warming breath, and plodded off in the direction of the pub.

The streets were empty, the shops and businesses closed. The feeble street lights made no dent in the gloom. The darkness felt palpable, dense as liquid asphalt. There was even a tang of asphalt in the air, probably smoke from the power station. She'd read that Longyearbyen, with its numerous research centers set up to preserve the Arctic environment and slow climate change, had the only coal-fired power plant in Norway. The pollution from the smokestack was described as a blight on the landscape when the sun shone. However ugly it might be, Dinah would rather see the source of the smell. In this infernal darkness, things not seen conveyed a sense of the sinister.

The light in the front window of the Beached Whale signaled that it was open for business. She crossed the street and peered in the window. Two men sat in a booth near the back and another man in a long shearling vest and a battered Soviet army hat sat at the bar talking to the bartender. She darted a nervous look down the dark alley where Fritjoe Eftevang had been stabbed and went inside. There was no boot rack and no sign. She pulled off her cold weather trappings and seated herself in a booth facing the door. She took off her mittens and blew on her hands for a minute.

The bartender came around the bar with a menu and handed it to her. He was a rawboned man with a ruddy complexion and a web of creases fanning out from the corners of his blue eyes. "British or American?"

"American."

"Good. I ran out of gin an hour ago."

"Do you have something warm? A hot toddy?"

"Will an Irish coffee do you?"

"Perfect."

He turned to go and changed his mind. "The dead woman a friend of yours, was she?"

"No. We met for the first time on the flight from Washington."

"Strange it happened here. Hasn't been a murder in Longyearbyen since the Germans occupied Svalbard in the Second World War."

Dinah didn't know whether to take that as a neutral comment on local history or an indictment of the American propensity to violence. She trotted out a lame cliché. "News travels fast around here. How did you hear about the murder?"

"It's a short grapevine." He went back behind the bar and picked up his conversation with the man in the Soviet hat. Their accents sounded more Russian than Norwegian, but they were speaking in English.

Dinah studied the menu and decided to pass on the brine-cured herring with raw onions, the whale in pepper sauce, and the seal stew. A bowl of tomato soup and a simple grilled cheese sandwich seemed to be the most comforting foods on offer.

The bartender returned with her drink and she ordered. Before he got away, she asked, "Did you know the man who was murdered behind the pub? Mr. Eftevang?"

"For about two hours. He sat where you're sitting, drinking aquavit and beer and spouting about hybrid corn they feed to livestock in some place in Africa and the price in some foreign money I'd never heard of. It was an off night or my customers would have told him to shut up and drink."

"Did anyone sit with him or talk privately with him?"

"Reporter asked me that. Thor, too. You know our policeman?"

"Yes."

"Like I told him, the man acted like he was expecting some-body who never showed up. Then about ten o'clock, he paid the check and left."

"Tobejas! Another one!" The man in the Soviet hat held up an empty beer mug.

The bartender stuck his order pad in his belt and went back to the bar. Dinah sipped her Irish coffee and wished she'd brought a book with her. Not the book of Norse myths. Something lighter, more hopeful and escapist. In hindsight, it would have been better to hang around the Radisson even if she had to go hungry. It was a bad night to be alone.

The door flew open and a gust of icy wind blew her hair back. A masked person in a puffy down overcoat the size of a blimp stepped inside.

"O…M…G!" He pulled off his cap and his ski mask and the cowlick spiked up. "Great minds think alike."

"Tipton." For the first time in too long ago to remember, Dinah laughed. "Did you come for supper?"

"There's a two hour wait at the Radisson and I'm famished." He doffed his coat and flung himself into the seat across from her. "What a day, huh?"

Chapter Twenty-five

Without the thickly-padded coat, Tipton looked like a gangly twelve-year-old again. He sat down and ran his eyes over the menu. The bartender returned to the table and he ordered a fish sandwich, a green salad with radishes, scallions, and cucumbers, and a beer. The beer surprised Dinah. She halfway expected the bartender to card him, but he didn't. Like Lars at the Kantine, Tobejas didn't seem persnickety about the rules and, after all, it was New Year's Eve.

After his beer was delivered, Tipton took a sip, wiped the foam off his lip, and turned his attention to Dinah. "You must be a bundle of nerves. How gruesome to look up and see a dead body. And then tearing off through the snow with that Aagaard bozo to find Erika. Ramberg should deputize you."

His friendliness surprised her. His idol, Whitney Keyes had accused her of being a mole for a rival campaign. She would have expected Tipton to take that as the gospel and shun her as a traitor, but he was all smiles and she was glad for the company. She said, "You seem well informed about the events of my day."

"Everybody has some tidbit of information. Whitney told me how you'd found Valerie and the police give away more than they should in their questioning. I don't think they have a lot of experience investigating major crimes here in Norway. Of course, it's pretty obvious now that Colt is the killer."

"I'd have thought you'd be defending him passionately and trying to salvage his candidacy."

"Oh, I would if all there was to it was a lot of idle gossip about a dead Norwegian protester and a pack of liberals squawking about his close relationship with Tillcorp. We could have rehabilitated Colt's image within three or four news cycles. But now there's a smoking gun. Can you believe he wrote that e-mail? But we hear it over and over again, killers are known for doing stupid things."

Dinah didn't doubt that Sheridan was capable of doing stupid things, but sending that e-mail went beyond the pale. "He says his account was hacked and you and Valerie tried to figure how the hacker got through the firewall."

"Yes. Valerie believed the hacking story, which I think was a little naïve of her. I ran a virus scan and didn't detect anything suspicious. The campaign's technology security is absolutely first rate. Even if Valerie bought into Colt's story, I can't understand why she didn't show the e-mail to the police as soon as she received it and let them decide. She's a lawyer. Lawyers are supposed to be sticklers about evidence and the rule of law and that sort of thing. And Whitney was adamant from the start that we cooperate fully with the Norwegian police."

Dinah reined in her sarcasm, but Tipton was the naif if he hadn't tumbled to Valerie's pash for Sheridan. She said, "If Valerie didn't believe that Sheridan wrote the e-mail or that he'd done the murder, she wouldn't have done anything to jeopardize his campaign."

"If she'd been more forthcoming," he said with a sniff of self-righteousness, "she might still be alive. Anyway, Colt's campaign is all over but the postmortem now. Valerie's murder and Erika's carryings-on are already fodder for the media. I got a text an hour ago from our campaign spokesman and *The New York Times* is already in full gloat."

"Who did the *Times* name as its source?"

"Oh, I don't know. Your Senator Frye is my best guess. But it could be anyone. Longyearbyen's become a journalists' hive and everyone's buzzing about Sheridan's involvement in the murder and his unfaithful rock-star wife. I don't think Norwegians are as used to this kind of titillation as we are."

The bartender, who was apparently also the cook and the waiter, brought their sandwiches and Dinah ordered a cup of regular coffee.

Tipton didn't want another beer. He paused between each sip as if measuring its effect on his blood alcohol level. He sliced off a morsel of the fish sandwich, took a tentative bite, and said, "Not bad for a greasy spoon at the end of the world."

"Mm." Dinah's grilled cheese tasted great. She considered ordering a second one to go.

"Was Erika loaded to the gills when you found her?"

"She had been drinking, but she covered it well."

"The mark of a true lush. I agreed with Mahler and Valerie. She was Colt's number one roadblock to the White House. She's good-looking and telegenic for a woman her age and her history might have appealed to a segment of independents and women who like the fact that the candidate's wife had some celebrity of her own at one time. But our values voters would never have gone for her, especially with her showing up tipsy at campaign functions and running off at the mouth about some lost child."

"You know about that?"

"From Valerie. She was privy to Colt's despair. She tried to persuade him to institutionalize her, but he wouldn't hear of it. And Whitney let his feelings cloud his judgment, too. This election is just too momentous to let feelings enter in. Of course, Whitney decided over a year ago to back Colt, before Erika went 'round the bend. Whitney is a fantastic tactician and an absolute master of the electoral map. He knows precisely where and how to rack up those two-hundred and seventy necessary electoral votes. And with his foreign policy expertise, he would have been an awesome Secretary of State."

All that and a bag of potato chips, thought Dinah. She tore apart her bag of potato chips with her teeth and ruminated on the political calculus of Whitney Keyes. What kind of feelings had clouded his judgment? Feelings toward whom and why? There was no question now that he detested Mahler. He may have resented Mahler's greater influence over Sheridan, but the antipathy ran deeper.

A man with your vulnerabilities. What vulnerabilities?

Keyes was the one who'd arranged this trip. Might the fantastic tactician have summoned Eftevang to Norway in order to embarrass Mahler? If Eftevang's ravings generated negative press back in the States, it would prove to Sheridan that Tillcorp was more of a liability than an asset and, perhaps, Sheridan would ditch Mahler. Keyes could have had no motive to kill Eftevang, at least not initially. But maybe his plan backfired and Eftevang threatened to tell Sheridan and Mahler who'd sent for him. Instead of ditching Mahler, Sheridan would have ditched Keyes. Keyes couldn't let that happen, so he set up a meeting with Eftevang and when the man wouldn't swear to keep his name out of it, Keyes retrogressed to his days in the Persian Gulf when killing was the short answer to a dicey situation. And when Valerie somehow found out that it was Keyes who had brought Eftevang to Longyearbyen, she confronted him and he killed her, too.

Dinah was willing to concede that she sometimes let her imagination run away with her, but the narrative was rolling and it all made sense. Keyes, himself, was the mole. Val neither liked nor trusted Dinah, but there was only Keyes' word that she suspected Dinah of working for a rival campaign. Furthermore, as closely as Keyes worked with Sheridan, he would almost certainly have known the password to Sheridan's e-mail account, or known enough to guess it. And except for that incriminating e-mail from Sheridan to Val, the case against Keyes was as strong or stronger than the case against Sheridan.

There was a definite whiff of pretense about the too-perfect Senator Keyes and the sly, malignant way that Mahler had told her to ask Keyes about Myzandia still perplexed her. Did Mahler know something unsavory about Keyes' foundation and its operations? If so, the vulnerabilities ran both ways. Tipton would brook no criticism of his hero, but when her coffee arrived, she hazarded a tactful query. "While you were being interviewed by the police, Senator Keyes and Jake Mahler got into a row. Is there bad history between them?"

"Oh, they've crossed swords once or twice before."

"Over how to manage Sheridan's campaign?"

"That and Mahler's love of the limelight." Tipton picked breadcrumbs out of his hairy, gray cardigan. "Val and Whitney both pleaded with him to stop giving speeches all over creation, crowing about the wonders of gene modification and stirring up the food purists on several continents. He was pushing Congress to kill a bill requiring labels on GM foods before we had worked out a position paper and talking points for Colt. Tillcorp had problems in Africa and we were all afraid if that story broke, it would taint Colt's image. But Mahler wouldn't let up. He acted as if he owned Colt and expected value for his investment." Tipton extracted a fleck of fried fish batter from his sweater sleeve. "Mind you, this is *before* we even have the nomination wrapped up."

"So Senator Keyes' grudge against Mahler has nothing to do with Keyes' health clinics?"

"Oh, I don't think so. Both Tillcorp and Whitney's Global Health Foundation have had to fight rumors of one kind or another. They have attorneys working full-time on damage control."

"What were the rumors about the foundation?"

"Some problem with the tetanus vaccine the doctors administered to the women in Myzandia, allegations that it was tainted."

"Tainted? Tainted how?"

"I don't have anything to do with that aspect of Whitney's life. All I know is there was a memo from one of his foundation lawyers about some hormone or other that caused spontaneous abortions. I think Mahler is the one who alerted Whitney's lawyer to the rumor, which didn't set well with Whitney. It wasn't true and Whitney saw it as, oh…provocation on Mahler's part. Like, he was calling attention to a false story to take the attention off his own scandals in the region."

A galvanizing thought struck Dinah. What if the rumor was true? Or even if not true, what trouble might it cost Senator

Keyes, legally and financially to defend against it? What damage would it cause to his prestige? Would stopping the spread of such a rumor be a sufficient motive to commit murder? She jettisoned tact. "Would Eftevang have known about this vaccine rumor?"

"Oh, he was in and out of Africa." Tipton seemed to realize that he was about to be mousetrapped. He drained his beer and, to Dinah's surprise, made a big to-do of ordering a second. She asked the bartender for another splash of hot coffee. She wasn't counting on much sleep tonight anyway.

The man in the Soviet hat paid his bill and put on his coat, another somewhat tattered relic from the U.S.S.R. He started for the door and she braced herself for another gust of wind. This time when the door opened, a framed photograph blew off the wall.

"*Skitt!*" The bartender grabbed a dustpan and a broom and began sweeping up the broken glass.

Dinah flashed to the legend she'd read about the mysterious pair who brought the Black Death to Norway. The man carried a rake. The woman carried a broom and where she went, all were swept away to their deaths. She wrested her eyes off the broom, tried to wrest her thoughts off death. "That's an unusual sweater, Tipton. I noticed it earlier. What type of yarn is that?"

"Oh, it's dog fur." He seemed delighted that she'd asked. "My mother knitted it for me from the fur of our English sheepdog. Reagan was my best friend from the time I was eight years old. Mother wanted me to have something to remember him by and she spun his fur into yarn. I have a vest and scarf, too."

The bartender returned to their table with Tipton's beer and a pot of viscous looking coffee. "No rush, but this is the last round. I'm closing early tonight. I promised my wife I'd be home before next year."

Tipton yakked on about Reagan the sheepdog and life growing up in Boston. In spite of the limitations of living in a bastion of liberalism, his mother was apparently an awesome political fundraiser for the Republican Party. Tipton had met all of the major figures in the party and two members of the Supreme

Court called him by his first name. He had decided at the age of fourteen to make his mark in the world of politics. Dinah was grateful for the diversion. She didn't want to think about death and unhappiness. The sound of a friendly human voice making small talk was comforting. Her thoughts drifted occasionally to Valerie, but she wrenched them back to the present and tried to ask intelligent questions from time to time.

The other two diners put on their duds and, being careful not to let in another gust of wind, said "*God natt*" and took their leave. Finally, with Tipton's chronicle of his ambitions pretty well covered and the bartender staring at his watch, Dinah acknowledged that it was time to go.

Tipton helped her into her pea jacket and she suited up with all the rest of the paraphernalia. Dressing and undressing had become a tiresome ritual. There were so many layers of clothing to put on and take off. Tipton held onto the ends of his cardigan sleeves to keep them from riding up as he struggled into his huge, puffy coat. He got one arm into a sleeve, but couldn't catch the other and writhed about helplessly. Like a little kid, thought Dinah.

She laughed and held the loose sleeve out for him. "This isn't the coat you wore when we toured the vault."

"I bought it today at that sporting goods store next to the hotel. If we're going to be here for another week, I plan to stay warm."

"Maybe you could lend me your old parka. I'd like to stay warm, too."

"It's yours." His arm finally found the armhole and pushed through.

"There you go." Dinah patted him on the back and a small chip of something red fell onto the toe of her boot.

A small red chip like…

Her heart lurched. She turned away quickly and slipped her balaclava over her face. Tipton was pulling on his gloves and didn't notice.

"Drat it." She tried to keep her voice nonchalant. "I have to go to the ladies' room. You go on ahead, Tipton."

"That's all right. I'll wait."

"No, really. I'll have to take off all this paraphernalia again and put it back on. I'll be fine. There's no one on the streets tonight."

"All right. I have a few memos to write tonight, so I guess I'll see you in the morning. Happy New Year."

"Same to you."

He opened the door and the wind rushed through like a freight train. Her heart was racing. She reached down and picked up the red chip. It was an acrylic fingernail. Fire-engine red. Valerie's color.

She studied it for several seconds. It must be the most elementary lesson a politican had to learn. You can't trust anyone. Valerie had learned it the hard way and now Tipton's best friend Reagan had come back from the grave to teach it to him.

She said to the bartender, "Do you have a telephone I can use? It's an emergency."

Chapter Twenty-six

Thor wasn't at the Radisson and he wasn't in his office. Neither was Sergeant Lyby. Dinah felt a rising alarm. Tipton had bludgeoned Valerie and it was odds on that he had also stabbed Eftevang and shot her. He had to be stopped and nobody who could stop him was reachable. Her hands were quivering. Who could she call? Who would believe her? Should she have picked up the fingernail? If she hadn't, Tipton would have. But who could say now that Valerie hadn't lost the nail in a struggle with Dinah? If Valerie's DNA was detectable, hers would also be there. Jerusalem, why was everything so hard?

She put down the phone. It occurred to her that she was utterly alone, at least until tomorrow. And what if she was wrong and Tipton *had* seen the nail fall out of his sweater? What if he had registered the no-doubt telltale look of horror on her face and was lying in wait for her somewhere out there in the darkness? She didn't understand why he'd shot her in the first place, but if he had reason before, he had ample reason to finish the job now.

"Miss, are you in trouble?" The bartender had cleared the tables and was unloading a tray of dirty dishes into the dishwasher behind the bar.

"Yes. I mean, I think I am. I can't reach Inspector Ramberg."

"Probably went home for the night to his cabin."

"Do you have his home number?"

"No phone out there. He lives more than four miles outside of town on the Longyearbyen River."

Dinah licked her lips. "Would it be possible, Herr…?

"My name's Tobejas."

"Would it be possible for you to walk me back to the Radisson, Tobejas?"

The creases around his eyes deepened. He rinsed his hands and dried them on the towel hanging from his belt. "With all these murders going on lately, I'll take my gun."

Tobejas turned on the dishwasher, gave the bar a quick wipe-down, and went back toward the toilets. He opened a utility closet and took out his coat and a rifle. "You seemed to be having a good time with the young man. What scared you?"

Doubts flooded her mind. The answer would sound ludicrous. Because an acrylic fingernail fell out of his sweater. She had no proof that the nail had belonged to Valerie. It could have belonged to some Norwegian sweetie Tipton had been cuddling with, or Valerie could have lost the nail while giving Tipton one of her bolstering little arm-shakes. But Valerie wasn't likely to have bolstered Tipton. She thought he was a kiss-up. Tobejas was staring at her, waiting for an answer. She said, "He dropped something that makes him a *mistenkelig*."

Tobejas flashed her a testy look. "Whatever that means."

"It's Norweg…Nevermind."

Tobejas zipped up his coat, pulled his ski mask over his face, and shouldered his rifle. "Let's go." He opened the door and held onto it until she was clear, then let it blam shut.

She shouted over the howl of the wind. "Aren't you going to lock up?"

"*Nei*. Murder's the only crime that happens in Longyearbyen."

He stayed close to her on the walk back to the hotel, holding the rifle at the ready and twisting his head around to peer down the dark alleys and side streets. The wind was blowing from behind them, whistling past their ears and scouring the street of everything that wasn't tied down. An empty cardboard box bounced down the street and passed them. A plastic sack flew out of nowhere and brushed across Dinah's eyes. Her heart skipped a beat. She caught her breath and swatted the bag away. It flapped up and away like a berserk ghost.

The blue lights of the Radisson came into view and she began to fret over what she should do once she was inside. She couldn't ask Tobejas to stand watch over her with his gun all night.

Something banged above their heads. Tobejas whirled around and raised his gun. Dinah cringed against the side of the building. Looking up, she saw a wooden signboard dancing in the wind.

When they entered the ambit of friendly light emanating from the Radisson, Dinah felt weak with relief. "Thank you, Tobejas. *Tusen takk.*"

"Will you be all right from here?"

"Yes. I'll be fine. The place is packed with people."

"Okay. I'll watch you until you're safe inside. Tomorrow, you tell Thor Ramberg he'd better do something about this craziness. It's starting to feel like the south side of Chicago."

Dinah nodded and hurried into the foyer. Before she removed her boots, she reconnoitered the lobby. There was no sign of Tipton. It was 10:30 and the Brits were partying to beat the band, literally. A lusty-voiced gang clustered in front of the blazing fire singing "Norwegian Wood" while the band played "Winter Wonderland." Several people were still waiting for a table in the dining room, including Lee and Rod. Dinah waved to Lee and he waved back. Maybe she should latch onto him and his partner. Who better to protect her than a pair of professional bodyguards? Mahler must have decided that he didn't need their protection. Strange since, presumably, he didn't know who murdered his attorney or why.

Dinah shucked her coat and thought about taking off her boots, but changed her mind. She couldn't picture a situation where she would have to flee outdoors, but better shod than sorry. She would remain ready to run until she was safely inside her room with the door chained.

On the off chance that Thor or Sergeant Lyby had left a number where they could be reached, she stood in line to speak to the desk clerk, a middle-aged man with an angular face like chiseled granite and a mien of supernatural calm. He was juggling the complaints of two other guests—a man whose cantankerous voice could be heard crackling over the telephone and a somewhat intoxicated woman flourishing a voucher that hadn't been redeemable in the dining room.

"I'm sorry, madam. The electronic code on the voucher does not match the number on the reservation. It's the tour company's responsibility to provide us with…"

"Call the company then." The woman had to shout to be heard above the noisy celebrants in the lobby and the band's manic rendition of "Stayin' Alive."

The clerk stuck a finger in one ear and spoke determinedly into the telephone. "No, sir. The hotel is unable to book a New Year's Day sleigh ride until we know what the weather will be. If you will call tomorrow…"

"Excuse me." Dinah stepped around the woman and interrupted. "Did Inspector Ramberg leave a number where he could be reached?"

The clerk shook his head. "No, sir. I have not seen the weather forecast."

"What about Sergeant Lyby?" entreated Dinah. "There must be a policeman downstairs guarding the crime scene, right?"

The voucher lady turned to Dinah. "What crime scene?"

"Will you hold a moment, sir?" The clerk put a hand over the receiver. "She means the fitness room, madam. There was a mishap earlier today. There are no police, but we have locked the door for safety reasons." He returned to the telephone, unflappable as a boulder. "If you call the desk at nine tomorrow morning, sir, we will know if the sleigh ride is possible. If not, the Svalbard Museum will be open. Or you can take a tour of Mine Number Three, which is interesting. It was the last coal shaft to be mined manually."

"Call Polar Travels," demanded the voucher lady. "I made this reservation six months ago. I'm not paying a thousand kroner for a dinner in Longyearbyen that I paid for already in London."

"Their London office is closed for the holiday, madam. I will ring them first thing on Monday."

Dinah was at the end of her tether. "Are there no police of any kind whatever who can be reached in this town?"

"It's New Year's Eve!" The clerk's equanimity was clearly raveling. "Like everyone else in the world except the employees of this hotel, they have plans. If you are ill and need to be helicoptered south to Tromsø, dial one-one-two. Otherwise, you will have to wait until tomorrow."

It crossed Dinah's mind to request that helicopter. She still had a bad feeling, a Nordic sense that the darkness was closing in on her, that it was inevitable, and she would have to face it alone.

She gave herself a shake. It was childish to be freaked out by a twerp like Tipton Teilhard. She knew what he had done now, so it wasn't as if he could sneak up on her. And she didn't have to spend the evening alone. Lee seemed approachable. Or she supposed she might even foist herself off on Senator Keyes, or Jake Mahler and Herr Dybdahl, or Senator Sheridan and Erika. A fraction of an instant's reflection and she rejected all of those possibilities. By now, she wouldn't be surprised if Brander Aagaard had been released on his own recognizance. If she knew which hotel he was staying at, she'd call him.

It was an hour until midnight but, behind her, a few members of the British tour group had already broken into a maudlin, off-key rendition of "Auld Lang Syne."

Should auld acquaintance be forgot,
And never brought to mind?
Should auld acquaintance be forgot,
And auld lang syne.

Those maniacs would be partying all night. All she had to do was make herself congenial and blend in for a few hours. Eventually, some of them would retire to the second floor and she would tag along until she could escape into her room and lock the door.

She picked her way back through the crowd to the big stone fireplace where the singers were holding forth.

For auld lang syne, my jo,
For auld lang syne,
We'll take a cup o' kindness yet,
For auld lang syne.

A soft, dumpling of a man with a thatch of gray hair that made him look like a chinchilla draped an arm around her shoulder, nuzzled her earlobe, and crooned. *We two have run about the slopes, and picked the daisies fine…But we've wandered many a weary foot, since auld…lang…syne.* If anyone had struck a match, his breath would have been combustible.

Dinah disengaged herself and moved into a vacant chair away from the fire. She tossed her coat across the back, but she was still too cold to take off her sweater.

We two have paddled in the stream,
From morning sun till dine;
But seas between us broad have roared,
Since auld…lang…syne.

If she hadn't been so preoccupied with murder, she might have a shed a sentimental tear for her auld lang syne. She wondered what Jon would be doing when the New Year tolled across the seas in Hawaii, but checked herself and banished the thought. As for her not-so-auld lang syne, Thor Ramberg, she couldn't let herself think about what he was doing or with whom. She was too angry. Even if he was no longer in charge of the investigation, even if he had no experience working a murder case, even if his superiors had it in for him, he ought to be here, the slacker. He should be here to see that no additional murders sullied Longyearbyen's pristine reputation.

And surely you'll buy your pint cup,
And surely I'll buy mine;
And we'll take a right good-will draught,
For auld…lang…syne.

Dinah harked back to all the clues she'd missed. Tipton's mother served on the Board of the American Council of Arts with Portia Warren. Why had she not made the connection? Zeb Warren was Sheridan's Republican rival. Apparently, Portia and/or Zeb had co-opted Tipton and turned him into a mole. He must have passed on the information to Warren that Mahler would be traveling with Sheridan to Norway. And for some reason, he had murdered Fritjoe Eftevang. He'd probably boosted the knife when he went into the kitchen to supervise the making of Keyes' sandwiches. And how easy it would have been for Tipton to send an e-mail from Sheridan's computer. He wouldn't have needed to hack into the account. He was the techie, the trusted security guy. He would have had Sheridan's password and could have gone in and monkeyed with the account whenever he wanted.

The band launched into "Norwegian Wood" and the chinchilla look-alike led his off-key choir in a rousing sing-along.

I once had a girl,
or should I say…

Dinah couldn't stand it. She wasn't feeling congenial enough to last through another forty-five minutes of this gin-fueled concert until midnight and the ultimate chorus of "Auld Lang Syne." It was too…fatiguing. Too emotionally…emotional. She picked up her coat and headed back toward the ladies room for an illicit cigarette. It had been a hellacious year and, if she wasn't going to be kissed at midnight, she deserved the license to do whatever else she pleased with her body, whatever else she deemed soothing and pleasurable. Anyway, this would be her very last smoke. Her birthday resolution hadn't taken, but at the stroke of midnight, she would swear off tobacco forever more.

She went into the ladies room and found it blessedly empty, but not quiet. She could still hear the merrymakers' voices raised to the rafters, butchering "Norwegian Wood." She rested her purse on the counter and dug around for the pack of Petterøes with both hands. Mittens, chemical warmers, chocolate mints.

Another New Year's resolution would be to carry a smaller purse and less stuff. Not every outing was a polar expedition, for crying out loud. She found the cigarettes at the bottom, slightly squashed, fished the matchbook out of the cellophane sleeve on the pack, and lit up. There was a chartreuse chaise longue under an Art Deco poster of a 1930's jazz club. She threw herself down and brooded. There were a couple of half-filled plastic glasses on the side table, one with a blotch of red lipstick. It reminded her of Valerie's lipstick.

She inhaled indulgently. Recklessly. Like a character in an old movie. Like Bette Davis in *All About Eve*. A Bette Davis quote popped into her head. "Everybody has a heart. Except some people." Wasn't that the truth!

She took a few more puffs, but the Petterøe wasn't as soothing as she'd hoped. It left a bad taste in her mouth. She dropped it into a plastic glass. The ember sizzled in the un-drunk gin for an instant and died. She laid her head back on the chaise, closed her eyes, and wished herself a Happy New Year.

"I wish I could…"

The door opened. There was a blast of "Norwegian Wood." She opened her eyes, but a brick crashed onto her head, ending wishes and music together.

Chapter Twenty-seven

Something was tugging at her, rooting under her back and shoulders, pulling on her arms, panting like a beast.

Bear!

Dinah came to with a convulsive jolt. She was lying on her back and somebody in a black ski mask was trying to take off her coat. She punched him in the face as hard as she could.

"Ow-oh!" He grabbed his mouth and toppled over on his back.

Pain rocketed down her right arm and into her hand. Disoriented, she rose up on her elbows and wriggled away from him on her back. Her head felt as if she'd been clobbered by a wrecking ball. It took her a second to regain her senses, to realize that her hands were naked and ice-cold, to comprehend that she was in a fight for her life.

She rolled over on all-fours and scrabbled to her feet, but her feet sank in deep snow. She clutched her injured hand. In the headlights of a car, she saw blood dripping from her knuckles onto the snow. She must have hit a tooth.

"Give me that coat." Tipton took off his ski mask and righted himself. He had his back to the headlights and she couldn't see his face, but he was wearing the parka he'd worn the day they toured the vault.

She looked down and saw that she was wearing his huge, down-padded coat. He had unzipped it and ripped open the

Velcro collar. She rezipped and thrust her hands in the pockets as she backed away from him. "How'd I get your new coat?"

"I put it on you so you wouldn't be recognized. The Brits helped me drag my drunken girlfriend to the car. But now I want my coat back." He slurred his words, as if he were talking through a fat lip. He moved toward her, miring to his knees in snow. He spread his arms to keep his balance. In one of them was a rifle.

"Where are we?" She tried to walk backward, but she felt like a fly on flypaper. Lifting her feet was a labor. They were weighted down by the heavy snow.

"Doesn't matter."

"Whose car is that?"

"Ditto."

She glanced around at the barren, snow-covered tundra and took another step backward. Was that dark structure sticking up in the distance the colliery beside Løssluppen Hole? That place was probably jumping tonight. If it was still night. She had no idea how long she'd been out. The year had probably changed. The weather had definitely changed. The wind had died. There were even a few stars. The only things that hadn't changed were the darkness, the cold, and the expanding depravity of a murderer.

She said, "I've already told Ramberg and Lyby that it was you who killed Valerie. The best thing for you to do is to make a run for it. You can go to Barentsburg, escape to Russia."

"You didn't tell the police. I heard you asking. They've taken the night off. Nobody knows where they are."

"I told the bartender at the Beached Whale. Tobejus, he knows what you did."

"If you complained to him about finding a fingernail in my sweater, he probably took it as sour grapes, the whining of a jealous lover." Tipton trudged forward faster than she could trudge backward. "We're just a couple of romantic young people who came out here to make out and lost our way. Unfortunately, you freeze to death before I can bring help."

"If that's your story, you can't shoot me." She turned around and trudged off in the direction of the colliery, if that's what it was. Of course, she wouldn't make it that far. Running was futile, but handing over the coat and lying down to freeze to death wasn't in her DNA. She was half Seminole. Seminoles never surrendered.

She slogged on, swinging her arms to increase momentum. Her face and hands burned from the cold and now both arms hurt. Her purse was still hanging around her neck. She could feel it swaying from side to side as she moved. Without slowing her march, she unzipped the coat part way and dug in the purse until she found her mittens and her balaclava. Her cap was in the pocket of the pea jacket back at the Radisson, but the balaclava would help. She'd read that fifty percent of a person's body heat was lost through the head.

Her heartbeat seemed inhumanly fast. The blood pumping in her ears drowned out every other sound. She no longer heard Tipton panting or the snow crunching underfoot. Working this hard, she would soon work up a sweat and when she stopped, hypothermia would set in. Tipton was also working hard. Maybe he would bonk first or have a heart attack. But she didn't hold out much hope of that. He was young and a lot stronger than she'd thought. Strong enough to stab a man to death. Strong enough to bludgeon a woman with a dumbbell and lift her dead weight onto the top bench of the sauna. She should have realized he was the murderer with the first words out of his mouth at the Beached Whale. How could he know she'd had to look up to see Valerie's body? The police wouldn't have described the crime scene for him in detail.

He caught the tail of her coat and tugged, but she bent forward and powered on like a draft horse.

"Stop! Stop or I *will* shoot you." He let go of the coat and she nearly fell face forward. "There are worse ways to die than by freezing, Dinah. After a while, you just go to sleep."

"You go to hell." She staggered on. He must have been sweating profusely. She smelled the pong of wet dog wafting from the sweater.

He jabbed the rifle into her back. "If you insist…"

She stopped, pivoted from the waist, and threw both arms behind her like a discus thrower. Her left forearm bashed against the rifle and knocked it out of his hands. Tipton dived onto the ground after it. She hurled herself on top of him and pummeled him in the face and ears and neck, aware of the absurdity as her mittens cushioned every blow. He retrieved the rifle with one hand, and tried to smash the gun stock against her head. She dodged the blow, but he managed to roll her off onto her back. She was spent. It was hopeless.

She was witnessing her own murder in a place and a manner that, even at this critical juncture, astounded her by its sheer improbability.

With her last ounce of strength, she jerked an arm free and reached for the gun. Tipton ripped it free. They wallowed for a minute like weary wrestlers. Dinah found the trigger, the gun discharged with an ear-splitting explosion, and then the earth gave way.

Avalanche.

They fell together, legs threshing, arms grabbing the air, rocks and snow pelting from above. Tipton caught at her arm, but missed. He plummeted past, slamming her sideways. Her back scraped against something hard and she slid to a bone-shaking stop astraddle some kind of a shelf or outcrop. Loose snow and dirt showered onto her head and shoulders and Tipton screamed.

When her heart rate slowed enough to allow thought, she blew out a cloudy breath and looked up. The headlights from the car illuminated a more-or-less round opening approximately five feet above her head. Tipton moaned and she looked down. He was nothing but a dark shape, perhaps another ten feet below her.

What was this? The freaking Well of Urd? The diameter of the opening was about two feet. Thor had said the area was riddled with abandoned mines. This must be one of them, or an air shaft for one of them. How deep was it? She couldn't make out whether Tipton had hit the bottom or, like her, was cleaving to a narrow ledge.

Wailing Jerusalem. What now?

Air shafts were sometimes planned as escape routes for the miners, weren't they? Maybe there were iron rungs or a chain or some kind of handholds above her. If there were, she needed better light to see them.

"My leg," moaned Tipton. "I think it's broken."

An instant ago, they were locked in mortal combat. Suddenly, they were accidental allies, she and her would-be murderer trapped in the same hole. If they were going to survive, they'd have to help each other. She would have to think about how much she hated him tomorrow. "Do you have a flashlight?"

"No."

Dinah had a small one on her key ring. She leaned all her weight into the wall behind her, took off her right mitten and held it between her teeth. With her naked hand, she unzipped Tipton's coat and felt around inside her purse for the light. She found it and, scarcely daring to move, she unweighted one leg and shone the tiny cone of light on the protuberance that had arrested her fall. As nearly as she could tell, it was some kind of a pipe. It looked to be about ten inches across and extended about a foot from the wall. It was encrusted with dirt and permafrost and debris. She didn't like to think how rust and the ravages of time had weakened it.

She slid her light up the wall behind her to the rim of the shaft and down again. The wall looked to be solid coal, covered in places with whitish hoar frost. There were no handholds. She shone her beam all around their prison pit, looking for any kind of bar or pipe she could use to climb out. There was nothing. Except for the coal seam behind where she sat, the walls appeared grayish-white and porous—a mixture of frozen soil and dust and lumpy agglomerations of ice. This shaft must have been plugged for years. If it hadn't caved in when it did, Tipton would have killed her. She could be one of the few beneficiaries of global warming. As the saying went, it's an ill wind that blows nobody good.

She shone the light on her wristwatch. It wasn't there. She took the mitten out of her teeth. "What time is it?"

The LED dial of Tipton's digital watch flickered. "Two a.m. It'll be hours before anyone finds us. We'll die of hypothermia."

"No, we won't. Use your cell phone." She ransacked her memory. What was that number the desk clerk had said was the emergency number? "One-one-two. Dial one-one-two. They'll send a helicopter."

He didn't answer.

"Tipton?"

"The phone's not in my pocket. It must have fallen out."

She smothered a sob. "I'll shine the light down there. See if you can find it."

He couldn't. He said, "Use your cell. You have one, don't you?"

"It doesn't work in Europe." A ray of hope dawned. "Did you rent the car? It probably has a GPS."

"I don't know. I borrowed it."

"From whom?"

"Off the street. Somebody left the key in the ignition."

People will come, she told herself. Tipton didn't know his way around and he wouldn't risk getting lost. He wouldn't have taken the car far off the beaten path. She felt certain they were near the Løssluppen. Some night owl leaving the pub late would spot the car with its lights on and investigate, or a party of cross-country skiers out for a New Year's Eve lark would notice. She pictured the owner back in town rounding up a posse to come looking for his stolen property. Maybe he would bring Thor and Sergeant Lyby. Somebody would come. It would only be an hour or two. She could survive for two hours. All she had to do was keep calm, maintain her balance, stay as warm as she could, and not go to sleep. She zipped up the coat again and stuffed her hands under her arms.

Her right hand began to ache. She wasn't sure if the pain was from the cold or from hitting Tipton in the mouth. She remembered the chemical warmers she'd bought at the church.

She put the flashlight in her pocket, the mitten under her left arm, and dug inside her purse again with her right hand. Pen, pad, iPod. She found a warmer and ripped off the packaging with her teeth. The jerky movement unbalanced her and she grabbed the wall behind to steady herself. When she brought her hands forward again, the mitten and the warmer were gone.

Keep calm, she warned herself. She adjusted her butt and grubbed around for another warmer. This time she was careful. She opened the packet without incident and inserted it into her mittened left hand. She found another, opened it carefully, and tried to squeeze the fingers of her right hand around it. They didn't want to bend. She forced them into a fist and stuck her fist in her coat pocket.

Tipton moaned. "Can you jump down here and help me straighten my leg?"

It was an effort to hold her revulsion in abeyance. She nevertheless considered whether going down might be an option. There might be an exit somewhere down there. But it was probably plugged by permafrost and, even if she could jump down without breaking her own leg, getting lost in the bowels of an abandoned coal mine was the last thing she needed.

Her neck and shoulder muscles had stiffened and her arms and legs were starting to cramp. "What time is it now?"

"Two-oh-five."

It was going to be a long two hours. Maybe she could goad Tipton to talk about his crimes. That should keep them from falling asleep. "Why did you kill Eftevang, Tipton?"

"Why should I talk to you?"

"Because you won't get out of this hole alive without my help."

For a long minute, the only sound was the idling engine of the stolen car above their heds. Finally, he decided. "I promised him some documents that I downloaded from Valerie's computer. He was going to name me as his source."

"That's it? He didn't threaten to blackmail you or shake you down?"

"No, but I would've been branded a leaker. No one who's anyone would have trusted me again."

"Did Zeb Warren or someone in his campaign ask you to dig up dirt on Tillcorp and Sheridan?"

"Promised me a plum job in his administration. A slot at the top. Very inside."

"How did you persuade Eftevang to come to Longyearbyen?"

"Told him I had something WikiLeaks would go for."

"What did you tell Mahler and the senators about WikiLeaks?"

"Only mentioned it was possible that WikiLeaks would use Eftevang to publish the Africa rumors. Both of them had a reason to be nervous."

"What did you intend to leak, exactly?"

"Tillcorp secrets." His speech began to slow and sound curiously apathetic. "Would've tied 'em up in lawsuits for decades."

He must be going into shock, she thought. That broken leg would make him succumb to the cold sooner. She would have to keep him talking. "And Tillcorp's secrets would've embarrassed Senator Sheridan?"

"No...political... distance."

"Between Colt and Tillcorp, you mean?"

"Mmm. Colt would've been tarred with the same brush."

"How did you hack into Valerie's computer?"

"No...hacking." He sounded increasingly stuporous.

"Tipton? Tip, wake up. How did you hack her computer?"

A speck of green glimmered in the dark below. "Two-ten."

"Hold on, Tipton. I'm sure somebody's looking for us as we speak. Why no hacking?"

"Hmm?"

"You said you didn't hack Val's computer."

"Didn't have to. She used the same password she'd used when she worked for Whitney."

"And you found incriminating documents."

"Hmm."

"What did they prove, these documents?"

He made a raspy, incoherent sound.

"Tip? The Tillcorp documents, what did they show?"

"Cows and pigs and chickens…"

"What about them?"

"Sick. Tested positive."

"Positive for what? Was it something the cows were eating that made them sick?"

"GM corn. Some new pathogen. Moving up the food chain. Mov…ing…up."

"Tipton?" She'd read that people have been known to survive a drop in body temperature to sixty degrees. He couldn't have dropped thirty-eight degrees this fast. "Tipton! Tipton, listen to me. There's a chemical warmer down there on the ground somewhere. I'll shine the light. Look for it and put it in your shirt. It'll warm you up." She took the light out of her pocket and shined it around the floor. "I think I see it, Tipton. It's about two feet from your left leg. Can you…?"

"Said the only way to authenticate the documents was to name the source. Stupid. Had to kill him. Had to…"

"After Eftevang's murder, did Warren tell you to frame Senator Sheridan?"

"My idea. Way better than a little dirt about sick cows." He coughed. "No way to spin a murder."

Dinah's insides felt shivery. The cold was eating into her bones and her backside felt like a frozen tenderloin. She hugged herself and contracted her glutes. "So you took the e-mail you'd written and you planted it in the room Maks Jorgen had rented. How'd you get the key?"

"Lying on the front desk. Easy-peasy."

He was playing with the flashlight beam, chasing it with his hands like a baby. She turned it off. "Where are the documents now, Tipton? What did you do with them?"

"Secret."

"Tell me. I haven't got anyone to tell."

But he seemed to be drifting into delirium. She repositioned herself, flexed her neck, and shone the light around the walls again. If she could stand up, her head would be almost even with the opening. And if she could reach up with her arms and gain some purchase, she just might be able to heave herself over the top. It would hurt like hell, but if she made it, she'd be free.

She took one hand out of the mitten, put the light in her mouth, and braced both hands firmly on the wall behind her. Slowly, she lifted her left foot onto the pipe until the heel was almost against the wall. Using her leg strength and scooching her back against the wall, she pushed herself up by inches. As she became more upright, she drew her right leg up and planted her right foot on the pipe. All she had to do now was turn around and hoist herself over the top. She took a deep breath, cautioned herself not to look down, and prepared to about-face.

Her right foot slipped. She threw out her arms, caught nothing but air, and landed hard on her left hip. She felt the pipe give under her weight and pieces of dirt and debris that encrusted it broke off and hailed into the well. She didn't swallow the flashlight, but she may have chipped a tooth.

"She had a cow," maundered Tipton, jogged awake by the shower of dirt and stones.

Dinah clung to what was left of the pipe and waited for her heart to clear out of her throat. Keep calm, she reminded herself. Someone will come. She took the light out of her mouth. "Who had a cow, Tipton?"

"Valerie found out I was working for Zeb Warren."

"You were Warren's mole inside Sheridan's campaign?"

"No more bein' a flunky. Gonna be a top policy advisor in Zeb's administration."

The darkest hour is just before dawn, thought Dinah, only dawn wouldn't come again until mid-February. The cold and the dark began to meld. They were inseparable from each other and from her. No one was coming. A feeling of finality settled over her. This was it. If he was going to die or if she was, she wanted to understand at least one thing. "Why did you shoot me, Tipton?"

"Hmm?"

"When I was coming out of the church, why did you shoot me?"

"Didn't."

"Yes, you did. Don't you remember? I was wearing Erika's parka."

"Didn't shoot Dinah. Didn't…"

"Tipton? Tip, wake up. If you didn't shoot me, who did?"

Chapter Twenty-eight

Should auld acquaintance be forgot
And never brought to mind,
Should auld acquaintance be forgot
In a hole that you can't find?

Dinah had been singing and talking to herself for a long time. Tipton had gone quiet. Nothing she said elicited a response, not that there was much to say at this point. The two of them were about to commit yet another crime in Longyearbyen. They were going to die.

The headlights from the car hadn't attracted any rescuers and, the longer she waited, the less hope she held out. She had scrunched both her hands into her one remaining mitten and periodically, as her writing hand warmed, she had recorded Tipton's confession in her notepad. It hardly mattered. Not even the cold mattered anymore. All she wanted was a comfortable place to lie down and rest. She felt like an endurance flagpole-sitter, only her endurance had run out.

Should auld acquaintance be forgot
And never brought to mind,

She waved her little flashlight around the dark walls in time with the music.

The girl you kissed fell in a hole,
She's in an awful bind.

Something white swept across the wall in front of her and a shower of snow sprinkled her face. She raised the light into the yellowish face and close-set eyes of a polar bear. It dipped its foot-wide paw into the hole and swiped at her like a cat fishing in a fishbowl.

Wailing Jerusalem! She shrank against the wall. Her eyes dilated on the thick, curved claws. One swipe and she'd be burger. Her nostrils filled with the stench of him but, pretty obviously, she smelled like a yummy snack to him. The bear made a fierce chuffing sound and stretched its long neck and fat paw farther into the hole.

She would jump. If she had to die, all right. She would die. She would break her bones and freeze to death at the bottom of this pit. But she would not, she *would not* be devoured by a polar bear. Her heart crashed against her chest like a caged thing. Hand shaking, she shone her light into the abyss. Tipton was awake and stirring. He was muttering to himself and taking off his clothes. His parka and sweater had been tossed aside and he was pulling a turtleneck over his head.

"Tipton, are you crazy?"

The bear gnashed its teeth and made a broad swipe with its paw. She leaned as far away as she could without tumbling off her perch and shone her light in the bear's eyes. They seemed to regard her with a mixture of irritation and interest. Not wanting to appear to challenge him, she turned off the light and averted her eyes.

"Please..." her voice fluted. She cleared her throat. "Please go away."

"Burning up," cried Tipton, naked from the waist up and tearing at his pants. It was as if he were preparing his flesh for the polar bear's pleasure.

What was the matter with him? Carbon monoxide poisoning? Maybe a fire was smoldering in a coal seam down there. Maybe the introduction of oxygen into the pit had ignited a fire.

The bear snarled and bared his fangs. Jesus, Joseph, and Mary. She donated every year to the World Wildlife Fund. Didn't they keep a list? Didn't she deserve some kind of an exemption? This was her private Ragnarok, an end so outlandish it must have been orchestrated by the gods. She'd always prided herself on having a kind of last-ditch courage, the spiritual legacy of her Seminole ancestors who never gave up and never showed the white feather. But it was one thing to be brave in the Florida sunshine with an edged weapon in your hands and a different thing altogether to be brave in a freezing hole, empty-handed, with a polar bear breathing down your neck.

She remembered the peanut butter cheese crackers she'd been carrying around with her since Honolulu. She reached into her purse, found the package, opened it, and began to throw the crackers up, one at a time. The first two fell down into the well, but the next one made it over the top. The bear retracted his paw. She managed to get another one out of the hole and allowed herself a grain of hope. Maybe he would be satisfied and go away. But in a minute, he came back and began to bounce up and down with his front paws, dislodging chunks of dirt and ice onto her head. She raised her arms to protect herself from the bombardment.

The bear continued to bounce and dig and snort. It must weigh over a ton. What if it fell in on top of them? She prayed it would miss her and land on Tipton.

A barrage of small rocks and ice rained down on her and jumping began to seem like the only alternative to becoming polar-bear chow. She calculated the distance to the bottom. If she suspended herself by her arms from the pipe, it would be only about a five foot drop. In his weakened state, Tipton posed no threat and if the carbon monoxide and the cold didn't kill her, there was still a chance someone would see the car lights and come to dig her out.

She sat forward and shone the light below her into the pit. Best to swing forward on the landing so as to avoid Tipton's broken leg. What was that word the kamikaze surfers yelled when they shot the curl? Cowabunga. She slid forward to the end of the pipe.

And then she heard the rumble of an engine. Had the car revved on its own? No. It was a different car. People had come. And barking dogs.

Karelian bear dogs?

The bear snorted and reared up on his hind legs. He towered over the hole. From her vantage point, all she could see was the lower part of his legs. The barking intensified, louder and more frenzied. The bear roared and bounced. Somebody shouted. Shots rang out. A flurry of ice balls hailed down on head.

When the noise stopped, she looked up into the bright, intelligent eyes of Crockett and Tubbs.

Thor's face appeared between the faces of the dogs. "Dinah? Are you hurt?"

"I'm too cold to know."

"I'll have you out in a minute. Hang on." He turned away.

"Thor?"

He looked back.

"Happy New Year."

Chapter Twenty-nine

Dinah wasn't really sick enough for the Sykehus, but she had plenty of scrapes and bruises and Nurse Vanya had softened since her last visit. She had recommended that Dinah stay overnight for observation and Dinah didn't mind the idea of someone clucking over her through the night. Her brush with death had left her feeling nervous and needy and afraid to be alone. She suspected that Vanya was lonely, too. There were no other patients in the hospital and no other staff and it was New Year's Day. They could keep each other company.

Vanya removed the thermometer from Dinah's mouth and Dinah asked, "Why would a person take off his clothes in sub-zero weather?"

"It's called paradoxical undressing. It's not uncommon in cases of severe hypothermia. I've seen it lots of times."

"What causes it?"

"Doctors say when the peripheral blood vessels become exhausted, they cause a rush of blood and heat to the extremities. A person who's hypothermic gets confused and fooled into thinking he's overheated. Hypothermia comes on faster if there's some other trauma."

Dinah nodded. In Tipton's case, there had been big trauma. By the time Thor hauled him naked out of that hole, he looked like a goner. Thor wrapped him in blankets, splinted his leg, and within an hour, he had been airlifted to the hospital in Tromsø.

Thor had promised to phone her as soon as he heard any news. She had told him about her discovery of Valerie's fingernail in the weave of Tipton's sweater and she'd recapped his confession. Her testimony probably wouldn't stand up in a court of law. The semi-delirious confession of a man who thought he was having a heat stroke inside of a freezing-cold mine shaft would be dubious in the extreme.

And the revelation that he hadn't shot her preyed on her mind. It threw everything into question.

"You were lucky," said Vanya. "That *tosk* stole Tobejas' car. When Tobejas walked back to the Whale after seeing you to the hotel, it was gone. Right away he thought it had something to do with the young man who frightened you. He called his wife to come and get him in the snøscooter and they went straightaway to Thor's cabin to tell him."

"It's very odd for a policeman not to have a telephone." Dinah didn't want to criticize the man. He *had* saved her life. But he'd been missing in action at the climax. If he'd been on duty at the hotel, she wouldn't have been addled and dragged off into a pit. He should be here right now. She'd told him that Tipton wasn't the one who shot her.

"Thor has a telephone."

"Tobejas didn't think so. He had to drive to his cabin."

"*Ja*, but it's the holiday. Thor wouldn't turn on his phone for work. He and the other policemen and women have their vacations, too. Three weeks in July and two weeks at Christmas and New Year. It's the law. I am the, what do you say? The skeleton."

Dinah smiled. "The skeleton crew."

"*Ja*. People who live here want to go south and visit their families. Only the crazy tourists and American *politikers* want to come here at this time of year."

A buzzer went off.

"Maybe another patient has come. Drink your tea and I'll be back when I can."

"Vanya, wait." Dinah was seized by a feeling of dread. "Is there a rifle somewhere in the hospital?"

"*Nei.* That would be silly." She hied off down the hall, chuckling at the silliness.

Dinah bounded out of bed, draped a blanket around her, and went to the door of her room. She didn't know whom to be afraid of or how to protect herself other than to hide. The main entrance and registration desk was to her right. She turned left and was ten yards down the hall, looking for an unlocked door when she heard Erika's voice behind her.

"Dinah. Where are you going?"

She turned. "Nowhere, really. Happy New Year, Erika."

"*Godt Nytt År!*"

Dinah walked back to meet her.

She carried a large white teddy bear with a red ribbon around its neck. She pushed the bear into Dinah's arms. "A keepsake. So that you won't forget our time together in Norge."

Dinah eked out a smile. Erika hadn't heard about her encounter with the polar bear. She couldn't know how deeply unlikely it was that she would ever forget her time in Norge.

"Here now, get back to bed." Vanya shooed them back into Dinah's room. "And after I'd gotten you properly warmed up."

Dinah climbed back into bed with the bear. Erika sat in the visitor's chair. Vanya trundled off and left them alone.

Erika looked down at her lap and rubbed her thighs. "The governor phoned Whitney and told him the murderer has been apprehended. I guess I was wrong about Mahler. He had nothing to do with either murder. But Tipton? I can hardly believe it."

"Just like in the books," said Dinah. "The least likely."

"I thought I would be your 'least likely.'" She pushed her hair out of her face and smiled. "Whitney gave us an abbreviated account. He said there'd been a fall and you'd been hurt."

"A few scratches." Dinah almost laughed at her imitation of Nordic stoicism. "I'll be discharged tomorrow morning."

"Then I'll tell you good-bye now. The governor has given us permission to leave and Jake has ordered the plane to be ready at six. We'll be back in Washington tomorrow morning. Senator

Fry is staying over for a day or two. He says the two of you will take a commercial flight."

Dinah toyed with the bear's ribbon. "Have you told Maks good-bye?"

"Yes."

"Is he being philosophical about it?"

"Maks is fine. He has written a new song. It's very good. I think it will be a big hit. He plans to cut another album with his wife."

"He's married? I thought he was incurably in love with you."

"I'm his romantic invention, the Fata Morgana glimpsed once and gone forever. Maks has a very nice wife."

Dinah digested this news without remark. She didn't understand marriage and it was beginning to feel as if she never would.

Erika said, "Colt has decided to drop out of the presidential race. He'll serve out his term in the Senate. In the meantime, he's going to use whatever influence he has to find Hannalore. Perhaps Inge will take pity on us."

"I wish you good luck, Erika. And when I get home, I'm going to buy the entire list of Fata Morgana CDs."

"I'll send you a boxed set. But you must promise never to play them when you're alone and drinking wine." Her hair fell across her face and she got up to leave. "Well, *adjø*, Dinah." She paused and turned back at the door. "There's a Norwegian superstition that if someone who likes you puts a curse on you, the trolls and evil spirits will see that you've already been cursed and they won't bother with you." She made a funny sound with her lips as if she were spitting. "*Tva tva*. And so now you have been cursed." She laughed—it was the first time Dinah had observed the phenomenon. It transformed her for a moment, and then she was gone.

Dinah tossed the bear into the chair Erika had vacated and closed her eyes. She was thinking about the missing Tillcorp documents and what Tipton had done with them when Vanya brought her a supper tray at 7:30.

"I didn't want to wake you, but Thor called. He asked if I would permit you to have a glass of wine. I said only if he brings enough for me. He will be here soon so eat your food. I won't put up with a patient who doesn't eat and then gets tipsy." She set the tray on the bed and stood back. "There is roast turkey and *tyttebær* sauce left over from New Year's Eve dinner."

"It looks wonderful, Vanya. *Tusen takk.*" Dinah dug her fork into a strong-smelling, gelatinous substance on the side of her plate. "And what's this?"

"*Lutefisk,*" said Vanya. "Lye fish. I made it myself. It is special. For the holidays." She had such a proud, expectant face that Dinah couldn't turn up her nose, although it was an effort to push a lump of the stuff into her mouth. "Wow."

"*Ja.* It's *godt.*"

The phone in Vanya's apron pocket rang. She answered, listened, and held it out to Dinah. Someone is calling you from Hawaii." She handed the phone to Dinah and left the room.

Dinah spat the *lutefisk* into her napkin. "Hello."

"Norris Frye called and said you were in the hospital. Are you all right?" It was Eleanor.

"I'm fine, Eleanor." Again the Nordic stoicism, but what was the point in describing all of her travails to Eleanor? There was nothing she could do, even if she were present. "I'm afraid I have bad news about your hapai banana, Eleanor. Now that it's been saved for posterity here in Svalbard, the Seed Savers in Hawaii are bound by an international treaty to lend it out to anyone who asks."

"Don't worry about that. You didn't I think I would send a real hapai to that ice cave until I knew the whole story, did you?"

Dinah laughed. "I should have known." She tried to sound casual and offhand. "How is Jon?"

"Don't worry about him either. He met a gorgeous Hawaiian girl over on Maui the day after Christmas and took her out last night. Today his head's in the clouds. Looks like we're gonna have a real Happy New Year."

Dinah felt a small shock of disappointment. She was glad that he wasn't pining away for her, but it was humbling to be so quickly relegated to Last Year's Number. Apparently, she wasn't the only one with fickle genes. "Aloha, Eleanor. I'm going to stay over in Norway for a few days. I'll come and see you as soon as I get back."

She had no sooner hung up than Thor walked in. His expression was somber.

"Did Tipton die?"

"No. He may lose his leg, definitely some toes, but he's stable and out of intensive care."

"Remind me," she said, "never to jump to conclusions based on your face."

The corners of his mouth turned up slightly. "I brought wine and good news to go with it." He set a paper sack on the chair with the bear and brought out a bottle of Tuscan wine and three glasses. "Vanya will come for her share in a while. She's treating one of the British tourists for frostbite. *Dessverre*, large quantities of gin and Svalbard's weather don't mix." He poured two glasses of wine and handed one to her. "*Skäl*."

"*Skäl*," she said and took a sip. It was a Brunello and very tasty. "Is there more good news?"

He gave the teddy bear a quizzical look and set it on the floor. "I have arrested the man who shot you?"

"Who? How did you find him?"

"Brander Aagaard has confessed."

"Aagaard! But why?"

"He claims he didn't intend to hit anyone. He's nearsighted. He thought he was aiming above Erika Sheridan's head, trying to frighten her away from the church. He thought she had gone there to collect something meant for him."

Dinah's thoughts sprinted through the chronology of events. Aagaard must have seen Erika in the street the night Eftevang was murdered and marked the color of her parka. When Dinah met him in the Kaffe & Kantine, he was lying when he pretended not to know whether it was Valerie or Erika who'd been out of the hotel the night before. He'd probably recognized Maks Jorgen, as well. Dinah had been wearing Erika's parka that day, but the café was dusky and smoky and she'd taken the coat off too far away for him to see it clearly. "The something he went to collect, would that be the package of documents Tipton had promised Eftevang? The evidence of Tillcorp's skullduggery in Africa?"

Thor's eyes glinted with satisfaction. He appeared particularly pleased with himself. "The documents are on a CD I found in his hotel room. I'm having it checked for fingerprints. Aagaard will testify that Teilhard left the CD for him in the church and told him where to find it. He will testify that Teilhard told him these were the documents he had copied from Valerie Ives' computer and promised to Eftevang. After the holidays, when the medical examiner in Trømso has returned to work, we will discover other evidence against Teilhard."

"And you'll keep your job?"

He sat down and savored his wine. "If I want it."

She ate a bite of her roast turkey, not sure whether to follow up on that or not. She mulled Aagaard's explanation. Something jarred. "He's lying, Thor. I was walking out of the church. If he thought Tipton's drop had gone haywire and Mahler or Sheridan had found out about it and sent Erika to get back the CD, he would have assumed she'd already found it and had it in her pocket. He would have been aiming to bring her down, if not actually kill her."

"If that's so, you're very lucky."

The repetition of that phrase sounded like a temptation to any listening trolls and evil spirits. Dinah reached out and knocked her fingers against the back of the wooden chair.

Thor said, "From the little part of the CD I have reviewed, there will be an investigation of the agriculture minister's connection to Tillcorp and his role in promoting their interests. The government will, what do you say? Clean house."

Dinah was too cynical to believe that Tillcorp would suffer any negative consequences in the U.S., regardless of how outrageous their actions had been. The scandal would be reported and then it would blow over and Tillcorp's public relations team would set to work to gloss over the whole ugly mess in Africa. They would tout their incredible scientific advances—fruits that could vaccinate and fish the size of a school bus, and they would prosper. She tried to remember the Bible verse, something about the wicked in great power thriving like the green bay tree. Jake Mahler may have lost one prospective president, but he had bought himself another. He probably owned the movers and shakers of both parties. Americans may as well get used to the taste of genetically modified foods. The country's amber waves of grain would all be patented Tillcorp products by the end of the decade unless there was some kind of a food revolution.

Thor said, "If you like, I'll take you out to my cabin tomorrow and introduce you to Crockett and Tubbs."

"I'd like that. Do you suppose there's a chance of seeing the northern lights in the next few days?"

He smiled. "You can never predict the *Guovssahas*. They are spontaneous and transitory."

Like human infatuations, she thought. But why fight it?